MW00773004

THEY
BLOOM
AT NIGHT

Also by Trang Thanh Tran

She Is a Haunting

THEY BLOOM AT NIGHT

TRANG THANH TRAN

BLOOMSBURY

NEW YORK LONDON OXFORD NEW DELHI SYDNEY

BLOOMSBURY YA
Bloomsbury Publishing Inc., part of Bloomsbury Publishing Plc
1385 Broadway, New York, NY 10018

BLOOMSBURY and the Diana logo are trademarks of Bloomsbury Publishing Plc

First published in the United States of America in March 2025 by Bloomsbury YA

Bloomsbury books may be purchased for business or promotional use. For information on bulk purchases please
contact Macmillan Corporate and Premium Sales Department at specialmarkets@macmillan.com

Library of Congress Cataloging-in-Publication Data.
Names: Tran, Trang Thanh, author.
Title: They bloom at night / by Trang Thanh Tran.
Description: New York: Bloomsbury Children's Books, 2025.
Summary: In Mercy, Louisiana, a town plagued by red algae
and vanishing residents, Noon finds a reluctant ally in Covey
and the two join forces to hunt a deadly creature
in the dark waters as a storm looms.
Identifiers: LCCN 2024036385 (print) | LCCN 2024036386 (e-book)
ISBN 978-1-5476-1111-9 (hardcover) • ISBN 978-1-5476-1112-6 (e-book)
Subjects: CYAC: Monsters—Fiction. | Missing persons—Fiction. |
Algae—Fiction. | LGBTQ+ people—Fiction. | Fantasy. | LCGFT: Fantasy fiction. | Novels.
Classification: LCC PZ7.1.T725 Th 2025 (print) |
LCC PZ7.1.T725 (e-book) | DDC [Fic]—dc23
LC record available at https://lccn.loc.gov/2024036385

Book design by John Candell
Typeset by Westchester Publishing Services
Printed and bound in the U.S.A.
2 4 6 8 10 9 7 5 3 1

To find out more about our authors and books visit www.bloomsbury.com and sign up for our newsletters.

For those who can't see themselves in mirrors

THEY
BLOOM
AT NIGHT

1

TODAY'S BODY IS SKEWERED through the old church spire, a gray-black whale peeling in fleshy wisps. Dead too long for food.

From between my fingers or with my glasses dangling aside, I am still sometimes too scared to see how life has changed. Trailers refurnished with fish and eels under sunken sofas, cardboard boxes soggy and broken into bite-size pieces, and bodies torn up by the crashing waves. I don't like to look, which means, of course, that I have to.

The bloom has claimed much of our town of Mercy, red algae spilling over the Mississippi and adjacent floods like entrails. Our boat cut through it easily, but the micro-plants are probably sticking to the hull right now. It should've been like any algae bloom—spill toxins into the water, kill a bunch of fish, ruin the local economy, and leave us to pick up bootstraps and get back to work—but no, since Hurricane Arlene twenty-one months ago, these red tides have become the longest-lasting bloom known to humans.

Worse, not all the animals die. Wrecked on the levee, the whale gapes in anguish, as if to scream, *Why me?*

"Cẩn thận nhe con," Mom says. Her eyes are trained on the riverside, searching for the outsize tree that flanks the fortune teller's home. Without looking, she reaches over and rubs Vicks under my nose to ward off the rotten egg stench on the breeze. The glob burns my upper lip.

I turn the three-spoke wheel, cautiously guiding our forty-foot trawler on the bloodred river. "It's 'be careful,'" I say, because that's our implicit deal: I learn how to steer a boat and she talks in English. They are the skills we each need to survive without the other. Just in case.

Brows pinching together, she mutters, "Be careful."

I steer our boat over the tombs lurking below, hoping that none moved again in the last storm. This close to land, anything can rip through the hull. The most dangerous stuff is always unseen. Mom should know; she spends most days staring into watery depths, searching for dark silhouettes. *Monsters*, people like to whisper.

It happens a lot actually—people claiming they discovered a new species or the southern Loch Ness, when really, this dead whale just washed up and became postmortem kebab. Maybe some deep-sea creatures got curious about the sun and swam up. Ninety-five percent of the ocean remains unexplored, so it doesn't surprise me to see strange animals. A two-headed shark is still a shark. I should know. Before, I wanted to be a marine biologist, though I probably would've ended up pregnant and stuck here. With most of Mercy abandoned due to off-and-on flooding, I never have to worry about being a late bloomer anymore. I am my best self in this apocalypse.

Mom is not.

"We only have twenty minutes," I say. "Mình chỉ có hai mươi phút thôi Má. Okay?"

The two moles on her left eyelid disappear in a scowl. Rushing at the fortune teller's is a sure way to annoy her, but right now is prime market hour. Our fuel gauge is way too close to *E* to risk missing the weekly trade, no matter the short distance to the harbor from here.

"It take how long it take," she says, pointing at the one tree that looms above all others. Beneath it is the tip of an old boardwalk, mostly covered by weeds. The smaller mole re-emerges at her left eye crease as she gets up, sweeping photos of our family from the counter into her bag. The plastic frames clank together. Anchoring as close and safely as possible, I remove the key from the ignition. It hangs from a silver necklace, a pendant to keep close. I turn the familiar weight in my fingers, counting một, hai, ba, as Mom taught me. Three times, a magic trick to forget all the bad things. It's more of a ridiculous comforting ritual than anything else. Mom pauses and, with a rare smile, helps put the necklace around my throat. "Đừng có lo." Both hands rest on my shoulders. *Don't worry.*

Mom never says "I am here for you," because she's still stuck in those family photos—in the memory of what was. She wants me to be a girl who sits down with her hair neat and smiles, though I have always been different. I *am* different. Under her hands, my sweater clings to my slick skin, itching me everywhere. I keep still, yet miss her when she lets me go. With a bit more fuel, we'll have an escape, for whenever we need. We can rejoin the parts of the US that forgot us as soon as the news stations left, or just go far from Mercy. But we stay.

On the deck, I open our freezer, where at least eight thousand pounds of large brown shrimp are layered in crushed ice, ready to be processed. I grab an already portioned bag up top, then the smaller sandwich bag beside it, and join Mom on the dinghy. A gentle wave helps us toward the fortune teller's porch. The entire cabin is dipped in the strangler fig tree's shadow.

Mom knocks on the door. "Chị Oanh ơi?" No answer. "Chị Oanh!"

This late in summer, the figs are fat, purple pustules that'll burst at the slightest touch. These trees used to only populate southern Florida, but it's tropical enough now to grow in Louisiana too. Some bats might come eat Bà Oanh's figs yet, then shit seeds elsewhere. Another cypress or palm will die under the strangler fig's embrace. That's romance; I don't touch it.

"Em vô nhe chị," Mom announces. Her knuckles are pale on the doorknob, and quivering. She opens the door. The algae that's laced itself across the cabin rips as daintily as a doily as the door opens. Fine red dust spills into the muggy air. Between the bloom's stench and the overripe fruit, I hadn't noticed her smell. Bà Oanh's body is bloating in the armchair she always sat in during our visits. Gasping, Mom leaves me at the threshold. The algae had found its way inside as well, seeping into damp wood. It resembles dried blood that can't be scrubbed clean— only blood isn't this orderly when spilled. There is no shape to the algae; it is just everywhere.

Rather than sobbing at Bà Oanh's feet, Mom cries and rifles through the woman's side table and drawers. She grows more frantic when she doesn't find a hidden fortune, a direction to which we can drive our boat next to find what she really cares about.

My dad. My brother.

They are out there somewhere, reincarnated and waiting for us to rescue them, according to her. Every family has their myths, and Sông is ours. It's like the spirit of the water, but its name doesn't mean ocean. We call it Sông for the rivers we've lived by. In Vietnam, we had the Mekong. Here, we have the Mississippi. Sông kept my dad's family safe during the perilous journey to the United States. During good shrimping seasons, my family thanked it for providing. During bad ones, they wondered if they'd mistreated the water, spat one too many times over the railing. To me, it was just metaphor, simile, and superstition. Mom has twisted it with her faith when my dad's and brother's bodies weren't recovered. She truly believes Sông birthed them again as some sea animal. More impossible dreams to catch within our nets.

"Nhung," my mother says, her eyes as brittle as pistachio skin. There is a question there.

Wake up, I can respond. *They are gone.* A fly lands on Bà Oanh's glasses. *She's dead too.*

I cover my nose, brushing a stray tear off my cheek. What's wrong with being swept in this a little longer, if it makes Mom happy? If it makes her want to live?

"Okay," I answer. "I'll help look." Setting our goods aside, the clock dwindling away light, I go through the fortune teller's ten-year-old receipts, yellowing magazines, and notebooks. Bà

Oanh had been haunted by the memory of her drowned sister. She didn't believe in reincarnated people or monsters, but she stayed because she'd lived in Mercy since she first came to the US. She never encouraged my mom's delusions. Lunar calendars and palm reading were her forte.

Her last fortune for Mom had been this: "Not the year for rat signs, Tiên. Bad luck will come and come again for your daughter. It'll be better if you wait on shore until the shroud passes. She should not operate cars or any other machinery."

Mom didn't listen, of course, because we had to be on the boat. She always held onto the hope that, next time, Bà Oanh would divine our family's location.

Eventually I make it back to the armchair, which Mom hasn't searched at all. She isn't good with bodies. People worth saving don't do things like steal glasses from corpses. I've always liked Bà Oanh's frames since the attached chain makes them harder to misplace. Her glassy eyes don't need them anymore. The flies I'd disturbed resettle on her forehead. I can see every blemish, every putrefying pore, every small cut likely from seashells on her feet, but no wounds big enough to kill. Maybe a heart attack or aneurysm got her in the end. Better than drowning. Many people drown these days.

I follow her sloping arm, to where it lies between cushion and armrest, so heavily covered in beetles and other insects that I almost miss the mini notepad. I tug it free. Five words are scrawled out: KHI NƯỚC CỨ DÂNG CAO. *When the water keeps rising.* An omen I know well. It's easy to imagine the muck-ridden river or the temperamental ocean waves breaking through the windows and ripping us apart. It always sings in a rush, but it is the day-to-day erosion that will end us. To me, *when the water keeps rising* means now. Like an outdated textbook, the phrase teaches me nothing new.

A laugh wells in my throat. I love the wild, open ocean where it's only us and the horizon, where no one can see me, but I don't want to trace the coastline looking for imaginary monsters again. Mom is overjoyed as she takes the notepad. For Mom, *when the water keeps rising* means every day is an opportunity.

I try to hold on. "We don't know if this is for us."

"Who?" Mom asks. "Who then?" I'm afraid she'll swallow all the carrion beetles with her lips open in argument. I let go. To the fortune teller, Mom utters "cảm ơn chị," as if the woman had written an epiphany destined for us as her final act before unceremoniously croaking. She leaves, slimy notebook hugged against her chest, the only weight keeping her from fluttering away. It won't be long before she takes us into the next storm. Even whales have been known to carry dead calves on their heads for weeks in mourning.

What's an ocean to a Vietnamese mother with a dream?

In those quiet moments between whatever's left of Bà Oanh and me, I open the plastic sandwich bag and put a dome of Vietnamese sponge cake on her lap. She had a sweet tooth, so I'd saved it just for her. The last of the freezer's frost has melted, making the crumps sloppy. It would've ruined the condensed milk she liked to dunk it in. I mumble a sorry, though I'm not sure for what. The way we barged in here, how I robbed her glasses? For my mom?

Here's the truth: my life went apocalyptic a whole two months before the hurricane swept through, when I lost my virginity in the famed shallows of Mercy Cove. Now more than ever, I can't look in a mirror. I am all the wrong shapes, skin flaking away to shell under prying fingers. My hair's as white as bleached coral, though for a time Mom made me dye it black. Now we just say it's stress-induced. She tells me these changes are from my imagination, but she puts me in thick sweaters and stiff jeans in this awful heat.

The taste of brackish water plagues my tongue as I linger at the door. On the dinghy, Mom hums and waves for me to hurry. My insides boil, which is unproductive because only one of us can be reckless at a time. Crying seagulls dive and snap up small fish breaking through the algae. I go to catch up with Mom.

Time bleeds this time of year, sun late into the day with skies like watered-down raspberry tea. This season used to bring back crayon-scented memories full of composition books and leaking glue. It had the slickness of a paper cut: sharp and quick, then pressed with humidity under a cartoon-themed Band-Aid. Outside, everything is beautiful, all at the cusp of rotting. There are no cicadas, only buzzing wasps that squeeze into figs to lay their eggs. September is close, a month of new beginnings.

I glance back at Bà Oanh's cabin, a place I plan never to return to, at the sliver of inside still visible. Light glints off the dead woman's yellowed teeth, made sharper by the blood-tinged foam dribbling from her nose and mouth. As the door closes, she suddenly seems to be wearing a smile.

2

THE BLOOM'S SCATTERED NEAR the harbor, streaking through a constant stream of fishing boats, and touched with oil. On the docks, the locals stop haggling to gawk at us. Of all trawlers, Mom and I go the longest distances into the Gulf of Mexico, where there is still a chance of hauling in shrimp. But really, the locals are just waiting to see if we've brought back the terrifying creature-thing rumored to be hunting in these waters.

"Non Bien Tien and Loony Noon's here!" a tall dockworker shouts. He flips a baseball hat back on his hair. The logo of an alligator eating its own tail is about as inspired as the nicknames they give us. In the early days post-storm, Jimmy's Gator Swamp Tour and Emporium, with its airboat fleet and crew members unemployed due to dying tourism, won a government contract to transport limited goods to towns farther south. How marked up the prices are doesn't matter, as long as the politicians don't have to think about us. We are the ones who chose to stay, after all. We deserve what we get.

Above deck, Mom and I find our way to the pier. A special crew waits for us as usual, and today Knife Girl is back. Despite being closer to my age, she lays out on a hammock and "oversees" Jimmy's henchpeople. Mostly, she reads a book and holds the pointy end of a knife between her white teeth.

"Finally," the tall dockworker says. "Jimmy woulda been *pi-ssed*. You Asians are always late."

I would've very much liked to push him into an algae mass, but someone else speaks first. "Shut the hell up, you disgusting skid mark." Knife Girl sits up in the hammock, small blade glinting in the sun before she uses it as a bookmark. She slips the whole thing into a cargo pocket. Her brown hair is parted in the middle and cut shaggily at her strong jawline.

Next to me, Mom has stopped humming. She does not like this change and, for all my curiosity about Knife Girl, I don't like this either. "We are late a lot," I say in what must be a betrayal to multiple cultures. I'll apologize to the entire continent of Asia later. A whiff of Knife Girl's sunscreen—Banana Boat—catches on the breeze, and something stirs inside me, a hazy memory, maybe, of simpler days. After a pause, Knife Girl introduces herself. "I'm Covey."

"Covey," I repeat. "Like a flock of birds?"

She raises a brow, then counters, "Noon, like the time of day?"

"Like Nhung," I say. "Something you can't pronounce." Since forever, Noon has been a placeholder for neighbors, teachers, and other kids. It is a favor to myself, honestly, since it saves me from correcting everyone's pronunciation or having to slap on the verbal equivalent of a participation sticker. No anger or

embarrassment flits across her face, just a flash of teeth that I
can't pin as a smirk or smile. We stare at each other.

"Why y'all call it *Wild Things* when it's one boat?" Skidmark asks as he ropes it to the docks.

Tilting my head, I consider the cursive Dad branded on the
shrimp trawler years ago. He'd wanted to name it Little Jay after
my brother, but Jaylen took one look at me and said no. *What
about this instead, after the book?* he suggested, and of course
our dad said yes. He always said yes to his son.

I ignore the worn paint again. *Wild Things*, his childhood
favorite. Not mine.

Moving into my line of vision again, Covey answers with
lazy confidence, "It's after the picture book. Yeah?" I nod, finally
noticing that no one's unloading our boat. Usually they'd be on
it, eager to get the hell out of Port Mercy. I look back at the girl.
Her eyes are an agonizing blue, the kind of ocean water that's
hard to find now. "Jimmy wants to talk to you both in person,
over by the swamp."

Dread hooks my gut. The harbor has always been our meeting place. The swamp lies farther inland, not safe for our trawler.
We'd have to take another boat.

"Nó nói cái gì vậy?" Mom whispers.

"Make him come here," I say loudly. "We aren't leaving our
trawler."

Covey's expression is hard to read. Her words, however, are
clear: "If you have no fuel, it gets left anyway." The next dock
not under Jimmy's watch isn't for hundreds of miles, with rules
and people we don't know. We would be stranded in algae-
infested waters trying to reach the next harbor.

"Ông Jimmy muốn mình tới gặp ổng," I say to Mom. She moves to argue. I tell her that we don't have a choice when we're led to a different boat.

The aluminum skiff bounces under our weight. Mom has fallen silent after rearranging my clothes to cover as much skin as possible. Covey controls the engine using a hand tiller to lead us down a channel off the bayou.

Things do their best rotting in daytime or deep in water. And this close to Mercy itself, there is simply more to kill. Animals that returned in low flood cook at its surface, a resting place for flies. Others sit drowned at the bottom. We hit the formerly dainty swamp off Port Mercy, where in some months there isn't even enough water to call it that. Now, patches of red algae float like cloudy fat on a pot of bún riêu. We pass stilt houses and houseboats. Somewhere, a woman's soft sobbing harmonizes with swinging wind chimes.

The sun begins to bake me brown. My mouth dries out. I want to reach into the brackish muck and catch a fish, any fish, and break its spine for fluid. Suck the eyes. It is a trick Mom's aunt told her about—how they withstood the dehydration while at sea on their way here decades ago. It barely works really, but I don't care.

I am thirsty and trapped. I need the ocean. I need to see no one else for miles.

Unmoving, Mom watches the only part of America she has ever known. From her world, she clings to the bench, squeezing until her knuckles turn white. At the next juncture of trees, the boat takes a hard right toward a shallower end.

A white man stands on the shack's porch, hand wrapped around a gun. He has it pointed directly in front of him. When our skiff bumps against the porch, he lowers it and turns his head. His hair is a deep brown, sweat-drenched and dripping down to a mostly gray beard. "Excuse me," James Boudreaux says with a bright, jolly smile. "I was just thinking about taking care of any potential interruptions." Our eyes follow his gaze back out to the tree some fifteen feet away, where a bird hovers over its nest, feeding its young. He helps Covey up first. "I hope my daughter has been a hospitable host."

Daughter? It makes sense that Jimmy would have his kid watch over his business. Plenty follow their parents into whatever trade—myself included—but Covey was always nose-deep in a book when she ought to be nickel-and-diming us on every haul. Next to him, she sighs. "We didn't get into it."

The word *it* snags on my nerves. *He's finally come for the boat,* I think as I pull Mom onto the creaky wood. We call *Wild Things* ours, but Dad had taken a loan from this man following the bank's rejection to purchase it. We owe more than it's worth now. The first time I met Jimmy was last year, when we brought in blue crabs. They'd looked normal on the outside but completely different on the inside. He wouldn't take our word for it.

"Wait," I had said, but it was already too late.

Jimmy snapped a living crab's shell open and exposed its body. The legs twitched once, twice, but he only added, "Let's take his little face off. It's distracting, huh?" His thick thumb peeled back the crab's black eyes in a gut-wrenching crack, then discarded the remains at our feet. The rotting sea had filled our nostrils.

The crab had no lungs. The feathery gills that should rise from either side, tasteless and icky, were absent; in its place, more orange roe and dark meat—what we break them for. Guts dripped from his fingers. It was unnatural. Wrong.

He made us bring in every fucked-up thing that wound up in our nets after that. He sold them to hobby collectors, rich people in dry places that mounted specimens to walls and kept the rest in thick tanks. Some he slipped to university scientists who happily ran tests on them. *No microplastics, PCP, MSG, the whole thing*, he'd report back gleefully. *Just more bang for your buck. Nature doing what food geneticists want to do.*

Now he has the same greedy look on his face. "It's very nice to see my best shrimpers again. Thank you for coming," he drawls as he lights a thick cigarette. Cherry smoke blankets us with his next words. "Tell me, what have you and your mom seen out there recently?"

He doesn't mean the sunrises and sunsets, a calm ocean rocking me to sleep, or the air so salty and cool I dreamed of floating in it. Anyone can tell him that. He wants stories and rumors: intestine-pink tentacles overcoming barges, impossible antlers riding a crest, and smudges swimming underwater, lost between one blink and the next. He wants to hear about the things that thrived while others died.

"Nothing," I say. "Just the same-old crap. The algae's getting wors—"

"Monsters," Jimmy cuts in.

"There are no monsters," I reply. Mom refuses to call them that. To her, they are gia đình. Family.

He blows out another sick, sweet breath. "Semantics, then. So what if it's actually a megashark or giant squid, or whatever messed up abomination's out there swallowing up people's lives and livelihoods. The problem is now it's here too. Right in Mercy, people are vanishing with no trace." He inclines his head toward Mom. "Tell her."

August has been full of bloated skies that refuse to rain. Of course, it would begin now. A soft drizzle catches on Mom's eyelashes as those moles vanish in wide wonder. A storm is always coming.

"You sure people aren't just getting drunk and falling in?"

He barks out a laugh. "One or two maybe, but there have been several cases and no bodies at all. Whatever it is, it's taking people whole."

"Or they could be leaving," I say. "This place sucks." They'd be far from the first residents to abandon Mercy.

Covey unfolds from her slouching. "Not everyone runs from a fight." I hate that she looks cool even for a second, and I hate it even more when Jimmy beams proudly at his daughter. "People have reported seeing or hearing things, then they disappear too."

Her dad picks up the spiel. "We can keep Port Mercy running for as long as we like, but that means Mercy has to stay on the map. Folks are terrified enough of storms, and this is the last damn straw. It certainly is for the government." He pauses for full effect. "A scientist has gone missing."

He explains how the lead botanist on their research team disappeared while collecting algae bloom samples, how annoying mishaps like these are costly to morale and bad PR for officials who want to keep the seafood industry thriving. "The government's gonna close the fishing season early. Some people will leave for less stingy places, and then they'll make everyone go. They're planning to designate this entire place a disaster zone."

"When?" I ask, mind reeling.

"September tenth." That's three weeks from now. "This is where you and your mom come in. You got all those other specimens. So you catch this one too. Dead or alive, I don't care."

I start to shake my head. Mom waits next to me, unaware (for the most part) of what we are being tasked with. It must be a shitty joke, but it's also my fault for letting my mom do whatever she wanted, for letting our reputation as monster hunters balloon out of proportion. The ocean's deepest part runs seven miles down. It is pitch-black, with pressure over a thousand times the surface level's. Of course, whatever can survive that depth can kill us. Of course, there is always something in the water.

There's a rush of excitement as I realize Mercy being a designated disaster zone would be the perfect excuse to convince Mom to leave. We don't have to listen to his demands.

As if he can read my mind, Jimmy adds, "If you don't take the deal, then my patronage ends here, and I'll collect on your loan. Someone will do what I ask them, for a boat like that. *Wild Things*." The name is obscene in his drawl.

The excitement plummets as I clench my fists so that I don't scream. Without our trawler, the only way out of Mercy is on a school bus refashioned for mass evacuation. And Mom will never agree when she believes our family is in danger. Seething, I ask, "And what do *you* think this monster is?"

"Now that's y'all's job to figure out," Jimmy says. "Don't care how you do it, but I want it contained. I don't give a shit about the scientist, or Mother Nature menstruating, people need to know the situation is under control. Once it's eliminated, it'll be safe. No reason to close up shop. That's how we get back to normal. Now don't keep your mother waiting. Translate."

"*He wants us to catch the animal,*" I mutter to Mom. "*Dead or alive. He'll take the boat if we don't.*" She inhales sharply.

Jimmy claps his hands together. "Do this and you'll get better rates on all your shrimping hauls. More fuel for your trips out there. Your debt will get knocked down by half."

This deal promises more freedom. We won't have to work so hard running nets across the entire Gulf and counting down the gallons of fuel. "*We can fake it,*" I say in Vietnamese, though once we'd brought back a faceless cusk—a deepwater eel with a bulbous head, hardly any eyes, and a tucked-under mouth—to Jimmy's annoyance. He'd known what it was immediately. I touch Mom's elbow. "*We'll find something weird and dead. We can stuff one of my fingers in its gut. After, we can stay out two weeks at a time. Or just leave. It'll be easy. It'll be better that way.*" Under their watch, I keep my voice low, urgent, but Mom recoils from me. Disgusted. The two moles on her monolids have disappeared in a bewildering stare, as though we don't know each other at all, and maybe she's right.

She would do anything to protect family, reincarnated or otherwise. I underestimated her.

Mom lunges for Jimmy's throat.

Like a moth to flame, I follow, desperate to grasp at her black hair. Covey catches me around the middle and shoves me against a wall, while the man easily gathers Mom up and slams her on the porch. I scream.

Sitting on her back, Jimmy holds her jaw closed. "I wrestle gators bigger than you," he says, his knees bruising her arms.

At my ear, Covey says, "It'll be worse if you get involved."

Anger surges at my pulse points. "Go fuck a screwdriver. I'm already involved." I fight against her strong grip as a low whine peels from Mom's throat.

"What did I do to deserve that, huh?" Jimmy *tsks* and shakes my mom against the porch. "See what you did to yourself?" His smile is cold as he regards me. "Tell your momma to stay put."

"*Don't fight*," I say instead.

Mom wails in response. "Trời đất ơi." When he lets her go, her arms flop to the side, oddly bent. She groans as he rolls her over with a dirty boot. Her thigh eases from a large nail jutting from the porch. The rust and blood meld together in one big mess.

"Get off." I shove Covey from me. Blood oozes from the hole in Mom's loose trousers. I apply pressure with my hands but she swats me away.

Jimmy plops down in a rocking chair. He points to the matching seat, then at Mom. "Sit." He wags a single finger at us. "Sit." I half-expect him to throw a treat.

Seething, breathing lungfuls of mossy air, I help Mom to her feet and onto the chair. I grip its back, digging my dull fingers in to stop the chair's squeaking.

"As I was proposing, ladies," Jimmy says, slopping government-issued Purell over his palms. "You have three weeks. This is a generous deal. And well, you Vietnamese know how to rebuild from nothing. You're resilient. You'll figure it out."

Less than a month to accomplish what we haven't over a year, or we lose everything.

Mom's crying cuts into my translation. Makes me repeat words. She's anguished. "We can't hurt them!"

"Con biết rồi," I say. A dangerous feeling thrums in my skin. My heavy clothes are too small to contain the shape of my rage, my desperation. I wish for claws and sharp teeth, a stinger to stab this man through. I imagine what it must be like to have a colossal squid's serrated grip to wrap around his smirking face and squeeze. "*We'll find another body,*" I try Mom again. "*We won't have to kill anything, I promise.*"

"Oh, by the way," Jimmy says, as if well-versed in all the ways to betray others. "My daughter will go with you. She's a great shot."

My eyes meet Covey's again.

I knew from the moment she spoke today, she was fated to ruin my life. She will report everything back to her crime lord of a dad. And she doesn't belong on *Wild Things*, the last space that's ours.

"Our nets will work fine," I say through gritted teeth.

The patience vanishes from his voice. "She's the best hunter around my place. You need a demonstration?" His hand hovers over the holster.

In English, Mom says, "No gun." With her bleeding leg steady, she snaps her fingers at Jimmy directly. "Okay?"

He raises his hands. "Okay then."

"That's fine," Covey says. Back at the shack door, she squats down to pick up another menacing contraption. "I'll take my crossbow."

3

IN THE BLUE-BLACK OF night, anything is possible—words float to the stars, animals leave their hovels, and Mom sings for me alone, drowning out the waves. The algae is no longer red but bioluminescent: bright turquoise sparks resulting from a chemical reaction inside the tiny organisms that make up the bloom. They share this with marine creatures, like *Atolla* jellyfish that use it as protection in the deep sea. I'd be captivated by how beautiful the water is, if not for the monsters lurking underneath that we must catch. And soon.

We're back at the harbor on *Wild Things*. Tomorrow, Knife Girl will meet us here to refuel the boat. Mom and I don't have a plan yet. We haven't spoken much at all, our energies depleted from the wild-ass turn of events. Mom lights incense for Sông, each smoky tendril a prayer. Cleaning Bà Oanh's glasses, I remember the smile I thought I saw. Perhaps she'd foreseen what was coming and could not stop herself from mocking us, though she'd never been unkind. It's a bad habit of mine, finding the worst in every situation, but no one has taught me to hope.

Our options are to search for monsters that probably don't exist but Mom thinks are reincarnations, to fake a monster under Covey Boudreaux's watch, or to drive toward the ocean horizon without enough supplies. I can't consider the alternative, which is to surrender *Wild Things* and leave this dying town for somewhere shiny inland. I can't see myself in a school uniform and following rules and eating cereal and living life and getting married and doing whatever people have written out for us. Then, I remember I can barely see myself at all.

It would be the perfect American story. To arrive with only the clothes on your back and make a home of it. Never mind that the first place Dad's family settled had been a fishing community in Texas, but once the boat people rebuilt too well, the Ku Klux Klan chased them away. Burned their boats. The line between exemplar and threat has always been thin. At the shack, Jimmy had called us Vietnamese people *resilient*, like it's an inherited trait rather than a forced behavior.

I mentally rehearse a speech about how we'll best Jimmy and keep our boat, but the words jumble, frustrating me. It shouldn't be this difficult to matter. I tuck Bà Oanh's glasses in a shoebox under the tiny sink.

My sweet brother once said I loved useless things: seashells, the oddly shaped buttons pulled from our dad's old shirts, and my own arts and crafts projects from school that I had finger-painted with messages such as *for you, Mom* and *happy birthday*. They were the neglected objects, the shit people would throw away, but how else can you keep happiness in a small box? Just yours; a treasure curated, permanent and safe. Not like everything else you might love.

Jay was (obviously) rude as hell, but I never faulted him for it. He got that from me. If he were here, Mom would listen. Not only because he'd be alive, but because our parents often treated my younger brother as a future decision-maker. Sons you get to keep, but daughters go away. Daughters marry into other families and take care of other mothers. They leave home and don't return.

I am not that daughter.

"Má," I say when we've finally settled down for bed. Usually I sleep on the bottom bunk and she takes the top, but tonight we cram on the two-foot wide space together—her sitting up because of her arms, and my head on the unhurt thigh. "Every month there's less shrimp. And now what's left is changing. I checked the fuel. We can get far enough away, then start over. Let's leave. No one would know until morning."

But Mom only pushes the bangs off my forehead, gently removing my glasses. The world is an immediate blur behind her. She takes a breath deep enough for her stomach roll to brush against my cheek. "Your dad and brother are here."

"You really believe that," I say, incredulous that so much has happened in one day and yet nothing has changed at all. Of course, I miss them. Their absence hurts me too, and imagining how they drowned makes me sick and angry and sad. But I don't get to give in because I'm the only one standing. Mom is always on her knees, praying or searching the water. "Why?" Some cope through faith, and Buddhists believe in reincarnation, but we'd stopped driving the hour-plus to temple long before Hurricane Arlene.

She doesn't respond. Her palm lays flat against mine. "Your hand's gotten bigger," she says. After cleaning up her leg, I'd put bandages on all my fingertips since the nails have fallen off in the last few days. The adrenaline over Jimmy's confrontation had numbed the pain perfectly.

"*Choose me.*" The words spill from my mouth in English, bleeding across the floor. I don't dare breathe for how close I am to ruining this. Asking to be chosen by my mom is like asking to be forgiven. Live with me elsewhere, even when I'm not the survivor she wanted.

The moles on her eyelids stay intact. "Con nói gì vậy?"

My heart stutters. Sometimes I wonder if she truly hasn't picked up any English or if the Vietnamese fishing community shielded her that much. Maybe she's pretending to not understand, which is an answer itself. Just like I am afraid to say those words in a language she knows.

"Never mind," I say.

If I was worth running for, we would've done it two years ago when she found me on that skull-shaped beach, the place I consider the heart of town. Mercy Cove was more popularly known as Chelsea's Cove, named for a high school senior twenty years ago rumored to have slept with fifty-seven people there during spring break. Sharp, steep rock brackets the cove. Fishermen rarely visited, though their kids made it the place to be. It was the perfect getaway, tucked far enough from town to throw parties with bonfires and cases of beer. Boys parked their big trucks in the long grass, dragging their girlfriends for a night under the stars. It was a hookup spot.

A trap.

My hands are coated in sweat. I hold onto Mom more tightly. Refuse to let shame wedge between us. Soreness twinges from thumb to pinky, and the bright smiley face on each bandage strains against movement. In response, Mom's beautiful voice shudders, then sings. The notes are long and deep, soothing, and I fall into a darkness that—with a flickering thought—reminds me of the deep sea.

Morning arrives in the form of a seventeen-year-old girl with a duffel bag and a wagon full of metal traps. By the time I see Covey at the harbor, I've already changed into long sweats and had a meal of fresh fish dipped in soy sauce. Raw, the only way my stomach will take food these days.

"You gotta turn over all your knives first. I have to check you."

"Seriously?" Covey drops the heavy duffel. Metal clanks inside. "We're hunting. It could be dangerous." Covey is wearing a simple pair of cargo pants and a loose tank that exposes her bra straps, and I can tell she has a lot of objects that could kill hidden.

"It's still our boat, so our rules," I say, and pop open the freezer. "The most dangerous thing around Port Mercy is your dad. You should know this." Even before Jimmy took over, the seafood industry was dominated by men. Hurricane Arlene didn't change that, except for making conditions worse for everyone else. At certain parts of the pier, I've felt their eyes following me. Some even brave a "ni hao," despite most Asians in Mercy being Cambodian or Vietnamese.

She doesn't argue with my statement. Methodically, she unsheathes hunting knives from her belt and the dagger from her boot. I stick those into the ice. Less willingly, she places the crossbow and a case of bolts inside the freezer. And though I hadn't planned on checking her bag, she swings it off her shoulder and loosens the drawstrings. She unearths a few changes of clothes, a shitload of batteries, and at least five paperback books. Covey looks more embarrassed by the books than the small ax she tosses into the freezer. She withdraws another paperback from her cargo pocket, slipping the small knife from its place. "Do you have a bookmark?"

"I'm not a library." The blade is narrow, less dangerous than some of our cooking utensils. "You can keep that knife."

Grinning, she closes the book around the knife. The remaining traps are moved onto the deck and tied down so they don't slip. Still easy enough to reach. Mom frowns; I'll have to make sure she doesn't throw them overboard when no one's looking.

Another hour passes while we fuel up and make sure we are well-stocked, in case of emergency. The injuries have Mom in a much more subdued state; she only attempts three tasks at a time and tells me to take over steering. So I lead us far away from the bayou. Traveling south, we pass areas of varying algae thickness, from carpets to only a smattering of red. Mom's out on the deck, awkwardly stirring the surface with a long fishing net, so she can peer down.

Covey watches the surroundings carefully; she probably hasn't gone this close to the Gulf since the hurricane. Suddenly, Covey leans close to me to say over the motor, "All the missing cases we're sure about happened in Mercy proper. In shallow areas. We have no reason to come out this far." She points back to the direction we came from. "Delgado went missing in town."

"Delgado?"

"Dr. Lucía Garza Delgado." She unfolds a photograph from her pocket. "The scientist who kick-started this whole thing." I slow down so I don't accidentally beach us. A rectangle drawn in blue ink encloses one of the few brown people in the team picture. A tiny scribble at the border notes *they/them*. Dr. Delgado is the youngest in their late thirties, with a buzz cut and wide grin. They'd put bunny ears on the scientist standing on their right.

"Where were they last seen exactly?" I ask. Mercy may have been a tiny speck two hours south of New Orleans, but the river and close access to the ocean makes the possibilities exponential for where a person can be.

Covey sighs. "I don't know. Different research points, I guess. We'll know more if we talk to their contact in Mercy." She juts her thumb toward town again. "Which is that way."

"We're shrimpers," I deflect. "And you can only shrimp in deeper water. Your dad hired us for a reason, so—"

"My dad is horrible," she says. "He's used to being the big man everyone listens to. He thinks if you bring some mutated fish that could plausibly haul off a human, we all just get a free pass. I don't take his word at face value." I flinch since she'd unknowingly called me out too. Every plane on her body is tense. He'd doted on her yesterday, proud over her willingness to fight, but I know better than anyone that looks are deceiving.

"Do you believe a monster is hunting people?"

Her answer is more reasoned than I expect. "I don't *not* believe, but first there has to be evidence."

This will be a problem, her investigative thinking. I had been relying on Jimmy's stupidity to match his bravado, at least to buy time until Mom's convinced to go.

"Delgado's team or the government must have combed over everything," I say.

Covey shrugs. "But we haven't searched, and it's your home, isn't it?" She says the word "home" so easily, like she's never been anywhere she doesn't believe she belongs.

"I'm not going back." The ferocity in my voice surprises me. I'm fine on the open ocean and dragging in some poor animal roughed up by the waves to fulfill Jimmy's extortion, but I don't want to set foot on land. Not back in the actual town, where the people I loved most—and some of the people I hated most—died. I've been living on rivers, the interconnected channels, sea, and rot-eaten planks around Mercy just fine. "Not yet. We do it our way first. A lot can happen in three weeks."

Covey *studies* my face—there is no other word as perfect as that for the intense way she looks at me now. My cheeks burn since I'm used to being disregarded. It's safer to be forgotten by everyone but Mom. "Sure," Covey says. "We can try your method for a few days, but then I'm radioing Jimmy if we don't turn around."

The threat hangs over my head, lacking heat. So few people use their parents' first names that I wonder whether she separates the man into Jimmy the Extortionist and Dad, and whether there are two versions of her as well, bad and possibly good. I don't know who I'm dealing with yet. I maneuver us to the delta where, after Hurricane Arlene, lighthouses were rebuilt with excruciating efficiency—all metal and bare. We usually stop at the southeast lighthouse to visit its keepers—Dad's old friends—but we won't with Covey.

"Is that what I think it is?" She points to a windowpane box the size of a coffin, crashed and slanted into mossy rocks.

Ah, yes. The fun little distraction some nonlocals added. A wind phone, like the one first set up in Japan after a tsunami took thousands of lives, where you are encouraged to speak to the dead. Even though the phone is broken, people visit it for closure. "Yeah," I say. "Looks like it'll wash away in the next storm though."

Covey glances toward the horizon, her gaze faraway. Not dreamlike, but close.

I can't help but ask. "You need to stop there?"

"No," she answers, voice more gravel than silk. "I never want to use it."

4

THE SALT CHANGES YOU, I'm sure of that. In the few pictures we have of Dad as a kid, he's so scrawny Mom joked it's a wonder he didn't blow away with the leaves. But you can see him changing the more trips he took with his own dad out to the ocean. The coarseness in his dark hair, the way he grew up lean but strong and broad-shouldered.

I had wanted the same for me. Eleven became twelve became thirteen, but not once did he take me with him on a trawling trip. Even in the summer, I had to watch him leave us while other Vietnamese kids younger than me—all boys—went with their dads to the Gulf.

Now it's just me and Mom, moving in tandem and spreading the trawler's wings, while Covey sharpens a knife. It was rough learning on our own when Dad and Jay died. Now green nets sweep the dark ocean, catching nothing, but it's not our fault. There may be less noticeable bloom in these waters, but that doesn't mean all's normal.

For miles in every direction, there is no one. Only sloshing waves and white foam, the first glimmers of iridescence when the sun sinks. There will be very few as brave, or rash, to come out here like this. It is by this strange ocean that I feel my first smile since leaving Port Mercy. The unused muscles ache inside my cheeks.

A few times on the first day, Covey tries to talk to us, but we speak only Vietnamese. Privately, I want to know what Covey sees in the ocean. I see kelp reaching upward and grasping at the surface, coloring the water brown. In some angles, they curl within sharp waves, like a girl's hair. I hate that I experience this alone, or almost alone, because Mom's back to searching for creatures in the water. She's not even doing it for Jimmy.

To ease the weight on her dislocated shoulder, I keep needing to wrestle the arm sling back on her. In one rare instance, Mom's eyes snap to me. *On* me. "Your head hurt again?" she asks. The tingling in my skull started that morning and worsened throughout the day. I try to play it off. "Không có sao má."

She waves me over to the captain's seat. "Sit down."

Mom breaks out Eagle Brand Medicated Oil, a tiny glass bottle of what must be the most valuable emerald liquid in this apocalypse. You can use it for colds, aches, sprains, and so forth. It's on par with Vicks. From the booth tucked on the side, Covey watches us over a bowl of rice, soy sauce, and dried shrimp.

My shirt's half off, covering my chest, as Mom rubs the medicine on my back. The coin's first stroke is always the worst, before you can establish a rhythm in expectations. It's a dollar coin, one of the things Dad kept for sentimental reasons. In my tiny treasure box, his two-dollar bills are folded in the shape of a heart. One for me, and one for Jay.

With the coin, she bruises my skin in deliberate columns, following my ribs. It stings, but Covey's eyes burn me more. Every plan or scheme to trick Jimmy, to escape Port Mercy, Mom has turned down—as if she hadn't heard his ultimatum at all, as if his daughter isn't sitting in the same room as us. Always observing. I bite down on my lip so I don't whine or argue with Mom again.

That night, I wake up from the pain in my back. The bunk cushion is too thin to support sleeping on my hip, so I toss and turn until finally I leave the cabin where Mom's resting. There's a small warm light on deck, like an anglerfish in the deep sea. The book light illuminates Covey's rapt face. I hate that I'm curious.

I look at the ocean instead, where there's a faint twinkling from algae spread this far. The weather's cool enough at night that I cling to my knit sweater, fingers careful not to dig into the bruises on my back. What do other people think of this view? To me, despite everything, it's beautiful.

"Is your mom hurting you?" says the girl behind me.

Her book is shut, light dim between the pages. I'm confused. Covey waves her mini knife at the sliver of bruise near my neck.

Her misplaced pity makes my sweater feel a million times heavier, like I might sink to the deepest ocean trench. "It's called coining. It's an ancient medical practice from Vietnam," I say more defensively than I mean to and with a few heaps of bullshit. "Don't talk about things you don't understand. I just can't sleep right now."

Covey's expression screws up in a way that indicates she's about to be rude too. "You know exactly what I mean," she says. "This isn't what you want to be doing either. We're searching for a needle in a haystack."

She's right. I glance at the horizon because I'm not letting her see it on my face. "I'm working on that," I say. "And my mom's the one who's hurt. Not me." Finality seeps into my tone; the conversation is over, as far as I'm concerned. I turn the key hanging from my necklace three times.

After quite a while, she starts to read just loud enough for me to hear. I freeze. Of course, she would've noticed how Mom helps me sleep after only a few days on *Wild Things*. Mom had begun singing to me in the months after the storm, because it seemed—to me—that the ocean was always calling. Luring me to a crest of a distant wave, frothing white as tonight's. Lonely.

I can't decide if Covey is kind, manipulative, or nosy, but she reads gently, as though setting out a bowl of milk for a feral cat. And I should leave, but I can't. I'm tired and Mom isn't awake to sing, and my back hurts. And so I sit with my legs dangling above the ocean, listening to a story about an imp who spins straw into gold in exchange for a miller's firstborn.

On the fourth day, we catch a massive fish. It's so deformed that we wouldn't be able to tell the species if not for its long, swordlike bill. By now, Covey has figured out our rhythm and, even when we don't ask, joins us in pulling in nets or doing household tasks. We lay the freshly dead swordfish on deck. It's longer than me and at least twice as heavy. It would've sold for a lot of money if it looked normal. There are dozens of little teeth inside its mouth, all of which should've fallen out once it reached adulthood. By some silent metric, Mom decides that it is indeed a fish and retreats into the cabin.

Messily, I use a cleaver to take its head off and inspect the insides. It has a sea salt smell. Absolutely normal, compared to those lungless crabs we brought in before. I sit on my heels. Swordfish is a pain to butcher, and it's not my specialty. I raise the cleaver. In pieces, it'll still be edible.

"Here," Covey says. "I'll do it." With her sleeves rolled, she uses her own knife to expertly take off the fish collar where there's rich meat, then the tail. She butchers the swordfish expertly, slicing through connective tissue. I am her silent helper, turning the heavy fish while admiring the shine of steel and muscle in her limbs as she breaks this massive animal down to usable parts. It's not her first time doing this.

It takes an hour for us to end up with oozy swordfish marrow and equal loin cuts so fresh and pink you'd never guessed it came from something *wrong*. We store what we can and deliver steaks to Mom for dinner. She sears the swordfish in a pan with too-old aromatics while I eat mine raw, mouth brimming with the sea and something like longing.

5

FLOCKS OF BLACK-TAILED GULLS have been following us for the last two hours, swiping at our nets with increasing fervor. The nets come up full for once. Jumbo brown shrimp, their eyes beady and black, stare indignantly in the face of death. The fish we keep too, slotted in the freezer beside Covey's crossbow. There are no monsters, which I have chosen to forget about most of the time. Among the bycatch is a gorgeous sea slug with a silvery, narrow body no longer than an inch and six dark-blue appendages that reach out like fingers. When Covey moves to the sorting table, I make room for her.

"Blue dragon," I tell her. "Its stomach is filled with gas, which helps it float on the ocean surface." Unlike the animal from yesterday, this one is completely normal, though it resembles clusters of blue crystals. I've not seen one in person before. When she reaches out to touch it, I catch her wrist. "Just because it's pretty doesn't mean it isn't venomous."

Surprise and a hint of embarrassment flicker across her face. "Gotcha," she says humorlessly, shaking my hand away. I use a small net to scoop the slug up.

Suddenly, the wind is screaming. The squall appears without warning. The torrent of rain is almost on us. Like ghosts, fat-bottomed clouds charge over the mirror shine of an ocean in pieces. The gust has increased but also changed direction, shifting us off course. My hat is the first victim, swept into the air. Through my boots and the boat's hull, I feel the ocean's powerful swell.

"Mom!" I yell, dropping the sea slug back in the water. "We need to get going."

She emerges, wearing one of Dad's thin sweaters, and smiles. My stomach drops. *When the water keeps rising*, Bà Oanh's fortune had said. Mom is giddy. She presses the sleeves against her nose, breathing in any trace of him, as though he will be here soon and she must compare. The nets sag heavily in the wild, jarring landscape. I'm afraid *Wild Things* won't make it. It wouldn't be the first time a boat's caught off guard.

My boots slide on deck, but I manage to stay upright. "I'm pulling them up," I tell Mom. Maybe it's not the right thing to do, but my dad isn't here to tell me otherwise. I have instinct, and this one tells me to run.

"I think I see something!" Covey shouts, eyes as dark as the ocean behind her. Inside the cabin, Mom stirs, straining her neck to look too, as if our family might crawl over the deck, limbs as sure as a crab's. "Stop, I need to get it in the net first." Covey has thrown open the freezer to get her crossbow.

I've paused craning up the nets. Rain slashes down, drenching our hair and clothes. I try to blink my vision better, but rain has rendered my glasses useless. The nets are dark masses on either side, the load indistinguishable. "You can't be serious. You'll miss." My hand touches the crane again. "Worse, you'll get caught up."

"Don't know 'til I try," she says, a hint of seasickness on her pale face. She searches for the case of bolts. Spilling the nets' insides and going is the smartest option, but of course Covey's afraid of losing it. Whatever *it* is. The black-tailed gulls have long left us behind.

"*She can't kill them, Nhung.*" Mom stands at the cabin door, more subdued now and looking like a teenager in the oversize sweater. Trembling.

"She won't," I lie. Ignoring Covey's command, I crane one net first. If she's as good as Jimmy says, she'll strike it regardless. Even if it turns out to be yellowfin tuna. The boat tilts too much since I'm still shit at the controls. Hundreds of fish flop uselessly on deck. I prepare to drag the second net in, glancing over to make sure Covey's out of my way—but Mom has disappeared from the cabin.

Her arm sling is abandoned on the floor.

My mother is standing near the bow of the ship, the sweater's loose green fabric flapping as a kite. Close behind me, Covey is realizing something that I didn't immediately see.

"She took my knife," Covey says, breathless. Her book—her *stupid* book—is missing its bookmark. The pages have become a sopping mess of smeared words.

"She wants to cut the net," I say in a panic, though the storm compresses my voice down to a whisper. Swimming in the ocean at strong tide is already insane, but Mom will do it with a dislocated arm and limping leg. I am frozen in place, all the English words I have yet to teach her bubbling inside. *Pomegranate; triangle; sign on the dotted line; enclosure; don't go in; don't leave me behind too.*

The water surges, redder than I've ever seen it this far out, as if the algae bloom has grown in these short minutes.

Covey is a blur as she rushes to grab Mom. Mom shrieks and turns the knife toward Covey. What is she doing? My stupor breaks and, with wind howling against me, I dart forward. I pull Mom from behind, both away from Covey and the boat's edge. Thunder rattles my teeth. We spin, a fucked up little dance in the rain, grappling within the bow's limited space.

Mom's face is tilted away, but I can imagine it screwed up in furious determination, and those three moles gone. Her arm thrusts back, smacking me square in the chest. My feet catch the boat's lip, which is too low to save me. My hands grasp for someone who is not there, as Mom fights for the knife. I am falling; that second without ground or cushion or body tethering to the earth is oddly freeing. Lightning arches its back, a shock of white amongst the gray sky. It is the last thing I see before water explodes around me.

The ocean reaches inside before I remember to shut my mouth. In a half second, my glasses are gone. Now I'm a rag doll in a giant's bath. All sense of direction is lost; up or down is the same. It's noisier than you'd think, your ears under pressure.

Too fast, I am swallowed whole. This void has no light, and it is terribly cold. My limbs have stopped struggling because I am being held, a fish against the butcher block, in the water's grasp. I think about the animal Covey prepared, knife cutting through fat and skin to reach its pristine guts—the curiosity with which we treated it—as the sensation of being inspected pervades all my senses. I am at the center of this cold, dark universe.

The edges of my vision lighten, and I see them. All at once there are hands—too many—attached to arms, I think. They must be attached to something with muscle because they clutch at my body, tearing at my thick clothes. The water's gone too deep in the sacs of my lungs, in my aching gut. No sound and still my ears ring, each word like a needle to a balloon. A headache implodes within my skull, pulsing with the ferocity of a door slam. And even surrounded by water, I burn.

Let us in let us in let us in let us in let us in let us in

I fight, but do you know what it's like to fight an ocean? Laughable, futile; this is how I will die.

Let us in let us in—

"Noon!"

We break into the light. The squall rages all around, and I am only deadweight and barely blinking, but there she is—her dark lashes dripping with water. Was it her hands that held me? Covey grabs onto a buoy my mom has thrown overboard, and somehow we make it up. I am alive on the deck and spewing red water—the taste of earth and rot and salt. Chunks of algae are wedged in my teeth. The grittiness coats my tongue.

"*Spit it all out! Spit it all out!*" Mom shouts as she takes Covey's place, hitting my back. Familiar, but I can't pinpoint it. It's all a dream I can't remember. Apparently sober now, she points at Covey too. "Spit it out."

But I had felt Mom's hands through my shirt, the heat searing in the cold, unnatural. To her surprise, I grab them. Then I lay my hands across her head, her face, her throat. Under rain and fat tears, her pulse throbs with fever. I turn to Covey. "She's burning up."

6

I PUSH *WILD THINGS* to go faster than it's ever gone, shaking off rainwater in every rough lurch. Behind me, Mom might have mumbled "slow down" or "save them." My brain's too much in a frenzy to tell.

Finally, we reach the delta where the three rebuilt lighthouses stand. I head for the southeast's dock; there's a small house farther in, where its keepers Vinh and Jenn live. Covey and I lift Mom under each arm and haul her on this imitation of land. The solid ground makes my knees ache, but I do it for her. Everything, I do for her.

My fist slams against the door.

Moments later, it opens. "Oh my god, please tell me you brought real rice," Jenn says, her long black hair in a bun. "If I have to eat one more box of Uncle Ben's, I'll die." The joke's funny; we complain about our postapocalyptic rice selections in at least 50 percent of conversations when we stop by, but Mom is completely soaked on my shoulder. The woman's eyes flick first toward the stranger—Covey—then back at Mom. "Hurry, come in. VINH!" she shouts over her shoulder.

Vinh emerges from the back, alarm crossing his tanned face, but scoops Mom's arms over his to help her to the couch. It is a relief not to have to be the adult here. Jenn leaves the door open as she speaks in fast Khmer.

"My mom and I are staying here tonight," I say to Covey in a shaky breath. "Go back to *Wild Things*."

"But—"

"Please," I say, and it sounds pathetic. She'd saved me and I can't even say thank you. I am one disaster after another. "Covey, they don't know you." At this, she relents, and I shut the door. Gathered around the sofa, we watch the number on the thermometer hanging from Mom's lips climb to 103. Jenn takes the cap off a Tylenol bottle and pops three in Mom's mouth. Vinh hands Mom a glass of water, which she drinks greedily.

My mouth still tastes of wrecked fish as I recount the story starting from our visit to Jimmy's. By the end, Mom is slumped asleep against the sofa cushion. "She was going to jump in to cut the net," I say, still dazed as I rub a towel against my cheek. "I got in the way." Phrasing it that way makes it seem less hurtful; I basically had done it to myself. Mom didn't push me in, even by accident. "Covey saved me. But I think Mom had a fever before all this."

"Jimmy Boudreaux got a big government contract to be a small dick," Vinh says, scowling hard, while Jenn gently rolls Mom's trousers up to mid-thigh. In before times, Jenn had been a nurse. It's partly why she's so respected in the area. The other reason is she's bright and funny in multiple languages. She's not smiling now though.

The wound from the rusted nail at Jimmy's porch is angry red but doesn't seem worse than a scrape.

"Please tell me she got her tetanus booster in the last ten years," Jenn says. "Tiên ơi."

I'm speechless, stuck somewhere in my own ribs, as she explains how there's no cure for this bacterial infection. It can get worse. Vinh suggests driving three hours north, to the closest hospital.

"No," Mom interjects, awake after all. She's folded over in pain. The fever would've been easy to hide from me. We don't hug or touch most days. The muscle spasms she must've done her best to withstand. Maybe the worst of it has only just started. "I can't leave the boat behind."

I close my eyes. Once we leave it, there'll be no chance to get it back. Her condition is not good. Jimmy's deadline, the entire area shutting down, will happen. "Jenn?" I ask. Mom doesn't like that I call them by their first names, but it is how they prefer it. Adding Chú or Cô is too much, and Jenn's Cambodian, though she's well-versed in Viet too after living here for so long.

"The better treatment is metronidazole through an IV every six hours at the hospital," Jenn says so my mom can understand. "The alternative is penicillin. I have that, but the second you get worse, we go straight to the hospital. This is serious."

At Jenn's side, Vinh adds, "It's what Sang would want." Dad's spoken name melts the determination from Mom's face. Vinh and Jenn had done their best to dissuade Mom of her delusions about reincarnated bodies. They've seen Mom through the worst of her grief. Remembering Dad with me is too different for Mom, I think, because I knew him only as my parent. But Vinh knew him as well as Mom did. Vinh was his best friend. The way he and Dad told it, it was inevitable that they would be almost brothers. Their dads came to the US around the same time and settled in Texas, forming one of the earliest Vietnamese American fishing communities. They knew the water almost as well as they knew their homes. They left for Mercy together. It was and is not perfect, but our families chose to live here.

Jenn gets spare clothes for us to change into. While she helps Mom, I slip into their modest bedroom to change. The wet clothes pool at my feet. I draw an oversize tee over my body. It is Wilder's; he loved his indie bands. I'm surprised Jenn would let me borrow it. It's probably one of the few things they brought from their trailer, but like the dads, Wilder and I were raised to be best friends. After getting dressed, I pace a circle about the living room, near the bare shelves where they still have photographs of Wilder from the years before he ran away.

Me and Wilder and at least a dozen rubber ducks in an inflatable pool.

Me and Wilder wearing twin Halloween costumes.

Me and Wilder on our first day of third and fourth grade.

Then came the later ones, middle school on, where Wil and I sat a distance apart. Me with a carefully arranged skirt, him with new, rowdy friends. To the camera, we shared a fake smile. Wherever he is, I hope he's okay. It's the homeliness, the domesticity, the way the frames have collected dust, whereas Mom's pictures of our family are freshly polished, that causes a different type of ache in my chest. Vinh and Jenn are stationary as they wait on the off chance their son returns. My life is on the go, chasing after dreams.

Soon, I will have nothing at all. I thought I could trick Jimmy and my mom at the same time. Fulfill a wish with a lie. But I let Mom go too far.

"I'm going to talk to Jimmy's daughter," I announce back in the other room. Not waiting for permission or a response, I step outside into the drizzle.

The tiny specks kiss my cheeks. Barefoot, I cross quickly on the metal island. The other lighthouses blink at the delta's fingertips, manned by a Mr. Williams and an elderly couple we affectionally called the Clauses. We know them, but we only shop with Vinh and Jenn. They appreciate the Café du Monde coffee and condensed milk we always trade for. Those yellow containers can brighten up any space, their kitchen and our boat included.

I hop onto the boat, frowning as my toes nudge against slimy fish. I narrowly avoid a live crab on my way to the cabin where Covey lounges on a bunk bed, reading as usual. At my entrance, she puts the book aside.

"How's your mom?" she asks. Her hair is mostly dry now, stuck in clumps. She's changed to her extra pair of clothes.

"Breathing," I say. "Jenn thinks she's got tetanus. You know, from the nail Jimmy slammed my mom on." Covey's expression doesn't change—no hint of shame. I'm learning that she will never apologize for her father's mistakes, the same way I won't for Mom's. And why should we, actually? "She can't travel in her condition. It's between me and you now, but you saw for yourself how there's nothing out there. Is there no way your dad will let us go?"

"But I did see something," says Covey. "I don't know what it was, but there was a flash of movement in all that chaos. It was big." Her convictions ping a memory of the water, of it swirling around me and the darkness that filled me. Of the deep, relentless cold, of being so close to dying and yet feeling like I've been seen. There were words and hands, but it must've been Covey rescuing me. "My dad doesn't do charity unless it's for church, and he gave that up a long time ago."

"And you?" I ask, exhausted and angry. I rummage through the cabinet for my box. "When did you start screwing people over?" I slip on the fortune teller's glasses. The world slots into place once more.

Color rises on her cheeks as she snarls, "I am not like my dad."

And she isn't; I know she isn't. Jimmy Boudreaux wouldn't risk his life saving me from drowning in the middle of a storm. But that doesn't mean she is innocent. "You just let him do whatever he wants, right? As long as you're okay." It's obvious she is important to him as family, no matter what she says. She rises above the rest in his eyes, and yet she falls in line, burying herself in distractions while others do the dirty work.

"What's your point?"

"You can talk some sense into him. Let us, everyone go. Mercy is done. The algae can have it."

"I can't get him away from this place any more than you can with your mom," Covey says, turning that stubborn look on me. She jumps to a question I didn't expect. "Why don't you know how to swim? Your family shrimp for a living."

Of course I should know how to swim, but no one has ever taught me. Dad did not want a daughter on his boat, and we work in the water, not play in it. I can't bring myself to admit that it was either a deliberate choice or a careless oversight by my parents. "I guess it isn't ladylike," I say, which only makes me look stupid.

"Well, you're definitely not a lady," Covey says, and my heart—despite itself—beats. "You're a shark. Like me. We're meant to swim but not inside tanks."

Is it a compliment or an insult? For one, my nose is flat with wide nostrils, so she should've been specific and said a hammerhead. Secondly, sharks eat their own siblings in utero. If my little brother is alive, he is the last person on earth I would kill.

Covey towers over me, but I'm not scared. "Compared to the ocean, Mercy is tiny. It's easier to trap something in a smaller area," she says. "We know the general area where Dr. Delgado was last seen, so we should start there. Us, alone. And if that plan doesn't work . . . we go our separate ways, before Jimmy finds out."

The implication in her words stuns me. I work my fingers into the tight knit of my sleeves and find that my lack of fingernails makes it much less satisfying. I hadn't expected Covey to propose screwing her dad over before I did. Nevertheless, I'm only experienced in chasing shadows or hauling in seafood. Every specimen we shared with Jimmy had been bycatch. "I shrimp. That's all I know how to do. I haven't ever trapped an animal."

"But I have," Covey says. "I know many different ways to do it."

I wave at the collection of knives and other sharp objects she's laid out during our absence. "I haven't noticed. Really."

She laughs too, but her words come out bitter. "You learn with a dad like mine."

I feel bad almost immediately, but I can't separate the two Boudreaux in my mind. Covey had restrained me while Jimmy threw Mom around at the shack. "Why should I trust you?"

"Because"—Covey hesitates, but only for a second—"I'm doing this for my mom too." All this time, I'd assumed her other parent wasn't in the picture, but now I can see the ghost haunting her. This moment feels like an omen, the cliffside to a steep fall. "She went missing three months ago."

Instinctively, I look toward the lighthouse where Mom is. I think about what it would be like if she disappeared—physically, without a trace. Three months this girl has been waiting for a chance to find her mom. I realize that's much longer than the scientist has been gone. There's no census of who decided to stay in Mercy after Hurricane Arlene, which means no one really knows how many people have vanished. "Did your dad look for her?"

"When isn't he watching over us?" Covey says. By the regret on her face, I know she didn't mean to give that away.

"Do you think he did something?" I ask.

"She thought he was having her followed again, because he was convinced she was cheating, but I was there that night she disappeared." Covey paces the small cabin. "No noise, except for a soft knocking. I thought it was like a tree branch." Her thick brows are drawn together. "She'd been running these daylong errands. I wondered what she was doing. Maybe there was someone else, but she would've told me. We always, *always* leave together. So, this is something I have to do without my dad knowing."

Her stoic mask has broken. There's distress all over the sharp lines of her face. She looks like a child. I wonder if she feels as trapped as I do. "You think she might be in Mercy," I say.

"It's all I've got to go on. I need every day I can get."

After a long pause, I nod. For right now, it is enough. "Okay. We do it your way now, since mine obviously was a disaster."

"But you know this"—she waves at the lighthouse and its singular island—"can't be our base of operations. It takes too much time to make the trip twice a day. If we run out of gas, which we will, we'd have to paddle."

"Then we camp close to Mercy," I say, without thinking any more about it. It's the logical choice. "We follow the trail of clues, starting with Dr. Delgado. We look for your mom too. We find them, or we find what got them. If neither, then that's it. We go our separate ways."

Covey nods her agreement, the truce solidified between us. A dull weight settles in my gut. Mercy was always going to come for me. I can't stay on its waters without paying respects to the town. It's always calling me home.

7

LAST NIGHT I DREAMED I was a boy. Like my dad, I had broad shoulders and a flat chest with a tattoo of a boat made of bones—the ink more green than black. My wide hips and anything seemingly extraneous had been carved away, left to stink on the carpet. There was a lump in my throat, the gentle slope of it bobbing every time I laughed. It wasn't a precursor to a sob. My brother was there too, smiling.

Our parents loved me.

With gentle hands, Mom shaved off my hair. Felt the shape of my skull, only slightly uneven from leaving me on my back too long as a baby. I whispered that I was sorry. She forgave me for being me. Then Dad clapped me on the shoulder and said we would go out shrimping together. He'd only taken Jay before, and I could've drowned in that senseless joy, of standing and finding myself tall, someone that could finally be seen in a mirror. A twin to my dad.

But when I glanced back at the pile of flesh with my stretch marks, I thought, that's me too. Can I be everything and nothing at the same time? Extra fat, extra parts, narrow bones. A shadow you know is there but whose shape remains unseen until it emerges on concrete. I want a body that's easy to manipulate.

What a gift that no one sees inside my mind. What a curse that no one sees inside my mind.

Maybe that's why I'm standing in front of the bathroom mirror, staring back at the girl with a shirt hanging around their neck. The reflection shows someone with white roots in their hair and fear in their eyes. This person is going home; they should be happy. But they're only smiling with their lips. She touches the edge of her rib, where a rash has bloomed at the edges of a perfect cut.

I don't remember getting it after I fell in the water, but everything had been so chaotic. No jagged skin or blood as you'd expect from an accident. Pink as the roses behind our old trailer, the rash colors my skin. It itches. It begs to be scraped off, pulled apart with a sick *crackle*, like Velcro on a teddy bear. Openable at any time to be stuffed or emptied. Maybe then, maybe then—

"You okay in there?" Jenn asks from the other side of the door.

"I'm fine. Head just hurts," I answer. There's no time for an active imagination. Nothing is fighting to surface from my body. After washing my hands, I join the three adults in the main living space. They hadn't liked the plan I shared over dinner the night before. Hearing about Covey's search for her mom made it more agreeable since she's less likely to sell us out to Jimmy. We don't have other real choices.

They need me and Covey to do this right. Jenn seems to be on the precipice of saying something, and I know it's about Wil, but she presses her lips into a line. Her favorite books, after which he was named, remain dust-free on a shelf. I imagine Jenn running her fingers over the author's name, too afraid to look at her son's pictures instead. They haven't spoken about him all night, but his absence is a pulse throughout their house. If Mercy shuts down, they can stay as beacons for passing ships, but it's unlikely that Wilder could find his way through the road closures. If they leave, they will not know where else to wait for him. While Vinh tests out twin satellite radios unearthed from a gray storage container, Jenn goes through the kitchen once more for anything that might be useful in Mercy, where electricity and running water remain unreliable.

I have to say goodbye to Mom. She sits on a lone chair by the door, packed bag at her feet. Immobilized by how her jaw seizes and the throbbing pain in her leg, she had to admit she's in no condition to travel. Truth be told, she'd been a liability long before these injuries. I have no one to blame but myself, having baited her to press on. Maybe if I had tried harder to wake her up to reality, we would've left Mercy. Maybe if I didn't squeeze myself into a box, she wouldn't have become so accustomed to not seeing me.

The rash twinges on my side. "*I'm ready to go,*" I say.

"*No,*" she replies as she struggles to stand. "*You're not.*" She puts the backpack over my shoulder. Mom tips a white sun hat decorated with sunflowers over my ears. We hadn't had time to dye my roots black. From her pocket she removes the key to our boat. I'd given it back to her since there's no use for it once we're on land or in the channels too small for the trawler. Gently, she puts the necklace around my throat, just as she had the day we found Bà Oanh's rotting body. She palms the key and reaches for me.

"I don't need it, Mom."

She shakes her head no. "*When you start thinking too much, you have to remind yourself to forget it all.*" Mom wants me to outrun the memories and worries; be less myself. At the same time, she's giving me the key to *Wild Things*, stranding her while she's healing. She's *trusting* me with Dad's most precious possession. More than that, she's showing that she is not going to leave either. When I return, she'll be here. Her hand feels papery thin and dry in my hands.

Together we stage the magic trick. "*Một, hai, ba,*" I repeat after her as we spin the key. Without fanfare or apology, my mother slips her arms around me. The pendant lays twisted between us. Her hug is tentative, then too sure at my ribcage, then it loosens again. She smells wild—salt spray, seaweed, just a hint of rot, and the last dregs of watermelon shampoo. I hold her too, the shock of the touch turning into something warm, fuzzy.

I soften against her, chin tucked into her neck.

"*You don't need to hurt them, con. They don't deserve more pain.*"

The sweet moment blurs at the edges as the ambush becomes obvious. Although I've made it clear how I'll do anything to save us, she's worried about our imaginary family. It's petty to measure the weight of our grief, the length of our recovery, when Mom's pain borders on a language of its own. How can I compare when she lived that many years with Dad? When the child she prayed for was ripped away? I lost them before I'd even stopped growing.

This is what I remember: Dad's nets spread in the spring grass, a river of the strangest green on green. His deft brown hands knitting fixes to the nylon. Jay and I would take turns diving onto the net, the coolest thing in the heat. It smelled as salty as the sea.

What I didn't know then: I was lying on something that had caused thousands of deaths. All so we could eat.

Mom releases me, tension now plastered across her face. She whispers, "*Never go back to the cove.*" The warning hits like a physical strike. I step back. Too ashamed by how she found me there, Mom never mentions Chelsea's Cove. We pretend I've never sneaked out to go to a cove party. There's no reason to bring it up now, unless she thinks I'm foolish enough to visit for nostalgia's sake. No, no, I'm overthinking it as always—she simply doesn't want me to search everywhere for the monsters.

"I'll do what I need to," I say. I'll become a shark if it means we get to live freely. Clutching the backpack, I leave. Covey's waiting on a skiff at the end of the docks, her traps organized as neatly as possible. The last thing I see when I look back at the lighthouse is Mom's disappointment, her closed eyes.

I've never been the survivor my mom wanted.

8

IT USED TO BE that standing on one side of the levee, I could never hear the Mississippi River. I'd thought my hearing was bad or whatever, but it wasn't. The sound blended into everyday life, like the old motor in Dad's truck or possums digging through our bins. It was the current of our lives, the background singer to Mom's songs.

All I hear now is the tide. It laps against the skiff we borrowed from Jenn and Vinh. It crackles with plastic—trash bags against cans against shipping packages. There's a slapping sound too, of some quick fish splitting the water, then disappearing before I can see it. The tide glows innocently. Covey and I don't talk as we row upriver toward Mercy, where dusk falls on us fast. My arms burn as I switch a flashlight on. "Let's just use the motor now," I say. "The place is close, and if we've got a light and this"—I wave at the bioluminescent algae—"they'll see us anyway."

Whether I mean *they* as people or *they* as monsters, I don't know. All that matters is my neck tingling with the sensation that something wants to find us as badly as we want to find them, and we're on a boat so small that a sneeze will tip us over. Sweating, Covey turns on the motor and follows the bright beam I shine on the riverbank.

The light catches on sunken boughs and reeds as thick as fingers, then the aging trunk of a black willow tree. Nailed to it are words and pictures stored within Ziploc bags. Some notices are new with fresh white paper, but many more are smeared with ink. Newspaper clippings curl behind plastic, having yellowed over time.

KAILEY, IF YOU'RE OUT THERE, FIND ME IN HOUSTON

LOST FERRET: Brown, long, likes cheese, friendly.
DO NOT kill.

Dads waiting 4 u in tennasee
NEVER ANSWER THE KNOCKS IN THE NIGHT
Rest In Peace, Babe! PRAY
GIRLS GUYS & GRANNIES: we are still open! go to—
Have you seen this dog?

Silver coins fill the tree hole, choking out any moss that may have spawned. A wishing tree rather than a well. It seems as futile as Mom's search of the wide open ocean, given how few people have stayed around. The Mississippi River touches ten states, all more livable than bloom-ridden Mercy. In the hurricane's aftermath, many escaped to these neighboring places and put down new, battered roots. And yet, some 700 people have held onto the hope that our loved ones will find us, hope that there is a heaven or a place to escape reality, hope that we can save someone else. It's all so fragile that we need sandwich bags to stuff them in.

It takes another ten minutes to reach the cabin I'm thinking of. It hunches over, partly blown in by weather, and the risen water cuts any leeway its stilt legs gave it before. Its boardwalk isn't much more than slumped wood drooping into the flood. The cabin doesn't look stable enough to live in, which makes it perfect. We pull in as close as possible to the porch and throw torn weeds and branches over the skiff so it's harder to spot.

I've killed the light, so Covey works under the moon, jiggling the door handle until it creaks into the sweltering night. Just days ago, Jimmy Boudreaux had hurt my mom on a porch not that much different from this one. And here I am, breaking and entering a shitty cabin with his daughter to investigate a series of drownings that may be an accident or the sinister activities of unseen monsters lurking in the water. Life is hilariously not funny like that.

"Fuck!" Covey curses right before I slam into her back and send us sprawling forward. There's a shift in her body, a turn that directs our fall to the side. The rain has cleansed some of the stale air away, but a hint of rot lingers and, frustratingly, her sunscreen up close.

"Why'd you stop so sudden?" I ask as I get on my feet.

Covey dusts her shirt and shorts off. The flooring is punched through by one almost perfect circle. The murky water is hidden under a layer of thick red algae, disturbed where it had swallowed Covey's leg up to the knee. "We should camp out in Mercy proper, don't you think? There're still standing houses there."

"No," I say too quickly. "We should stay on the water, where it's easier to go." It is a half truth, since the bigger reason is I'm not ready to step foot back in town.

For a second, her brow furrows, an argument brewing behind her eyes. But then she peels off the boots and walks barefoot to the other side of the shack. Someone has stripped anything useful, cleaning out drawers and cabinets. Flannel blankets are piled by a couch. In the rear room, there's bed springs but no mattress. A cross hangs above the door. This was someone's fishing cabin. In my old life, I probably rode my bike past their actual house.

Eager to distract myself from the dread churning my stomach, I unpack the bag Mom put together for me. I've never been this far away from her, so she's thought of everything. It's meticulously organized, with a whole gas stove, portioned food, porcelain bowls, extra clothes, and two pairs of chopsticks. There are candles too, since batteries are valuable. I light several on a side table, careful to remove errant paper and anything that might catch fire. It smells strongly of pine trees, a real Christmas-in-the-summertime occasion.

While I set up for dinner, Covey flicks on the radio. The sound is fuzzy as she flips through the channels. She settles on the tail-end of a weather report.

—cast models project that the tropical depression will gain wind speed as it curves northwest from the eastern Gulf. Residents

of Plaquemines Parish are encouraged to make evacuation plans early in the event of its transition into a hurricane, as road conditions remain battered after the historic Hurricane Arlene. Here with us, the governor—

I switch the radio off since a weather forecast isn't exactly mood-improving music. "We're fucked as it is," I tell Covey. "I don't need a report on it."

"Then it's your duty to talk," she says, taking an oyster from the open cooler. "It's creepily quiet around here."

I listen, and of course, she's right. There are no cicadas, frogs, or birds, only the river swelling beneath us. "Alright then," I say. She's slipped a knife into the gray shell, flicking the meaty body loose and into her mouth. "Oysters are alive as you eat them." Covey waits for the punchline, swallowing slowly, but my smile widens. I can feel sand between my teeth. "Especially when kept fresh. That"—I point to her knife wedged in another oyster—"cuts the muscle attaching them to the shell but it doesn't kill them right away." I run my fingers over my throat, then sternum, and stomach, a trail of sweat soaked through the sweater. "They're alive and screaming all the way down."

Taking a long breath, Covey sets both oyster and knife down. "I really didn't need to know that. You're a menace."

I pluck the meaty body out of its shell and slurp it down, quelling the emptiness in my gut. "Don't you hunters have a code? Honor the whole carcass or something?"

"You really think my dad had a code? He'd catch alligators for their skin, and just toss the rest," Covey says as she works on another shell. "My mom had one. Don't kill anything that can smile." It's the first time since the lighthouse that she's mentioned her mom. She looks embarrassed to have shared such a tender detail.

"Well, I guess I'm giving too much credit to the man who coined 'double the crab, double the yum,'" I say. Jimmy had made up the ridiculous slogan for the malformed crabs we caught last year.

Covey lets out a bark of laughter. The sound's so sudden and unexpected that I flinch. "I told him it was a shit idea. The toxicology stuff from the science teams says the algae doesn't produce the same kind of toxins found in red tides, so he's convinced this bloom is different from other ones. Like evolution on steroids, but for seafood you can immediately buy at $29.99 a pound."

The bloom had started innocuously, just a hint of red after Hurricane Arlene, until we woke up one day with it choking ponds and bigger waterways alike. It'd been unprecedented, how quickly it spread. Accusations were thrown all over the place—it was an experiment gone wrong, it was a foreign intervention, it was us sinning. I knew it couldn't be humanmade because for a long time, everyone still wanted to make money. More shrimp, more fish, more everything to fuel the billion-dollar industry. Only now, whatever's happening in Mercy is enough to scare officials away.

"Our first stop should be the scientists' camp," says Covey, "then the Oliviers'."

At the name, my ears perk. "The librarian?" Mrs. Olivier is nearly seventy years old and has lived in the parish all her life. For the short time I attended ninth grade, she allowed me to hide out in the library during lunchtime. She's the only adult to have asked what was wrong, though the words could never come out of my mouth. After I dropped out, she even mailed me a sweet letter.

Covey nods. "Yeah. When the science team first set up in Mercy, she was their guide. They used the school gym." The gymnasium had been the school's pride, and despite all our sports teams being terrible, most of our funding had gone to remodeling it the year before the storm. At least someone got use out of it. "Of everyone, she probably knows most about what they were up to and where. That'll help us decide where to set up the traps."

Over our meal, we talk more than we did in the entire four days on *Wild Things* together. Our next move decided, I tell her about other weird sea facts just to witness her disgust. She responds by reciting every single book-better-than-movie adaptation. It may have been forced at first, but then it becomes natural to talk over each other about nothing at all. Eventually the exhaustion of the last day and a half catches up—almost drowning, Mom's fever, our deal—and we curl up in separate blankets across from each other. I scratch my ribs and try to untangle the nerves that rise in the absence of distracting conversation.

I listen to the rippling water beneath and around us. I imagine the many veins—canals, rivers, streams—that connect people to bigger bodies of water. There are sawtooth masts rising from the ocean floor, like darkened shark fins. Centuries of shipwrecks are collected down there, haunted houses big and small, and every storm drags more into it, creating whole underwater cities. Mercy was drowned, then revived. Released from the ocean's grasp but with a promise: *soon*. I can't predict what we will find there.

drip
　　　drip
　　　　　　　drip
　　　　　　　　drip
　　　　　drip

The water runs steadily, each tap like a finger digging inside my head. I squeeze my eyes shut and roll over, cheek against a rough pillow, and try to ignore the twin pulses.

　　　drip,　　　*drip*

"Jay, did you leave the faucet on again?" I mumble. He's always rushing back from the bathroom at night to our shared room, fleeing from the dark. With still-damp hands, he would pull the blanket over his head, the fabric darkening in spots.

drip drip drip

If we leave it, Mom will scold us in the morning.

Drip.

No answer.

Drip.

He is dead.

I open my eyes. I am not in our old bedroom, and he is not curled on a mattress on the floor. There's the fresh pain of remembering that twists deep inside my head, then right on my mouth as I choke on a silent scream. So much of the cabin is a blur, but I see it. I see him.

From the hole in the floor, my little brother watches me. He is all soaked, wrinkled skin and no eyes, but he's watching me.

drip,   drip

I scramble all around for my glasses. I slam the pair on my nose and turn around immediately. The water's surface wavers, but it is empty, bodiless. It crackles with bioluminescence. Covey's curled up on the opposite side, snoring softly, as if this is only happening in my mind.

Water droplets glisten on the wood, then smear under my shaking hands. The algae is blood-red and rotten on my fingertips, *real*, but that doesn't mean I didn't hallucinate. Whatever it was, it'd been small—as small as a drowned little boy.

Why would I see Jay now, after all this time?

Chest tightening, breath loose, laboring, I rush as quietly as possible to the tiny bedroom in the back. I don't shut the door but I go as far away as I can from the shack's gaping wound, pacing back and forth in front of the dresser. Mercy has always brought out the worst in me. Alone, especially. Already I am falling apart. I am pathetic. I am stupid. And god I *itch*. From the rash on my side to my shoulders, all drenched with sweat, to my neck which pulses intensely. I want to tear everything off, and I *am* tearing my sweater off, when my fingertips touch something wet. Like a flower, the side of my neck blooms. It gulps in air. I tamp down a scream.

I look in the mirror above the dresser, where the reflection of a girl has lifted a ridge of their skin. Red capillaries pulse underneath, desperate for water, like fresh trout on a butcher block. My eyes are just as desperate. Confused. The wet arches of this new organ shudder, yet I am breathing through my own wide nostrils. The gills slot back into an undisturbed neck when I let them go.

This is all wrong. I am dreaming. I am still the same teenage girl from before.

I close a fist around my necklace, Mom's simple spell on my dry lips. "Một, hai, ba." It's time to forget and not overthink. I hold on to the mantra with all my strength, the key cutting into my palm.

9

BY SUNRISE, I'VE DECIDED I am sane but stressed. And although I most definitely do not have gills, because humans do not have gills, I stick a large medicated pain patch on either side of my neck. It soothes the tenderness there, and the hint of menthol reminds me of home. Mom likes to say I've had an overactive imagination since I was little. Before Jay was born, I had insisted on sleeping in the same bed as her. The darkness was watching me, as it always had from the crack in my closet before a light switched on, during that dreamlike state of fading away. In those precious seconds, coats would become monsters. Multiple heads sprouted from the shadows, and spindly fingers crawled through blank space for my throat. In the dark, you can never be sure you're alone, or maybe being alone is what makes it worse.

Whatever reaches from the other side would only find you.

I think about the ocean and the seven miles down to the deepest part of her. How light doesn't reach beyond 3,280 feet.

I think about it the way people imagine their favorite place, like a garden where you know exactly which rocks the frogs hide under, but that too is a trick of my imagination. I had fallen in the ocean but certainly not that far. Few humans have ever explored that deep.

The hole in the cabin floor sits innocently as ever when Covey and I leave to check out the school. She's said nothing about last night or the minty additions to my neck. Being a geriatric weirdo has its advantages. And since I'm local, she also needs me to get around Mercy. Covey and I trudge into town by way of a broken levee. The lowest areas have at least a half foot of water above it, strewn with garbage, but patches of dry-ish land dotted the landscape. The algae closer to the port has been thick and persistent, but here it is wild, growing lace-like across the buildings, similar to the fortune teller's place. My uneasiness grows as more familiar places pop up. Everywhere I look, there is only need—a desperation slipping back over my bones, as comfortable as a too-warm coat. Even now, this place holds memories. Power.

We pass a rainbow-painted food stand that had opened only in summers. Wilder and I would save our quarters up until we each could buy a small snowball, his red and mine blue. We'd trade bitefuls until our taste buds couldn't tell cherry from raspberry. We stopped when adults started calling them *dates* and other kids teased us about *kissing* through our plastic spoons. My chest wants to split open. I overthink and drift away; this is why I need a magic trick to forget.

"Is it ridiculous that the thing I miss the most through all of this is the dollar store?"

I come back to reality. "What?"

A dreamy look has settled on Covey's face. "The knick-knacks, the half-off almost-expired milk that's perfect for pancakes, and greeting cards with bad art and even worse jokes." It's hard to take this sentimentality seriously when she has her crossbow slung over a shoulder "just in case."

"I guess I would kill for Sour Patch Kids or a Warhead right now. Maybe even Smarties," I say, a white lie since even the prospect of death can't compel me to eat those dusty pennies.

"Do you think it's picked through?" Covey asks. Her eyes drift upward to my sun hat. "We can look for some hair dye at least, if you want."

So she's noticed my white roots after all. I tug on the choppy ends which are brittle from repeated dye jobs. "Won't change anything anyway. I've gone prematurely gray for good." I gesture at our surroundings. "Stress." Not a complete lie, of course. My hair had turned white overnight, a few weeks after returning from Chelsea's Cove. I'm glad for an excuse to change the subject when a brick building with blown-in windows comes into view. "There's the school." There's an abundance of rippling American flags and rusting tables. The Oliviers live across the street in an old stilt-style house that made Mrs. Olivier's commute easy when school was still open. Now there aren't enough school-age kids to justify running it.

We push our way through the heavy outer doors closest to us. It's the wing for the elementary grades, so crafts projects plaster the walls. Lights dangle from the ceiling haphazardly, and the septic stench from red algae pervades the halls, despite the building's being dry. I lead us down the corridor where it'll branch off to the gymnasium. The hair on the back of my neck rises, but it's just the googly eyes from the poster boards following us. "This place is creepy," Covey says, dodging loose macaroni and fuzzy balls that have fallen from their respective projects. We pass classrooms with alphabet rugs, handsome wood cubby shelves, and clear toy boxes, all neatly abandoned.

The gymnasium is a different story. It's barely recognizable from my school days. Tents section off the large space into makeshift labs and sleeping quarters. There are refrigerators, microscopes, and several machines I can't name. Cards are spread out on a fold-out table in a casual sitting area. The generators must have been dragged off by residents when the science team left in a hurry.

Strangest are the tanks sitting on the far back wall. We wander in from the outskirts. The largest tank is taller than me and full of murky blue water. At the bottom are tiny, spotted cream-colored blobs that, upon closer inspection, I realize are jellyfish. An array of marine animals fills the smaller tanks, but they share one trait: none are moving. In these artificial environments, where everything from temperature to the pH level must be maintained, they float listlessly.

"They left them behind to die." My words are colored in hurt. I place a hand against the largest tank with the dead jellyfish. A small sign affixed to the front with tape reads *Mastigias papua*. "These are special jellyfish," I say, memory jogged from a TV show. "They live on the opposite side of the planet in this lagoon. Papua? Palau?"

Covey bends in half to squint at the gelatinous globs at the tank's bottom. "What are they doing here then?"

Plenty of jellyfish—cannonballs, moon jellies, and sea net-
tles to name a few—live in close proximity within the Gulf of
Mexico. It would've been easy to catch one far out from the
bloom haunting our shores. So why go through the effort of
transporting jellyfish from halfway around the world? Their
research activities must've required the *Mastigias papua* for
them to spare no expense. I rack my brain for what the TV pro-
gram said about these jellyfish—something about constantly
floating back and forth at the surface during the day, then down
at night. A peculiar movement pattern . . .

"I thought they were here to study algae," Covey adds, her
thinking scowl on.

"I mean it's all connected, right? Paleontologists often work
with geologists to study fossil records and rock layers. All things
in nature are connected. Oceans have plants and the animals
that eat them or live around them," I say. Despite my sound
reasoning, I'm unnerved by the dead animals too.

"There's another tank under this sheet," says Covey. It had
escaped notice with all the wildlife rotting in the other tanks. Her
hand grasps the sheet, then yanks it away. "What the fuck." We
stagger back, sheet forgotten on the ground. Red is splattered all
over the glass, obscuring the view inside. It appears viscous, as if
the innards of an animal found its way outside. Imploded.

Could another animal have done whatever happened in the
tank? And what could it do to us?

I pick up a thick bristled brush lying on the ground. "Let's
see what was inside," I say, approaching the tank. It's piqued my
curiosity, despite the ghastly scene. The scientists had been on
the pulse of something before they got scared. My neck tingles

underneath the medicated patches. What if there is some truth to the rumors about monsters? What if—

I squash the thought with a count of một, hai, ba.

Covey hovers close, crossbow tilted at the tank's lip.

A chair screeches behind us.

Whirling around, we watch a seat at the folding table pull away. The difference is miniscule, attributable to a strong gust if we'd been outside on a porch or if the tablecloth moved at all. The darkness shields whatever's lurking beneath. Covey notches a bolt in. "Stay out of my way," she mutters to me, which—*rude*. I have no interest in being impaled.

A splotch shoots out from the table, and Covey's bolt immediately follows. It misses, and she recovers quickly, following the shadowy mass. She's much more sure-footed on land. I take the other route, holding the brush as a weapon, and glimpse the creature skittering from desk leg to desk leg.

It's bulbous and thick-skulled, moving as quick as a snake tongue. Limbs spread far, then retreat. There's a sheen to its reddish pink skin. On either side of its rounded body, large gills flare open and closed.

Covey's shoulder blades are taut as she takes aim. This time she will not miss.

"Wait!" I yell. The bolt quivers, as if about to rocket away, but she—surprisingly—stops. My fingers have curled over her shoulder. It's warm. I let go immediately. "It's just an octopus."

Her face shifts from concentration to pure "what the fuck." *What the fuck, indeed.* I glance at the series of tanks where one is, in fact, empty. The octopus had escaped, maybe when it realized it would starve. I move toward its new hiding spot.

"Don't touch it," Covey warns.

"An octopus can only live out of water for a max of sixty minutes. This one has no idea where it's going." I roll my sleeve high and grab a bucket to fill with water. A neon-yellow Post-it is stuck on the tank's front, FRANK spelled out in big block letters. I drag the bucket toward the noisy animal. "Here, octo, octo," I coo. It squirms in place, as if embarrassed for me. I tip the bucket over to leave a wet trail and then refill it. It takes a while for the octopus to emerge, crawling across the ground in a freaky display of muscly arms with powerful suctions to reach what must feel like an oasis in this gymnasium.

As much as I like octopi, I don't know what their tank conditions should be. They also have venom in their beaks, which is sort of like a mouth made of jagged shells, so handling it any closer is a big nope. "What should we do?" I ask.

"I mean we could eat it."

She withers under my gaze. Most people don't know that octopi can solve mazes, get themselves out of jars, and yes, escape tanks. They're intelligent.

"We will finish searching this building. We will go see Mrs. Olivier. Then, maybe, if your traps have caught anything at the cabin, I'll bring a snack back *for* Frank."

Now that we'd expended all our nervous energy on chasing an actual octopus around, calm has overtaken me. Drawing close to the large tank again, I finally see that it's not blood or guts stuck to the sides at all. It's algae, but different from the wet carpet on our waterways or mosslike growth on land. I scrub the side of the tank with the brush until there's a square window to look through. The center, for lack of a better description, resembles a brain. There are rivets, and dips, and pale polyps in the mass occupying the tank. "Coral reef," I say. "But it's all bleached out . . . I mean, I don't think it's the same kind of algae?"

There's a question in Covey's expression.

"Coral reef get their color from algae that live inside of them. When it's too hot, or the ocean is too acidic, they die like that. The corals get stressed and expel the algae but that's not what is on the inside of the tank." No book or show ever talked about being able to see that type of algae at least. They are tiny organisms. Coral reefs are diverse ecosystems of their own; to section some into an aquarium is sacrilegious. They're already dying at an accelerated pace.

"I think the only answers we're gonna get will be in what else the scientists left behind." Covey points to the filing cabinets and stacks of paper. We decide to focus primarily on Dr. Delgado's desk, which has its own gargantuan mountain of notebooks. I notice that they like stickers—they're stuck on everything from their computer to notepads to to-do lists. I pocket a working GPS unit.

Everything that looks remotely interesting gets shoved in my backpack. In a folder titled LABS with a sticker of a butterfly wearing glasses, I find a list of nine locations. Some documents already have specimen findings. The lingo is difficult to understand, and Delgado writes in a very mad-scientist type of shorthand, as if they can't keep up with their thoughts. But near the bottom of the list, an unexplored place: Mercy Cove.

10

WE'RE MULLING OVER THE list as we cross the street to the Oliviers' stilt-style house. I try to keep my face neutral any time Covey mentions Mercy Cove. She wants to check out all the locations eventually, for any trace of Delgado or the thing that may have taken them. I press my fingers around the key on my necklace. I don't have to think about it now. We still have Mrs. Olivier to question, yet it feels like I'm in a funnel. Mercy had patiently waited for my return to spring everything on me.

We trudge up the rickety staircase. Laundry as dry as cardboard hangs on a sagging line across the deck. After untangling ourselves from the clothes, I knock on the door. There's no answer at first, and I'm afraid we'll find what we did at the fortune teller's, but a scraping noise draws nearer. Mrs. Olivier's middle-aged son, Travis, opens the door. He blinks several times as the sun casts a glow on his deep brown skin. His face doesn't register who I am, but he recognizes Covey from his work at the harbor. His eyes flicker to her crossbow, then back. "How can I help you?" he asks. There's a humming sound deeper in the house.

"We're here helping out my dad, you know, about why the research team left so suddenly." So she isn't telling him everything. I stay silent. "Mrs. Olivier was their guide. We'd love to chat with her."

If it'd been only me at the door, Travis surely would have turned me away. But Covey had mentioned her dad, and no one denies Jimmy Boudreaux what he wants. Travis lets us into the dark entryway. There's a vase of fake flowers on a nearby table, collecting dust. "Listen," Travis says. "You can talk to her all you want while we're still here, but I'm sure you've heard about the early season closure." Covey doesn't deny it under his steely gaze. "Help me convince her to go. She needs 24-hour assistance and it's not gonna happen in Mercy."

"Is she sick?" I ask, suddenly guilt-ridden that I didn't know how she was doing to begin with. I keep zero contact with anyone on land, Mrs. Olivier included, though her letter is still folded in my box of small treasures. I never answered her.

"She's not all there like she used to be," her son explains. "The dementia has her memories shot and her patience clipped. It's terrible. And if I don't have a job anymore either . . ." Her illness must be the reason Travis shifted to deckhand duties under Jimmy's watch rather than looking for higher-paying work on commercial trawlers in another state. In a sparse beam of light, beyond dusty motes, his face is grim, lined with missed sleep. He's exhausted. "Just know that not everything she tells you is gonna be reliable. Not anymore."

Covey nods. "We'll talk to her."

Travis waves us into the room down the hallway, a living space that's seen better days. The wall to the left has been pinned repeatedly with drawings—in marker, pencil, paint, and in a variety of styles and skills. The few boasting the phrase BEST TEACHER suggest all were gifts from students. Mrs. Olivier sits in an armchair in the middle of the room, only her cloud-white hair visible. "Ma, Jimmy's daughter Covey is here to see you and, uh . . ." Travis pauses, probably unsure which part of "Loony Noony" is my real name.

"Noon," I say, "one of your old stud—"

"Nhung! Oh my god, I haven't seen you for a such a long time." The cloudlike puff shifts until we can glimpse her brown eyes. "Come, come in closer." We cross the room and slip around the armchair. Mrs. Olivier immediately sets her knitting down and drags me into an awkward half-sitting embrace. "I'm sorry I don't have anything to offer you. We've been short on things."

"Not our fault," Travis says, with a look directly at Covey before moving on. "I'll be in the next room packing. Shout if you need me."

Mrs. Olivier *tuts*, but she radiates a familiar warmth. "Oh, you shouldn't be seeing me dressed so plain," she says, almost shyly. At school, she always came dressed in her version of a uniform: shift dress, cardigan with a shiny brooch, and dark tights. It feels wrong to witness her in a nightgown, with large bandages wrapped around her forearms. This close, I can count the sunspots that have made a home on her skin, like whirlpools. I can see each bulging vein in her hands. She looks so much older and smaller than she did two years ago.

I sit on a perpendicular loveseat, but Covey stays on her feet. She's probably expecting a giant squid to come flying out from the china cabinet. "We have a few questions about the research team that stayed inside the gymnasium, if you don't mind," I say, since I'm sorely lacking in the small talk department. But then again, I never talked during those lunch periods hiding in the library either. It wouldn't have been a haven if I'd been forced to.

Mrs. Olivier picks up the knitting needles. "*Mmhm*, sure, dear. They were so secretive about everything, but I'll help where I can."

"There was a Dr. Delgado on the team," Covey says. "Did Dr. Delgado tell you anything about going out to collect samples? If it was different from their usual trips, I mean."

Rather than knitting something, Mrs. Olivier is unravelling it piece by piece, so far done that I'm not sure what the knit was to begin with. "Well, I suspect it had something to do with the missing people."

That piques our interest. Jimmy hadn't mentioned that the officials or research members were conducting investigations. "Why do you say that?" I ask.

"They came and asked me about it. After all the weeks I spent telling them something strange was happening out there. Lucía listened. Asked me where people were seen last or where people told me they saw things. *I* saw things too, mind you."

I shuffle the folder from my backpack and open it up to the list and case notes.

"Does it look like anything to you?" I ask.

"Yeah, those are some of the places I told them about. Don't recognize the other places though."

"We just came from the gymnasium where they did their research activities. But we found a lot of unexpected equipment." Covey chooses her words carefully. "What was Delgado's area of expertise?"

"All of 'em have a specialty, which means all of 'em argued about a lot of things and different methodologies. Most of it welcome, but . . . Their supervisor is a transphobic piece of work," Mrs. Olivier says. "Absolutely disregarded Delgado's findings in everything." Mrs. Olivier squints as if the motion will uncloud her memory. "Delgado studied coral reefs? Some type of clam . . ."

That explains some of the tanks in the gym. "Covey," I say. "Coral reefs aren't actually plants. They're animals."

"So?"

"The info we got from your dad isn't all right," I say. "Delgado must've been a marine biologist, not a botanist." Which lends more weight to the argument that there's something monstrous in Mercy, I realize. Maybe the boy in the water wasn't so imaginary after all. "Mrs. Olivier, you said you saw stuff too. What kind of things?"

She doesn't answer right away. She scratches at the thick bandages around her forearms. Then, with a shaky breath, Mrs. Olivier says, "I don't know how to explain it to you kids."

I try to coax her. "Please try. I'm listening."

Mrs. Olivier smiles, but it's only a motion. "Have you ever had a nightmare in which you have to fight back?"

A shiver of déjà vu runs through me.

"A dream where you are attacked for no reason, and there comes that moment where you know you'll die or be hurt in some irreparable way." She has edged the knitting needle underneath a bandage, scratching back and forth. "And you, who have never fought anyone or hurt anything, suddenly find a violence in you, and you react with that violence. Your body knows. That primal thing wakes up, given the right stimuli."

Though Covey squashes her immediate skeptical expression, her left brow remains higher than the other. She's done listening now, choosing to pace instead while she pieces together the clues that make sense. Me—I'm still on the chair because I do know that feeling. I can picture the nightmare—all dark, all hands, and the desperate, *desperate* hope that you'll survive, and the conflicted fear that you'd kill to save yourself, and that it'll be who you really are.

Mrs. Olivier talks faster. "I think we've woken up something in the ocean. I really do, after all this time. The things it's seen, the things it's showing us. The bloom—"

I rise, concerned at the way her eyes turned wide and glossy, and the small patches of blood deepening on white bandage, and turn to call for Travis.

But Covey has stopped suddenly in front of the wall plastered with drawings. She grips a notepad paper, then yanks it clean off the pin. Someone has rendered a flock of birds in pencil. They are mid-flight and arching toward the paper's edge as if a whole world awaits beyond. "It's my mom's," she whispers. She holds it out to me, nail grazing the signature at the bottom. *M.B.*, where the *M* resembles a turned-around three and the *B* is a straight-up eight. "I'd recognize it anywhere. Mackenzie Boudreaux."

My heart leaps for her. "A covey," I say unhelpfully. Her mother had drawn a covey, a flock of birds, probably thinking of her daughter. Another scribble indicates it was drawn this year, but it doesn't narrow down the months. Mrs. Olivier rambles to herself about memory and instinct, though she's not given a detail about what she's witnessed.

"Where did you get this?" Covey asks. "When did you see her?" Her patience short circuits and immediately the girl's kneeling at the armchair, staring into the librarian's face.

"I don't . . ." Mrs. Olivier trails off, eyes unfocused. Mrs. Olivier had been a beacon, a guide, for people coming to or staying in Mercy after the storm. "I really don't remember. So many—so many kids give me these things. I love them all, but they're not really here anymore. Not the same way. I—"

"Covey," I say. "You know what Travis said. You can't force it."

"But my mom—she *knows* that if Jimmy ever found out she went around his place of business in secret, and unsupervised, he'd . . ." Covey is pale but snaps back to herself, with the gaze of someone who's revealed more than they meant to. "I'm so sorry," Covey says to Mrs. Olivier. The air seems to have vanished from the room. I want to ask Covey why she is afraid when we've found a real clue about her mom's whereabouts.

At the doorway, Travis says, "It's time for her to rest." His frown is pronounced. He's annoyed we'd riled Mrs. Olivier up rather than convinced her to take care of her health.

Abashed, I turn to leave, but a hand snatches my wrist. The grip is much stronger than Mrs. Olivier seems capable of. Only a slight tremble betrays her exertion. Unkempt nails dig into my skin. Her eyes are a cold splash of water, the pupils too big. The sensation of falling nearly buckles my knees.

"Never answer the knocks in the night," Mrs. Olivier warns in a flat voice, a distant wind of her former self, as her son peels her away from me.

11

ON OUR WAY BACK to the cabin, Covey folded and unfolded the notepad paper as if she might catch the birds in flight. Despite the revelation that her mom visited Mercy in secret, we didn't broach the topic. The tension in Covey's shoulders suggested she needed time, and I have my own worries. Mrs. Olivier's nails had left crescent moons on my skin that I couldn't help but trace as I wondered how her deterioration happened this swiftly. I thought about what she said about nightmares and fighting and discovering violence. On the old map of Louisiana spread out before us, Mercy Cove's skull shape taunted me too: *What are you willing to do to survive?*

A lot, I think, or else I wouldn't be here with Covey.

We've pinned all nine locations on the map, which is a little too small to be exact. At least half the list are noted in coordinates, which makes sense since Dr. Delgado wasn't a local and needed the GPS unit. They had been collecting samples—likely animal, given their expertise—at these places, but most of the locations don't directly touch any bodies of water. Maybe Delgado just had to see for themselves where people went missing or reported hallucinations. We will have to too.

Every time my fingers graze the skull-shaped cove, the desire to scrape off my rash-wrecked side grows. Luckily, there are eight places to check out before that beach. Like a scientist, I refocus and record observations from the gymnasium: the tanks, the dead animals, the bleached reefs, and sticky algae. Frank, the octopus that gave us a heart attack, had escaped for good by the time we returned with snails. "I don't get how they can pack up and leave living creatures to die," I say.

From behind me: "Darling, anything can be left."

The cold voice surprises me. I turn and watch as Covey assembles one of the metal death traps. Her expression is hard to read.

"It's what my dad said after my mom disappeared," Covey explains, not looking at me. The "anything" in this case is their daughter. It's shit behavior, even for a shitty dude, to tell a kid they can be discarded. What had he been saying to Mack, his wife, then? My breath is stuck in my throat; I don't know what to say. I miss the moment when Covey shifts the conversation. "If they're giving up on Mercy, what does it matter if a few fish die?"

I snort. "One day they'll give up on Earth too, all the people on it, and go to the moon or Mars." Now that the news has stopped running reports from or about Mercy, they're probably extolling the efforts of billionaires to build commercial rocket ships again. Never mind that there is green here to protect. And from my quick visit through Mercy, people.

Covey finishes with the first trap, sets it aside, and reaches for another rigid cage. "Oh, *gross*." She hastily pulls her hand from the trap. A long, long piece of snakeskin is pinched between her thumb and forefinger. "It must've been rubbing on the rough metal. Do you think it's still around?"

The skin is pale white with diamond cut-outs for the scales. No telling when the snake shed that. Nature will go wherever it wants since we're the ones who plopped boxes down everywhere to call home. "Lots of animals shed their skin. Ours just comes off tiny cells at a time," I say as some attempt at comfort. "The natural world is way weirder than that."

"What do you mean?" Her brows are raised; she still hasn't gotten over the oyster thing, but of course she's too curious to ignore me.

I grin, doing my best to channel evil energy. "I mean animals are fucked-up normally. For example, salmon spawn once in their lifetime. They go back to the place they were born, do it, and spend so much energy doing it, they literally start to rot from the inside. Most last just a few days, but others can live for weeks. There are eyewitness accounts of salmon literally throwing up decaying organs. People call 'em zombie salmon."

Covey rakes a hand through her hair. "God I can't believe Sex Ed was right all along. You have sex and then boom! You die."

I laugh. At first, I'm not sure the foreign sound came from me at all until I realize that I am *still* laughing. That makes me laugh more, which makes Covey laugh, and tears sting my eyes, because *why is it so funny?* Maybe because I know more than I should about relationships in nature but not at all between people. That of all the classes I'd ever sat through, Sex Ed had been the most useless. I suspect schools used it as an excuse to scar teenagers with the half-century-old video of a hair ball giving birth.

As sudden as the laughter comes my mother's voice. "Nhung." I stop laughing. "Nhung." I grab the radio from my bag and answer her. The rush makes me dizzy, as if I'd switched planes of existence. I haven't thought to call her for the last day, too uncomfortable and busy. Without reading the moles on her eyelids, I can't tell whether Mom's angry or disappointed. My mouth is close to the plastic. Covey looks away, marking where we'll leave the traps.

Mom's fever is less frequent now, but the spasms haven't improved. She wants to know if I've killed anything. I touch the bandages I'm too scared to remove from my neck and say no. It's somehow worse to be far away, then suddenly anchored to the weight of my guilt. It doesn't matter now that it is nighttime; there is nothing to share over the radio static when any moment she can switch it off.

If I ask her whether she's ever seen Jay in the water, of course she will say yes. Sông saved them.

If I tell her about the changes I've seen in my body, she will tell me that it's all in my head—or worse, that I'm a growing girl.

So I hold on to the key to *Wild Things* and talk to her until the conversation fizzles out. "Nhớ cẩn thận," says Mom. *Be careful.* We hang up.

"What's her take on all of this?" Covey asks right after.

"I didn't tell her anything."

She stops writing x's on the map. "Why not?"

"Because I'm not giving her any ideas to return to Mercy while sick as hell." That's a partial truth because I can't explain the things Mom does or says. I don't want anyone to judge her. I bounce a question before Covey can push further. "The drawing of the covey was pretty good. Is your mom an artist?"

"It was just a hobby," she says, then cuts herself off. "Wait, no. I sound like Jimmy. She really does love to draw. She used to set up a booth at local weekend markets before he made her stop. She even illustrated the silly books I wrote and kept them at her booth. You couldn't even *read* my handwriting . . ." Her cheeks are flushed with pink. I wonder if she's held in all the ways she misses her mom over the last three months and now, given the chance, her yearning spills from a dam. No one is here to say she doesn't matter. Covey picks up where she left off, more composed this time. "She doodles without thinking all the time. It's why I'm not sure if the drawing is a clue or if she made a pit stop at the Oliviers' or what."

"It's a covey," I say. "It's *you*." I say it without thinking, because I am not one to give false hope. That's how I know I mean it, and now we sit in this painfully awkward earnestness when I shouldn't care at all. We mumble something or the other; we finish our map and mark the places to either search or leave a trap.

When we finally lay down to sleep, the hole in the cabin floor glimmers, the iridescence shining bright as the water shifts gently. I turn and watch the mold-eaten ceiling. For a long time, neither of us speak.

But then Covey cracks open a book and reads aloud. I'm thrown back to that night on *Wild Things* when I couldn't sleep from the coining bruises and she read loud but not enough to startle me or wake Mom. I make a noncommittal *huh* because I'm sure I dreamed it. I don't even remember the story from the first time—only how her voice blended with the ocean waves. She grumbles, "Don't be weird about it. It'll help tire me out too."

Like a switchblade, her tongue is sharp when she wants and hidden when she wants.

She's made of knife-points in other ways too: long fillet arms, a butcher's wedge of a torso, and paring knives for collarbones. She is exactly the girl you dream of cutting your teeth on, figuratively and literally.

I am not thinking that. She is the enemy. I am not thinking that.

I shut my eyes and exorcise my thoughts. Without Mom, it's too easy to let others close. I forget, seconds at a time, that it's normal to laugh. To mistake this for a long-awaited sleepover between friends is naive. The story Covey tells me is sad, closer to the fairytale version of "The Little Mermaid" rather than the mouse one.

The beginning is similar enough: The Little Mermaid falls in love with a human prince. So desperate for love, and acceptance, she makes a terrible deal with the sea witch for the ability to live on land. Through a brew, the Little Mermaid gains legs but loses her beautiful voice. If the prince returns her love, then she'll be able to stay at his side. She will be granted a soul. If not, she will die.

Only he does not fall in love with her. He loves her dancing, though it feels like knives on the soles of her feet, and her camaraderie, though it's his voice alone during their conversations. He will marry another girl.

The Little Mermaid doesn't know what she's truly lost until it's too late.

While Covey reads to me, I wonder if all myths share roots. Maybe people across different cultures and times yearn for the same things—love, companionship, safety—and accept that there is a cost with the universe to get them. Like my family and Sông. If Sông saved my family repeatedly, what has it taken from us that we don't yet know?

In the story, the Little Mermaid's sisters exchange their hair for a dagger that she must kill the prince with. His blood on her feet will restore her mermaid tail. But when she finds herself standing next to his bed, she cannot kill him. She thinks she is in love. At dawn, she throws herself off the ship instead. The Little Mermaid turns into foam. She returns to the sea whence she came.

12

IF THE OCEAN IS where I feel best, and Covey the swamp, then Mercy is somewhere between—the flooded areas masquerading as a body of water meant to house something living. Maybe it's what people call a liminal space, belonging neither to one nor the other.

I am alone today. Or rather, I left without telling Covey first. Close to three days have passed in that cabin, and we'd established a routine: rise at dawn, eat, check the traps set at the locations we've covered from Delgado's list, explore the next one, eat while I tell her horrible facts about different ocean creatures. At night, she reads to me. I've become familiar with her cadence—how she pauses dramatically before a plot twist, gives her opinion. She would say this is stupid of me, and I would agree. This fourth set of coordinates landed right in Magnolia Springs, a trailer park named for all the white-flowering trees planted along one border. Coincidentally, it's also where my family's trailer was. There's a tether between me and this place, pure muscle memory; the consequence of being born and raised in Mercy. I must see it alone first and process whatever emotion I'm meant to have.

After storing the skiff along an expanse of rock, hidden under driftwood and long grass, I hike over the small levee to a long lot of trailers. Hurricane Arlene had decimated the property, wrecking through metal and wood alike. It'd always been full of kids running around after school, jump-roping on the single concrete patch at the end of the lane, but no kid has been here for a while. The guilt over leaving Covey asleep in the cabin subsides upon seeing the damage to my old neighborhood.

Of the trailers that didn't get blown away, more than half are spotted with algae and mold. Others have open cavities. Insulation spills out from soggy walls, and furniture litters the outside. Newly installed units are perfectly boarded up, the long nails driven deep into windowsill, and transformed into tombs. Like the Oliviers, more folks have packed up to leave in anticipation of the season closure. Ours was one of the closest to the crumbling levee. Rosebushes—dying now—bolster the back, and the trailer's supporting beams are cracked. The algae has made a home here, thriving where it shouldn't be. I walk through the muck until I reach our place. The door is gone. The wood-paneled walls hide the red haze that's overcome everything.

Go in, I urge myself, but my feet are rooted in mud. Living in Mom's grief day in and day out made me believe I'd be alright, but it's different when you choose to walk through your old life. This home is a reminder of everyone I've lost. And is it not fucked up that I prefer the ocean and being away from all this? Mom has her fantasy world of reincarnated beings; I have mine, in which I never have to hurt. The losses are abstract. If I see a lurking shadow at night, it's only my subconscious. I don't want to dream about Jay as a ghoul in the water again.

Returning to the cabin is the most logical option, but I don't want to yet. It's my first moment alone in two years, without someone else in the next room. I decide to visit the house Delgado surveyed instead. The paths I used to take with my bike are still there but cracked through. I wander the neighborhood and find a strangler fig that has cannibalized a magnolia tree. Barely any parts of the original tree can be seen behind the new thick roots. A tendril has grown straight through the tire swing that Springs residents hung up years ago. Wilder and I spent many afternoons pushing each other higher and higher under those white blossoms.

I stop at the Phans' double-wide trailer with sage-green trim and rickety steps that basically disintegrate underneath my boots. And though I lack the courage to visit our trailer, I'm determined not to let this trip go to waste. I grip either side of the door, a foot up for leverage, and pull. I spill onto the floor, then turn on a flashlight.

Picture frames hang on the walls, crooked. The handsome family of five had taken pictures at the mall photo lab with various props. Large dice you can sit on, a fake barn, a plain white background, Easter Bunnies and Santas—I can trace their ages through each setup. Our families weren't close, but I saw the kids out enough. Which ones told Mrs. Olivier they'd seen something strange? Or did they go missing? Delgado's notes didn't specify, and the ill feeling in my gut warps into guilt. How do I not know what happened to them?

The flashlight sweeps over the floor, showing muddy tracks and leaves scattered farther in. I follow, hoping for any indication that the Phans evacuated, rather than the alternative. The hallway is long and empty, punctured with doors to other rooms. Junk litters the floor. No one's lived here for a while. I pass by bedrooms with dusty bunk beds, then stop at a sunlit area.

Angels look down from every surface. They come in ceramic, plastic, and porcelain. The material apparently didn't matter to them. Some have fallen on the ground, others are crushed to pieces, and still some hold miraculously to their ledges. There are cherubic faces with giant, blushing cheeks, then others of inhuman beauty—ready to curse any passerby for their sins. Algae grows on them too, digging in the crevices of carved wings and facial features. These angels are bloodied warriors guarding home.

Mercy had a small and thriving Vietnamese Catholic community, but I hadn't known the Phans were this religious. Stepping back, I accidentally knock an owl-shaped clock off the wall. It breaks, spilling corroded batteries everywhere.

There's a shift at the edge of my vision. "Hey!"

The deep voice is a punch to my chest, moments before it even registers in my mind as belonging to someone I know. On instinct, I lower myself on the floor.

"It's better if you come out now. I don't like being surprised."

The Phans had a stern way of speaking without yelling that got their kids in line. Even if it's been a while, I know their voices. This is not them. This should be possible only in a nightmare.

"I have a gun and I will shoot."

"Okay," I say. "Just—don't." I shuffle from my hiding spot, dazed as I jump down through the back door. The impact of the ground zips up to my knees.

"Noonie?"

He's wearing a smile, and it actually is warm and so very happy to see me. I want to be a peach pit. Let him tear into my flesh now, and I'd be poisonous in every bite. I want, desperately, to be different from who I was at fourteen, but standing here, I can't say that I have changed much. I'm wearing false bravado, a cape too large for my shoulders.

Where's my sea witch to turn me into a creature fearsome and powerful?

Where's my dagger?

Coming closer, Aaron pulls the sunflower hat off my head. Teasing. "Thought it was you," he says before adding, "Oh snap. You're going white already." He yanks it down on my head, too hard. "Everything's all kinds of fucked up now, huh." The brim grazes my ears. I shudder. "How have ya been?"

It doesn't matter that I stay quiet. Aaron's always known how to fill the spaces in our conversations. The more he tells me, the more nauseous I get. He's still living in Plaquemines Parish but a few hours up. Even there, people are riled up about the bloom. He's apprenticing at a mechanic shop where they're definitely underpaying him. "You think I want to be back here?" Aaron asks. Jimmy needed capable hands, you see, and Aaron needed a job to make quick money. He's searching for whatever rabid animal's dragging folks off. Working his ass off for days now. "I don't want to stay in this or that shithole town.

I have a girl waiting for me back home. She's graduating this year, and then we're leaving."

I turn my head up.

"What? Don't look at me like that." Aaron smiles. "She's seventeen. It's legal."

The sensation of my feet leaving sand. The water in my hair. The weightlessness and burden of my body all the same. If you're not careful in Chelsea's Cove, you'll get pulled into the tides beyond the cove. A boy named Rithy died that way in seventh grade after being goaded into a dare by high schoolers. So, I held onto Aaron and didn't let go. And now he's maybe hurting a girl I don't know.

Does that make it my fault?

I don't know how to swim. I don't know anything useful, I'm finding.

"You're here with your mom and Covey right?" he asks. "Jimmy said y'all would be out in the Gulf searching, not around here." His palm rests on the gun at his hip.

"We haven't found anything," I say. My voice is too high. I try to adjust. "I just wanted to check out Mercy. My old house. Then fuel up and go." It's a lie since we have five locations remaining to scope out, and it's my first time being untruthful to him. At fourteen, I hadn't known you could be too honest.

"Better get all hands on deck!" Aaron chuckles. "There's a storm coming, ya know? All season nothing, and now it happens all at once. Not sure what Jimmy thinks you'll find out there anyway. He needed Covey out of his hair. That girl's real annoying." His hand slides away from the gun, then blocks the sun from his eyes as he looks down the street. The bend on the road that eventually led to his house is barely visible. "Anyway. Thought I saw tracks coming in here, but it was just you or probably everyone abandoning ship. I'm gonna get going. Good seeing you."

Aaron gets into a mud-splattered pickup truck and drives off, a cloud of exhaust in his wake.

Blood is pounding in my ears, drowning out the birds that have come to feast on figs. And though the world is red-tinged, the sunlight is still soft gold. The brightness is overwhelming when I tip my head back. The sensation returns—sand vanishing from between my toes—and the sky seems to exert pressure. I feel small.

I find myself back in our family trailer. I try again what Mom told me. Squeeze the necklace. Say the magic words *một, hai, ba* and forget, but it tastes wrong. The key hangs against my chest. It'd be easy to fall over.

I can't be present in my body like this. My muscles act; they yank the hat from my head and throw it. It flops into cobwebs, the sunflowers shadowed. I want to scream out of frustration and disgust, but I'm afraid of what sound that'll make.

There are pictures here of my family too, the ones Mom didn't grab because they were too grimy or broken, or maybe it's because of the way I look in more recent ones: eyeshadow smoked sloppily on her eyes, concealer dotted on the mole to the left of her mouth, and never smiling with teeth because an uncle once told her they were too crooked. The paint and eyeliner make her someone else. And yet the moment she goes to take it all off, her tiny bones won't shake free of the mask. It sticks, like salmon skin on a poorly greased pan.

I was a girl then, and someone's secret girlfriend. *His.*

I retch into a dark corner. My breakfast—the uncooked white flesh of an unfortunate catfish caught in Covey's trap— splatters on the carpet, each flake resembling a maggot through my tears. I wipe away snot and bile. It's pointless to cry when it's all in the past. Mom even lied to Dad and said I had food poisoning that night, not wasted on too-sweet drinks. No one else knows what I did. Even if they had, Dad's too dead to be ashamed. Aaron is not here for me. He's here to hunt for Jimmy. Was Covey in on this? People's eyes always dart over me, as though they can read everything wrong with me.

I stalk the halls of my old home, breathing the stale air that has filled it. Dad's cheap guitar is still here, the strings snapped. Most of the furniture has been misplaced. It's both familiar and not. There are deteriorating bills and unwanted ads, pamphlets in support of book bans that Aaron's mom slipped inside neighbors' mailboxes. A life long gone. Laid down in the hallway is a horrendously pink pen with bright feathers and a little triangle tag that says #1 SISTER. The tag has faded since Jay brought it home from a school book fair.

I've sunk down to my knees, broken plastic to my forehead as if I might pray. His love is something that I know, and I miss it, despite mashing every memory to a pulp.

That's when I smell wet fur, something animal like pork rind. It thickens the closer I move to the bedroom I shared with my younger brother. The scent's distinct from the algae, and it doesn't smell dead the way corpses do. Maybe fate has a hand in today's impossible sequence of events. *Suffer, and you will receive in return*. I don't believe in that at all. I nudge the door open. It slaps against a small bench on the other side.

There is a hazmat suit, neon yellow and stark, crumpled on the wall straight across from me. In nature, bright colors are a warning to *stay away, I'm dangerous*. The blue-ringed octopus, a tiny baby maybe five inches big, has enough poison to paralyze the diaphragm of over ten humans, suffocating them to escape. Man-of-war jellyfish—which are not actually jellyfish but many organisms banded together into one form—have venomous tentacles under their cute, sail-shaped heads. Lionfish carry a neurotoxin in their bold spines that causes swelling and extreme pain.

But a hazmat suit is a choice. The research team had been studying the algae like anything else to put under a microscope. The suit is to protect them from whatever's around us. What's protecting us from this place? I breathe, eat, sleep, *live* in Mercy, as hundreds of others still do. Whoever is inside the suit doesn't move when I shine my flashlight into the panel over their eyes. The dirty fingerprints make it impossible to tell if it's Delgado.

Standing a foot away from the body, I reach and with my sleeve, rub away the smudges. What I find stuns me.

Since the team photograph, Delgado's hair has grown out a bit. Half an inch and dark brown. Their face can be described as peaceful, despite the narrow objects jutting out from their ears and subsequent bleeding. The blood has browned, crusting over pallid skin. How long have they been here? Heart stammering, I tilt the bulging helmet to get a better look at their ears. Pencils are lodged deep inside, the thick kind made for little hands to easily grasp, probably from the elementary school and never meant for this kind of violence. *What the shit.*

There was no reason for Delgado to return to Magnolia Springs, much less my house, when the Phans' was the target and, according to the notes, already sampled. Was the scientist dragged here to be killed? All this time, we've been chasing a monster in the water—not a murderer. And why would any killer bother to put protective headgear back on a victim?

I'm in a fever dream, where my childhood bedroom is all wrong. Violated by blood and algae and strangers.

I need someone else to witness, and it can't be my mother. I have to get Covey.

As I back away, turning at the last possible moment, I'm hit with déjà vu. The fortune teller's dead smile, the carrion beetles and flesh flies scuttering all over, the drippy foam from her lips. This is not that; this is somehow much, much worse.

13

"COVEY, I SWEAR," I say. "Delgado was right there, slumped over." We are standing in my old bedroom in Magnolia Springs, the body in the hazmat suit absent from where it should be. I was gone maybe thirty minutes. Covey had been waiting on the shack's precarious pier when I returned. She was pissed to be left behind, and the tension in her jaw has not eased up since. Especially since my claim about finding the missing scientist is proving false. All traces, including the rancid pork rind smell, have disappeared.

"Maybe you got the trailer wrong," says Covey.

I shake my head. "No. I can find my way here in my sleep. *Pencils* were shoved in Delgado's ears. No one can survive that, can they? This doesn't make any sense."

Her blue eyes are curious but pitying, as though viewing me in new light. "Mrs. Olivier said people saw strange things, but I don't buy it. The toxins from algae blooms can cause hallucinations. Why did you come here alone?"

"This is my family's trailer," I say. "I needed to see it alone." Though I hadn't been alone in a sense—Aaron was there. But his name is impossible to say. He's my nightmare in the flesh, and what if she thinks he wasn't real either? Or worse, what if I did imagine it, as I had with the gills in my neck. She peers around the room, taking in the mildew that has settled in the bedding. Firetrucks for Jay, butterflies for me; a different time.

In all fairness, Covey does check the Phans' and surroundings outside. She finds a set of footprints too large to be mine. A dragging gait that leads to and disappears on a rock path. I've scraped my knees there more than once.

My agitation increases with every passing moment. Covey is seeing the worst of Magnolia, possibly the worst of me. "I have no reason to lie to you," I say.

"Except that you very much do," Covey counters, getting up from surveying the mud. "You want to get away from Mercy. The sooner, the better."

"So do you," I say. Heat builds inside my thick sweater, slicking my neck. "Do you know an Aaron?" The words slur together in my quickness to spit it all out.

Her eyes narrow. "Why?"

"He was here."

"Why did you wait to tell me?" The question is innocent, and yet it cuts deep. *Your fault for being misunderstood*, I think she's saying. "He's a creep. He's, like, in his twenties but wants to be cool so bad."

It's a small relief to know she saw through his friendly mask. "He'd left before I found Delgado. He said your dad hired him to find the monster in Mercy. We cover the sea, he covers the land type of thing. Don't tell me you didn't know."

"Shit," says Covey. "No."

"Maybe he got the body," I say. "That's logical, isn't it?" She doesn't have a response for that because Jimmy had sent Aaron without consulting her. There's no telling what else we don't know. Her dad has great joy in keeping special information from people. Still heated, I pull myself up into the trailer. "I'm grabbing a few things, then we can go."

In the relative privacy of the dark hallway, I breathe. I head back to the bedroom where I'd dropped Jay's #1 SISTER pen. There were two tracks belonging to those giant tires, and only one fresh from when Aaron backed out of the lot. He hadn't come back, I don't think. But if Covey's gonna call me a liar, I'll give her just a little white lie. One of omission. Kneeling to pick up the pen, I swivel at the sudden motion at the corner of my eye.

A broken mirror lies against the bureau. My reflection is all fractured glass. I hate it. My gums are sore as I grind my teeth together.

Mirrors show a *you* that no one else sees, and you begin to wonder if either is really truly you. Although I know better than to fall for it, I still think: is my nose too wide? Too flat? Is my hair too this, or that? Are there gills on my neck? Have I lost my mind? Am I a girl enough—the right kind? Going through life invisible is easier, but the temptation is still there to stand before a mirror and call the worst monsters to you.

Candyman, Bloody Mary, Nhung, Nhung, Nhung.

Believe me, I want to beg but cannot, the words all gummed in my throat.

We spent the rest of the afternoon visiting locations from Delgado's list and checking traps. The first place was a one-story brick house, the small pond out back basically a pool of blood due to algae crowding its surface. Covey approached the large decorative stone used to subtly mark where we left the trap, but it came up empty. We've snared nothing but squirrels. The next location to scout was farther out on the bayou, a crashed houseboat called *Seaz the Day*. It's tricky to map out, given the ample trees and wreckage. Our mood is brittle by the time we leave.

This mood continues into the night, though there are still moments when our eyes meet and we know we are in over our heads. She reads the shortest story aloud before bed, then sleeps before I do. It takes forever for me to drift off, and yet in no time at all hands are yanking me from sleep.

Eyes flash in the dark, shining partly yellow from the dim flashlight. I blink into the globe of light that has broken the darkness around us. We are dazed fireflies cupped in a kid's palms. My head is pounding, and I cannot tell the difference between the banging in my head or the one that comes from outside.

Covey's face is not idyllic. "Shhh." She helps me to my feet as my world spins. My confusion grows.

Knock knock knock knock

The steady beat is not at our door but someplace farther away.

Knockknockknockknockknockknock

My eyes dart at the hole in the floor, where the vibrations send ripples of iridescence across the algae. Covey marches toward the entrance.

"Wait." I sidestep the hole to cut her off. "Don't go out there." There's something I ought to remember about knocking.

"Whatever's making that noise might actually be what we're looking for," Covey says. "I should've stayed up to lay more traps. Maybe it followed us here." I wake up more at that statement. Covey hadn't seen Delgado's body, the dried trails of blood from their ears, or that haunting sour smell. A dead body cannot hunt. She worries her bottom lip and snatches up a hunting knife laid out on a table. "I have to look." She opens the door before I can stop her.

The pier's long red tongue is bare as usual and sinking in the same places. The wood creaks under her weight, then mine. The moon has risen full, so we don't need flashlights to see which patches of mold-eaten wood to skip over. The water laps calmly underneath, suddenly too relaxed, too normal. "Deceptive" is the descriptor I want, but that's a human word or else reserved for the possum that plays dead.

The girl has walked out with just a knife, ready to strike at whatever imaginary monsters or—worse—people come to take. Maybe it'll be Aaron. Despite the absurdity, I search the murky riverbank for any flash of yellow hazmat suit. There's no sign of the caustic color amid the iridescence. I follow Covey almost to the end of the pier. A single patch of water glistens on the wood, shaped like nothing at all. Unusual in that the wet print

is by itself, just as if something had reached over the pier's edge
and rapped on the surface. A shiver works its way through me.
I snap my fingers to get Covey's attention, then gesture back at
the shack, where we can at least pretend we're safe.

KNOCK. KNOCK. KNOCK.

The sound assaults our spines, and we whirl around to see a
new wet patch on the wood, glistening moon-silver. Not there
from before. That's enough to kill whatever hubris brought
Covey out here. She rushes us toward the shack. My flip-flop
catches on an uneven plank, and I stumble forward, certain to
fall into the water if not for Covey heaving me by the shoulder.
She's drenched in nervous sweat too.

"At least watch where you're going—" Her own scream cuts
her off as she is dragged away and into the water. Covey's head
smacks against the pier with a nasty thump, and I scream too,
grasping at the space she stood. The whole of her disappears
into the murky water, leaving the world eerily silent.

An ugly, monstrous thought accompanies the shock: it
would be simple to let her drown. Letting this one clever obsta-
cle go makes it easier to return to the lighthouse and escape
with Mom. Covey had implied my experience at the trailer park
was from the algae toxins' neural effects, but the only hallucination I've had is that we can be friends. We should not trust each
other at all.

Yet, in the hollows of my chest, a tender seed has been
planted. Her doubt wouldn't have hurt me that much if I
didn't care.

The entire universe seems to hold its breath.

I dive in.

14

THE RIVERBANK IS SHALLOW, but I'm short. My feet barely graze the mucky bottom, and I'm struggling to stay afloat when all I know is how to dog-paddle. I let myself sink to look for Covey, eyes strained against algae and reeds. There's a flicker of movement to my right, as bright as shiny scales on a fish. Holding onto the pier's planks for added support, I emerge and suck in as much air as possible.

The water parts gently on the surface, softening the violence beneath it. There's no other sign of a monster, so I plunge back down. My vision is all murky green, moonbeam, and red. Covey has minutes—if she hasn't been ripped apart already.

Though I kept my lips tightly shut, water rushes in. It pries the spaces between my crooked teeth. The world comes at me full volume. The knocking is no longer a rhythmic beat. It is a voice.

Let us in let us in let us in let us in let us in let us in

Like before, the water has me in its clutches. It embraces me, holds me still, welcomes me. I fight against the river, a current too strong for where we are. I am a small thing in its domain. A burning sensation spreads from my side to my lungs to my head. I black out.

There's a girl hanging on to a thick oak branch. The sun's out and strong, shining right into my face. A spring day, a school day, but we've played hooky. "Mommy, I'm scared." Her thin arms tremble with the effort to not let go. Her fingers dig into the bark; bits fall and hit my face. I'm aware that I am her mother and not at the same time, though I can't quite remember who I'm supposed to be.

"You climbed up there all by yourself," I hear myself say. "Covey, you can do this."

The girl takes a giant breath in. The tree rustles in the wind, leaves flitting away.

I open my arms. "I'll always catch you, honey!"

Before letting go, she screams, "Mommy!" Her dark blond hair is a halo around her small head. I am filled with love and panic because what if I can't save her? What if she hurts herself because of me?

But she falls right into my arms, and I don't let her go. "I got you."

We break through the hole in the shack. Air fills my chest in big gulps. There is no oak, no little child, only me and Covey huddled close. Glasses gone, water burns my eyes, blurring the world into vague shapes and colors. My brain has seemingly dissolved into mush. I feel for the wood, then heap her aside as best as I can before hoisting myself in agonizing inches until I lie next to her.

She isn't moving.

I turn her on her side until water trickles from her mouth. "Wake up," I say as I lower my face close to hers. "Wake up!" It was Covey, wasn't it? In my dream or vision or messed up hallucination. I'm ready to do CPR but she jerks forward and spits up water on the floorboard. Her eyes are bulging and bloodshot. "Thank fuck."

Her trembling hand touches my brow bone. "Why do you look like that?" she asks in the barest whisper. Bile, or water, rises in my gut. I pull away, as though burned, and she rests, exhausted from trying not to drown. In moments, I am on my feet and running for the back room to look into the dreaded mirror.

My neck is incredibly tender, the two bandages missing, but it's the eyes that catch my attention. Not brown but a dark squiggly slit in the center. When I blink, the illusion disappears. I grip the bureau hard, disoriented. The algae bloom's hallucinogenic effect can be real, and so can the monsters. They are not exclusive truths.

Mirror-me is not me, but I'm starting to not feel like myself either. I jumped in, then woke up back at the shack. I saved Covey, but I don't know how.

Cursing, I rush to the other room and shove the old sofa over the hole in the floor, in case whatever hunted us the first time attempts another round. While Covey sleeps (with me periodically checking that she's breathing), I keep guard and try to remember what happened. It's all a hazy dream; I'm sure I saw a young Covey and her mom. Maybe it's just from talking about her mom, but she's never mentioned being stuck in a tree before. There's no way to ask without raising more questions.

Right before dawn, Covey wakes. Still sopping wet since I didn't want to change her, she curses her pounding head. "I thought you didn't know how to swim," she says.

"I don't. Guess we got lucky. Or instinct kicked in." I wait to see if she brings up me looking different, but she doesn't. She starts to peel off her clothes to hang on the fishing line I've strung nail to nail across the room. I turn away. "Do you remember what grabbed you? I couldn't see anything."

"No. Just cold. Not anything I've . . ." her voice trails off, then picks up again. "Why does it have to be knocking?" She rustles through her backpack.

Because I've thought about this, I'm ready with an answer. "Why not? We're humans. We see a door and we think it's meant to be opened." Horror movies always start that way, with haunted houses, bloody basements, forbidden vaults and tombs. "We see a lock and we think about how to pry it open. The more you're scared of the shadow on the other side, the more you want to open the door, right?"

"So you're saying you're a masochist."

I turn toward her. She's fully dressed. Though there had been a hint of teasing in her tone, she's frowning now.

"If we're going to keep doing this together, you need to promise me something."

"What?"

"Don't jump in after me—or after anyone in the water. You don't swim, Noon. If you die *stupidly* trying to save me, I'll laugh at you forever. You got lucky this once. Don't fuck with the unknown."

In one week, she had saved me and I saved her, even if it makes her mad. I actually like that she's a little pissed at me. No one has ever told me to put myself first. I give my best nonchalant shrug. "You knocked your head hard, didn't you?"

Covey rolls her eyes. "Just listen then. I'm sorry for how I reacted in Magnolia Springs."

It's hard to believe that all happened yesterday. Me running into Aaron, finding Delgado's body, which then disappeared. It feels as if months have passed. "It's fine," I say.

"No, it isn't," she says. "Didn't you tell me that nature is stranger than we know? This is obviously something no one anywhere else has dealt with before—even if the government, universities, rich people, my dad keep trying to make it quiet. Anything strong enough to drag me can drag a dead body. I should have believed you."

The sun has risen, shards of light between broken wood and windows. This time, I'm the one who reaches out. Past the tiny curl of her chopped hair, right to the notepad paper clipped on the fishing line to dry. I finally notice the symbol on the bottom edge. "Covey, the drawing," I say.

Covey's sunburnt pink as she swivels around to look at her mom's drawing too.

"That's the seal for the Sharp family. They owned the one supermarket here. Had their own brand stuff." Two *s*'s comprise the symbol on the paper, one inverted. It had the unfortunate visualization of buttocks, the way the bottom curves wide. It's the Sharp ass, Mercy residents like to say. "I know where they live."

15

WE WAIT UNTIL THE bright afternoon to leave the cabin, back
on the skiff. The circles under our eyes are twin dark masses,
and despite being literally attacked last night, our mood is
good. Covey's mother had left a direction for us. The Sharp
mansion sits on land handed down generation after generation, alongside water. The house itself had been rebuilt to be
bigger and grander, even as the Sharp family grew smaller.
Rumor had it that each of their five Great Danes had their
own room.

But the outside of the mansion isn't really how I remember it.

Today, algae and moss have made pastures of the brick. It
is stained green and crumbling in places. The entire first floor is
underwater, of course, though they'd for many years tried to
build up the riverbank. There are *a lot* of wrecked boats outside the mansion. Fancy speedboats with aerodynamic noses,

clumsy dinghies, even sailing boats—their sails ripped into the water. If the skiff were even twice as big, we would have problems getting close.

Covey asks the obvious question. "Who builds a mansion on a coastline that's been disappearing for decades?"

"The same kind of people who want a house on the moon or Mars." Rumor also had it they invested a large sum of money in spaceships, after all. "We can enter there." I point to the far-left window, the glass almost all smashed through. We keep our pace slow by the broken boats. Twice I think I see a face in the water, hollow stare trained on me, but it ends up being trash. The lack of sleep's dulling my senses. We tether the boat to a windowpane and leave most of our things behind, in case we'll need to run fast.

It takes a bit of maneuvering to get inside without gashing our thighs open, but we land safely on the other side. The ground is strangely solid beneath my feet, more so than the wood in the cabin, where I could always hear the faintest rustle of water. Sometimes, it seems I'm still hearing it now, the river refusing to drain from my ears. We are in a long corridor with cracked eggshell-colored walls. The rug reeks of mold. Despite the many windows, it is oppressively dark. Covey has armed me with a knife, which I hold like a stick. I'm more likely to gash myself than anything.

Covey switches her flashlight on, then draws too close to me. "Did you lose your glasses?"

My free hand reaches up and finds nothing at the bridge of my nose. They must have slipped off when I dove into the water last night. I should've noticed. I've worn glasses for at least ten years. "My vision is not that bad," I lie, though I'm already grabbing a spare from my bag. "I wear them for fashion."

Her gaze homes in on my pineapple-print sweatshirt. I'm offended—it's an excellent, cheerful shirt—but point taken. The tortoiseshell glasses make my vision worse, as it's not my prescription, but I don't take them off. She carefully leads us farther into the house. I push the door to the first room, but she enters before me. A gigantic bed sits flush against pale-pink walls, the sheets dragged off the mattress. At the center, a large stain blooms, darkening to the color of red wine. Black ants linger at its edges and flies zip around the room, angrily claiming their space. "What the hell," Covey mutters, shining her light right on that damning spot.

I'm thinking of a young Covey, a kid who trusted her mom completely to jump from a tree, though the vision is likely fiction. If we believe the notepad to be a clue, we must also believe Mack has been here. Seen this stain, or else . . .

"We should keep looking," I say.

Covey reaches the same conclusion because she pulls a knife from her boot, keeping it raised ahead of her flashlight. The next two rooms have been ransacked of any valuables. Only echoes remain: a silver brush with hair-choked bristles, a half-chewed dog bone, leather shoes creased in the middle. The next chamber is large and the walls are bookcases, packed with complete collections of encyclopedias. A second-level loft sits above those bookcases with handsome desks. There's a mattress at the center of several turned-in armchairs. Velvet curtains are drawn completely shut on the opposite wall.

Despite the grisly scene from earlier, Covey brightens as though she's arrived in a toy store. She immediately goes to the closest bookshelf, ignoring all the reference materials from the bottom to pull out a leather-bound book. She tucks the knife behind the cover and flips through. There are a lot of words flashing by. "Why would you have so many boring books in one place?" she sighs, taking the blade before plopping the volume down. She reaches for another. Her priorities have gone out the window.

Despite the warning bells in my brain and my lack of interest in the written word in general, I walk next to a bookshelf and feel along their spines. Mrs. Olivier would probably be thrilled to see books too, but I hope Travis has convinced her by now to leave Mercy. Here is the one place that doesn't smell like moldy rug. It smells like an oil lamp and something warm. This place could fit our entire trailer inside of it.

Paper crunches beneath my shoe. I bend down to inspect the neon green candy wrapper.

That's when a floorboard squeaks behind me. *I fucked up*, I realize as cold metal rests at the back of my skull. "Don't move. Is it just the two of you here?"

"Yes," I say. The weapon doesn't budge from the base of my skull. My eyes nearly bulge out of their sockets as I try to see without moving. The bookcase has cracked open; feet with toenails half-painted sparkly blue step out. Covey's disarmed by an accomplice before my captor nudges me to stand up, pivoting around to keep the weapon trained on both of us.

"Nhung?"

This voice, I know it.

This face, I know it.

Neither is a nightmare.

He's grown taller since I last saw him, and he favors his mother in looks. His name tumbles from my mouth. "Wilder!" For a moment, neither of us knows what to do. Then all at once, the glass breaks and we're in each other's arms. Solid, warm, and real, my childhood friend in the flesh.

The girl with the bat and Covey are staring at us. "You know each other?"

Wilder gives me one last squeeze before standing back. "We grew up together. Practically in each other's backyards. This is Noon—you still want to be called that, right?"

I nod, stuck between stunned and deliriously happy. He's been so close and far at the same time. It should've been easy to see each other before this.

The girl sets her bat down and grins. "I'm Saffy." Her smile is brilliant even in the dark.

"And this is Covey," I say since she's busy being reunited with her knife. I glance at Wilder, teeming with questions, but say instead, "We're working together, investigating the missing persons cases and what's been dragging them off."

Saffy opens the curtains on the back wall, allowing sunlight to spill into the library. "Maybe you can help us with Rosa." Covey and I look at each other.

Wilder explains, "She went out for food supplies several days ago and didn't come back. We're anxious, obviously." He taps a photograph pinned on a corkboard. A dark-haired girl with deep-set eyes smiles shyly at the camera next to a younger-looking Saffy.

"We haven't seen her, but first, we came because of this." Covey hands over the notepad paper. The pencil has faded considerably since being dried. "My mom drew it. She's missing too, and we found this at the Oliviers'. Mrs. Olivier's been having memory trouble, so she couldn't tell us more. Noon said this stationery belongs to the Sharps."

"Mack is your mom?" Saffy asks. "She was helping funnel some supplies and stuff to us, since we didn't feel safe visiting the harbor."

Surprise crosses Covey's face, so this must be news to her as well. "Do you know where she is?"

"We haven't seen her for at least two months," Wilder says, leaning on an armchair. "We kind of thought, well, that Jimmy had something to do with it."

The man's reputation is widespread, clearly. The two wear expressions befitting people who just stepped in shit. Covey has deflated from the hope that soared only moments ago. "It's not ruled out," I say so she can process the disappointment. "But Covey was home the night her mom disappeared, and there didn't seem to be any signs of . . ." Murder? Maiming? There has been enough evidence about their tumultuous marriage, but I'm not sure Covey even knows what her dad is capable of.

Saffy covers for my awkward hesitation. "Why don't we get you both settled in and chat more after?" She gestures to a connecting door. "I'm sorry this is rude, but y'all look awful. There're plenty of rooms, but we like to pair up for safety."

Remembering the blood from earlier, I ask, "What happened in that pink room?"

"Oh, you mean the jam stain," she answers. "We try to make it seem like the house is haunted or just really messed up. In case people want to get close."

Wilder salutes. "Saffy's the boss with smart ideas." Playfully, he turns to me. "That's got to be sweaty as hell. You want some new clothes?"

Instinctively, I pull my sleeves to cover more skin on my hands. Mom picked this armor. I am tired and sensitive, I realize, over the way Wilder speaks—as though we've never lost contact the last two years. I feel his absence so much deeper now that he's in front of me—no longer an idea or a memory, but a person who truly doesn't know what has happened in my life. I don't know what he's been through either. I thought it'd be enough to know that he was safe; turns out I wanted more.

I shove that hurt away for another time. After grabbing our belongings from the skiff, we follow Wilder and Saffy to a different area of the mansion. The room they've given us is grand, complete with a gated fireplace on one wall and a piano hugging the windows. A tall, golden portrait has been placed over the mantel. He must be one of the Sharp ancestors, given the old-fashioned outfit and absolute shit of a smile.

I should call Mom. I should maybe even tell her to relay to Vinh and Jenn that I found Wilder. Covey could've died last night and somehow, I blacked out and saved her. While Covey collapses on the bed from exhaustion, I sit by a window and grip the radio. It doesn't make sense that my best friend is sitting in another room and I'm here, with a girl carrying a knife. Maybe I wouldn't have been so alone the last two years if Mom and I spent more time looking for the living than the dead.

It doesn't feel real when Mom picks up the line, breathy and asking about whether I'd listened to the weather report.

A storm is coming, she says again. *The water will rise.* A premonition for when our reincarnated family will come, even though there are bigger, real problems, like a monster stalking us. Like the gills on my neck and strange eyes. Like Aaron back in Mercy.

Mom and I are in different worlds.

I chew on my shirt and listen. She never asks if I am okay.

16

IT'S EVENING BY THE time someone wakes me up. I don't remember falling asleep, but I'm curled around the radio, half off the loveseat. Maybe Mom heard the fatigue in my voice, then sang me to sleep. Maybe I was just impossibly exhausted between the attempted drowning and unexpected reunion and slept like a brick on my own. Heavy with sleep, I turn to eye the source of the noise. From what I can see, a tawny brown cat is kneading Covey in the stomach, one tight jab after another.

"Noon!" Covey whisper-yells again. "Noon!"

"What?" I say, the cushion soft against my cheek. This is luxury, compared to *Wild Things* and the shack. Sleeping twelve more hours sounds good right now.

Covey doesn't agree. "The cat is making biscuits on me."

A heart-shaped locket glints on the collar around the cat's neck. It obviously belongs to Wilder or Saffy. "So?"

The girl is truly horrified—even more so than from last night's knocking at the shack. Covey jerks her head at the cat.

"Its glowing green eyes are daring me to move so she can murder me. Get her off!"

"Come 'ere." Lazily, I do a rubbing motion with my fingers that the cat very pointedly ignores.

Covey gapes at me. The cat continues making biscuits on her stomach, nails scratching into the fabric. It's going to be full of holes later.

I prop up on an elbow. "Are you scared of cats?" Reluctantly, Covey nods, and I laugh—I really laugh so hard I choke on my spit. "Oh my god. I can't."

She's offended by my lack of care, then looks hopeful as I get up on my feet. Her blue eyes are wide with appreciation but narrow as it becomes clear I am going straight for the door. It's hilarious to see Covey being incompetent for once. My cackling stops as a noxious, burned smell slips inside the room.

There's no smoke, but immediately I pick the cat off Covey, and we head into the hallway. The cat meows grumpily in my arms, which is too bad, because if there's a fire, I'm carrying her out. We follow the fumes, which grow stronger and stronger until we reach a spacious dining chamber.

Wilder and Saffy are arguing over a portable stove. From a corner, a generator powers all the tiny lights blinking around us. It's unexpectedly warm and homey. Even the burning pot smell. Several bags of noodles and seasoning packets are empty next to them.

"How do you burn ramen noodles?" I ask as the cat hops from me to the table.

"So you met Sandbag," says Wilder when the aptly named rotund cat curls up where dinner will be served. "And uh, Saf's a bit of an obsessed experimenter?" He means it kindly because there are only the usual suspects in the pot.

Saffy throws her arms into the air. A few noodles swing from the ladle. "My nonna was an excellent cook. So were my parents. This should be genetically impossible!" She sighs, regaining her composure. "Anyway, it's still edible."

We gather at one end of the expansive oak, bowls literally smoking. Their satellite radio is on low in the background, reporting on the various news around Plaquemines Parish. Wilder picks from potted herbs on the windowsill, dipping them into water, before sprinkling cilantro onto the noodles. "That's gourmet as hell," says Covey.

Saffy swats the green leaves away. "Babe, that's soap."

"We can't just waste herbs!" Wilder says, piling it on his bowl. "You know, plants literally cry when you cut them. It's just too high-pitched for people's ears. I have caused distress to put food on the table."

At the word *ears*, I stop eating. The noodles are a gummy mass in my gut as I picture Delgado in my bedroom, pencils in their eardrums, then gone—just like that. I don't understand how this mansion, Wilder, and Saffy are so *normal*. Noticing my hesitation, Covey decides to fill them in on the last few days of our journey. From the boat, to my old house, until the shack where an unseen creature targeted us, she covers it all.

"We still aren't sure what Delgado was sampling at all these places," says Covey. "Mrs. Olivier basically said they're not a botanist, so it can't be algae."

"Technically, algae are not plants," Wilder says. "True plants have structure: roots or a stem, leaves, flowers, that kind of thing. Algae are plantlike in that they photosynthesize, but they're organisms, really." We stare at him. He shrugs. "They can live on their own or be in a symbiotic relationship with another living thing."

Saffy points her chopsticks at Wilder. "He likes plants, and when the bloom stayed around, let's say he went down a deeeeep hole in the library."

"Is that why you're named Wilder?" Covey asks, as though her name makes a lot of sense.

He grins. "Do you have a moment to speak about my mother's lord and savior, Laura Ingalls Wilder?"

"No!" Saffy and I yell at the same time. He cracks up while we send "you don't wanna know" vibes at Covey. Second to collecting creepy dolls, idolizing an old book series without accepting criticism is unhinged obsession.

As his laughter dies away, I remember something. "They had coral reef in one of the tanks, with a bunch of red algae. There were also those little jellyfish, remember?" I glance at Covey. "I watched a documentary about them once. They swim around a lake in Palua to feed something else *inside* of them, and that thing also gives them energy." I feel dumb for not connecting it all before.

Excitedly, Wilder asks about all the other animals kept at the makeshift research station. He confirms the giant clams as another potential symbiosis partner for a type of algae. As for Frank the octopus, "no idea."

"Okay," Covey speaks up. "Explain symbiotic relationship. Please."

"It's like a friends with benefits situation," Saffy explains. "Let's say it's two people who would never, ever hang out with each other otherwise, but then when they do get together, it's perfect. One person gives *A*, the other person gives *B*, and *at least* one person's getting off."

It's not how I would explain it, but irritatingly, it is a very good example.

Wilder raises his hands. "Team Neurotic Kids with Very Specific Interests high five!" Saffy and I give him his high fives. He turns to Covey. "Now you look left out. What's your specialty?"

Covey squirms, apparently embarrassed to be put on the spot. She whispers, "Serial killers."

Saffy gasps dramatically into her hands. "You're a true crime girlie, oh my god."

"No, no—"

I jump in and clarify for her. "She wants to be a writer."

"Oh, that explains everything. Gotcha."

Flushed, Covey sets her chopsticks down and puts the conversation on task. "You think that's why Delgado had the hazmat suit on?"

"I mean it would make sense, if they think these red algae can live in a human body," Wilder says. "But these relationships happen naturally over time because it's mutually beneficial. The algae blooms that happened in lakes and coasts before were just toxic, which yeah, you shouldn't touch either."

It feels as though I'm on the edge of something horrific. It's confusing, and frustrating, to try and untangle the threads of information that the adults have fucked up. "This doesn't explain why Dr. Delgado had pencils shoved in their ears," I say.

Behind Wilder, the radio broadcast wraps up with a weather update that confirms the tropical storm Mom and Aaron warned me about. Wilder reaches to switch off the radio, but it bursts back to life, staticky at first, then filled with a familiar timbre.

My mother Grace Olivier has been the librarian at Mercy High for forty-seven years. She disappeared last night and may be in mental distress. She is not a danger. She is five-foot-five and one-hundred-seven pounds, last seen wearing a nightdress. She's seventy-three years old and may act confused when approached. If you went to Mercy High, you know my mother. She is not a danger to anyone.

Travis is replaced by a more robotic tone, giving additional information on her. I go through a somersault of emotions. Covey and I had just visited her. Confusion had plagued Mrs. Olivier toward the end, but she'd been okay. Right there, where Travis could watch her. How did she leave? Did someone—*or something*—take her, as it had tried with Covey? Maybe it'd gone to the Oliviers afterward.

If you have any information on Mrs. Grace Olivier, please report to the Mercy Harbor main office or your nearest emergency responder.

We sit in the wake of news that shouldn't surprise us. Almost everyone here is missing someone. There's the coming storm, too. If it strengthens to a hurricane, it'll eat a few days out of our deadline with Jimmy. It means being prepared to drop everything and leaving Mercy sooner than anticipated. Maybe that's a good thing, if the red algae is somehow invasive to our health, but it's not a good feeling to know you are giving up on finding someone.

"So," Saffy says slowly. "Who wants dessert? It's just a chocolate cake mix and whatever replacements we've got. I had to make it on the stove, which was a real nightmare. It'll go bad soon, so we gotta finish it off."

We're dedicated to feeling better and loving dessert, it seems, because we say yes enthusiastically to what must be an interesting rendition of cake—if Saffy's burned noodle lump's anything to judge by. Somehow, I get wrangled into helping with the cake while the others shuffle through the radio channels for any additional information.

I'm taste testing an expired jar of very vanilla frosting when Saffy says, "You and Covey should stay as long as you like. You can't go back to that cabin."

All evening, I'd been stunned that the mansion could operate so cheerfully in a place where loved ones can go missing. I watched my childhood best friend and Saffy exchange inside jokes. Saffy knew Mack, but she doesn't know me and Covey. I don't know her either. "Why are you being so nice?"

The question is rude, but Saffy looks thoughtful as she tucks her auburn hair behind an ear. "You know Wilder is petty and cautious enough for an army. I just think if this is the end of the world, why should I be careful with my heart?" She removes garish candles in the shape of a 1 and 7 from the cake and plops them aside. "It's more fun this way, and it makes me feel good to be around people."

I don't deserve to have fun. Safety has been the most important thing to me for a while. I made mistakes in my past life, and

I can't let Mom see me like that again. My heart is off-limits. Thankfully, Saffy fills in my quiet.

She tells me she's from the Northeast. She met Wilder little over a year ago on a bus route. "Even shelters that are supposed to be trans-friendly aren't always trans-friendly," Saffy says. "My only crime is being born poor, and if I'm going to be punished for it, I'll do it at my own pace. I want as many happy days as possible. Don't you?"

In the day we've been at the mansion, I've come to understand why Wil said Saffy is the boss. It's hard to be strong but kind; idealistic but not a pushover. I like her, even while fearing the heart on her sleeve.

Back in the dining room, Saffy scoops cake into our bowls, still slick with an umami sauce, and we reuse utensils too. I'm acutely aware that this cake was meant for someone who isn't here. We eat more quietly than before. The bottom is burned to a crisp and stuck to the pan, and dry crumbs roll off the sides where we haven't frosted well, but the inside is good.

Sweet and savory, then bitter enough to remember. The perfect birthday cake.

17

TRAVIS ISN'T HOME THE next two days, so we can't ask him about his missing mother. Poking around the harbor yielded no results about Rosa; no one wants to admit seeing a teen girl who's gone missing. Covey and I checked our traps, but she has caught nothing besides an errant rabbit too decomposed to eat. In the time we pretend that all's normal, Saffy valiantly cooks bad meals and Covey reads us stories. All the while, the storm and Jimmy's deadline draw nearer. I get lost in the mansion more than once a day, stuck inside rooms within rooms until someone rescues me.

That's how I end up in front of a large whiteboard.

FUCK-IT LIST CENTRAL

WILDER	SAFFY	ROSA
Texas	Make the perfect roux	learn how to ice-skate
Boy band member		see the aurora borealis

"Instead of a bucket list, because we're one hundred percent not going to die any time soon, we keep fuck-it lists," Saffy had explained when she found me there. "Just fun stuff to cross off at the end of the world. Anarchy. Sex. Et cetera."

She invited us to keep fuck-it lists, too, scribbling our names below theirs. But I haven't thought that far into a future for myself. I'm trying to make it through the next week and a half to somehow save both Mom and the boat. I stood there, marker in hand for an embarrassingly long time, until Saffy said, "It's okay if you don't know."

So, I repeat the embarrassment on my own. Today, I slam the marker down, having written nothing again, and dart into the hall. I swing the flashlight beam back and forth, agitated by the lack of progress and the pulse in my ear. The headache persists, no matter what I do. It must be from the drop in pressure that comes before a storm, or maybe it's all the recent events adding up, proving that I'm in over my head. Delgado should have left behind a mad-scientist type of journal with all their hypotheses about the bloom and animals.

I assume I'm lost again, until I hear voices—Covey's gravelly tone and Wilder's more upbeat one—drifting down the hall. Before I can make my presence known, Wilder says, "Noon is like a corpse flower." I stop, just beyond the dining chamber's cracked light, my own beam shut off now. I should feel guilty, but all the hairs on my neck are raised in anticipation of my old friend's judgment. "They bloom once a year, release all those putrid, smelly feelings—"

My irritation bubbles over immediately, because how dare he talk to Covey about me as if I am still the same person. Yet it feels as though he's let someone in on a secret—true or not. "Can I talk to you?" I say, interrupting in the grandest fashion: an unintentional door slam.

Surprise flits across their faces. Wilder recovers quickly and, with a small smile, gestures for me to follow. "Yeah, come on the roof with me." He'd assumed correctly that I meant him. We haven't been alone since our reunion, and now I suspect he's been avoiding me too. Covey is scowling. I don't want to know what she asked that prompted Wilder to deem me a *corpse* flower.

He leads me to a vacant powder room, then climbs out the window. He balances on a trellis and goes up to the roof, popping his head over to see if I'm coming. I glance at the still water below before pulling myself onto the trellis. I'm far less graceful than Wilder, who's clearly done this a million times. This flat section of the rooftop has been set up with a blanket, binoculars, and a juice box. "I watch the stars sometimes," he says and nods at the spot next to him. I sit down. The tree line obscures much of the lateral view, which means people would have a difficult time seeing us, but the sky is completely open. "Here," says Wilder as he offers me half a peanut butter and jelly sandwich. "Sorry we're so bad at cooking."

The crust crumbles too easily, but the rest is relatively soft. "You still death grip your sandwiches," I say without thinking as I turn away from the dusky horizon. His thumb has left an imprint in the white bread. He used to do this with every handheld food—bánh mì, hoagies, even with gỏi cuốn, he would accidentally tear into the delicate rice paper.

He chuckles. Wilder curls his shimmery nails into a claw before shaking the goofiness away. "You know, about that convo earlier—"

"I don't wanna hear it," I say, the sandwich's sweetness overwhelming on my tongue. I hold it in my lap and exercise my aching jaw. "I thought you'd be farther away, where we couldn't meet." He and Saffy had mentioned supply exchanges, so he must have known I was still here through the gossip at the harbor. More important is the fact that he knows that Jay and Dad died. I'd assumed he was somewhere else, ignorant about how the Mercy we grew up with is still clinging on in the worst of ways through people like Jimmy.

"I was, at first," Wilder says defensively. "I went as far as Baton Rouge, but it's hard. World isn't built for runaways." He twists a knob on the binoculars. "I didn't come back to Mercy until several months ago."

My tongue kneads against the sore gums. Over and over and over, but it never gets better. Just something swollen to prod and for sugar to decay. I think maybe it's my wisdom teeth coming in because I'm that age, but they shouldn't be so far up. Wisdom teeth are lodged in the back, where a dental surgeon sometimes drills them into pieces. Takes them out chunk by chunk. That would be less painful than this conversation.

"Then why didn't we see each other until now?" I squish the sandwich even more. "I was always with my mom before this."

"Exactly. And your mom would tell my parents. When I left, I didn't fully get that I would end up having to leave it all. You end up missing one birthday or big event, or whatever, and you just get embarrassed. I heard about your dad and Jay. I couldn't even think about what to say that would make it better. I'm sorry about that."

Despite the hurt, I understand. Many days passed where I wanted to be away from Mom's grief, which filled every corner of the boat cabin. Even memories aren't safe. A glimpse of a picture or smell is enough to catapult us into the past when Dad and Jay were alive, then rudely snap us back to reality. I share this grief with Mom, and yet no words have ever made us better. A sigh rattles my chest.

Wilder sets the binoculars down, and the world seems to darken around us with shadowy treetops and dim stars. "What I was trying to tell Covey earlier—*no*, listen." He leans forward to catch my eye. "Corpse flowers. They bloom once, yeah, with all those goopy smells, and people line up to see 'em. And it's like you, when you open up. Once you see it, you never forget what it's like to be next to someone who feels that much all the time. It's like you."

I can't help the skeptical scrunch taking over my face, but I let him talk.

"I'm a really simple person by comparison. If something's not in front of me, I don't worry about it. I take it day by day. You're important to me, okay, even when we're not around each other."

Hearing it softens the knot in my chest. His eyes are brown and honest, though he phrases everything with attitude. I sniff and say, "So I melt down and it's cute." Panic confuses his expression, but then he spots my crooked smile.

"Let's be truthful then," Wilder says. "The complete truth. The history of Wilder and Nhung." He pauses for drama, then taps my palm. "Before I left, I was a little in love with Danny Trần, but I was a lot in love with you."

The confession befuddles me for a second. "I was a lot in love *with you*," I spit out. "It was so weird. We literally crawled around in diapers and suddenly I wanted to kiss you? I thought it was because people kept teasing us whenever they saw us. Subliminal messaging."

"Or our actual parents trying to pair us off," Wil adds. "It's like the flip switched when we turned ten, didn't it? I know you get it. Sons carry the name on. If you're anything less than a macho man, then you're not a man at all."

"Yeah." I set the sandwich aside. The way Dad treated me and Jay became increasingly different as I got older. Others began to comment on me and Wilder too once we started middle school. What was innocent before was suddenly cause for teasing. When our families got together, we started to sit apart, but I saw the subtle tensions between him and his dad. The clap on his shoulder. "Is that why you ran away?"

Wilder lets out a bitter laugh. "I asked my dad straight up if he wanted a son who was happy. He said he wanted a son that didn't make him sad. That's as good as disowning me over some piercings and nail art. Add being bisexual on top of that, and they were going to have an aneurysm."

"They knew?"

"Oh they knew. I had to get away from all his shit. Like the brainwashing got to me. Made me so angry. I had to go away to be my own kind of boy, man, whatever."

I'd failed my best friend in many ways. Withdrawing because I was afraid of what others would say. Not prioritizing us over rumors. We were both reduced to boy and girl, and he'd been fighting his parents alone. "I'm sorry I didn't do more," I tell him.

"Hey, my dad is a whole forty-something-year-old dude. I didn't expect you to stand up to him," says Wilder. "I wasn't what you needed either."

I want Wilder to tell me everything that has happened since he left, but to ask this is also to offer myself up—to pry apart my ribs and let all the ache come in. There's a name fresh on my body, needling its way into my stomach lining. Making me sick.

What if all that's left of me is what Aaron abandoned on that shore? Gross, disgusting, and stupidly naive.

Then there's a feeling that has burned its way through my bones: *What if I'm not a girl at all?* Everyone seems to know who they are and who they want to be. Saffy's a girl, Wilder's his own type of masculine, and Covey is herself and a lesbian. I'm encased in skin that isn't always mine, clothes that aren't me. I am in a funnel of consequences, and I don't know what'll happen if I escape.

Wilder plops his chin into a palm. "Do you want me to kiss you now?" The question rips me from my worries. I'd forgotten how straightforward he could be.

I think for a moment. "No, I don't. Not anymore."

He nods. "I feel the same. Actually, in general I'm pretty neutral about all the touchy stuff. But I see you as my friend."

In another life, we would still love each other that way. We wouldn't have made the choice to run so hard from each other. But this isn't bad either, being side by side after the fact and quietly loving one another anyway. *Choosing* to love him in a different way. It makes me think a future is possible. Every crashing emotion can be lifted eventually. The worst will die away and some good will come. We have survived to be together again.

We sit comfortably in our silence as the misunderstandings sort themselves out. After a long time being bitten up by mosquitos, I'm ready to call it a night, but my eye snags on telltale luminescence of algae being disturbed. "Wait," I say. "Something's out there." I point at the outlying darkness beyond the mansion's backyard.

Wilder is sleepy but raises the binoculars to his eyes, adjusting for a few moments. Then, he curses, "Holy shit. It's Mrs. Olivier." He shuffles the binoculars to me.

Through the magnified lens, I can barely focus on her. She is an outline with silver hair, shifting side to side as if disoriented. "We can't scare her away," I mutter to Wil. "Go get Covey and Saffy. Tell them to be quiet."

I watch Mrs. Olivier the entire time he's gone, studying her movements. After several agonizing minutes, my friends join me. Wilder squeezes my shoulder to let me know he's there. Covey's wary with her crossbow, squinting for any animals that might be tracking the librarian. For some reason, Saffy has wrangled Sandbag into a carrier backpack. She mouths, "I'm not leaving her behind." The implication is, of course, that we might not get to return.

We climb down onto a raft, paddling as quietly as possible across the fifteen feet to dry ground. Mrs. Olivier's moved some but not by much, each step hesitating. Is she looking for her house?

Her lilac nightgown is blotched with some kind of fluid, like oil.

A twig breaks under one of our feet. Spurred by the noise, Mrs. Olivier runs.

18

MERCY COVE MERCY COVE Mercy Cove

The site of my assassination, where everything between me and Mom went from bad to worse. It was supposed to be fun, the party I sneaked out to. I was a Big Girl, fourteen and fresh-faced.

That's where Mrs. Olivier is taking us.

She's faster than should be possible, since just the week before, her bones cracked with the tiniest movements. We would lose her entirely, if not for the bioluminescent algae: step-by-step, a flicker of blue in the distance. She doesn't look back, or else she'd see us too.

Chelsea's Cove is on the very outskirts of the town itself, tucked away by unkempt paths of fern. It's beyond the levee, far from any civilization—the perfect place for partying. I'd heard the wild stories before Aaron brought me here.

Two juniors skinny-dipped!

Dana is such a slut giving it up

God I still have sand in my undies

They rush ahead, unaware of how my legs have become lead. Sweat stings the rash on my side and dampens my clothes. I can barely breathe in the humid air around us. *My mom told me not to come here*, I can try, but then I'd have to explain what happened to me. I shouldn't think only about myself.

"This was on Delgado's list to sample," Covey says to Wilder. I'd forgotten completely in my terror. I thought I would have more time to prepare.

Stop, I can plead to Wilder, *remember when we rolled down levees together?* We can tuck our elbows in now and barrel right through ant hills and dandelions. Remember how to laugh, how to be young and not yet fuckups. Instead, we carefully descend the levee, ankles itching from the long grass. It thins the closer we get to the beach. Soil becomes silt, sinking beneath our shoes.

There are dark rocks, as wet as open skulls. Shiny, glistening heads breaking the sand. Tendrils of seaweed reach from the shore, as if climbing toward some distant destination. There's rot blowing on the wind, of course—this close to the ocean teeming with algae—but underneath there's a sour greasiness. The ground is littered with bottle caps and glass, remnants of another time. Broken seashells edge from the sand.

Mrs. Olivier does not hesitate. *Crunch* goes the glass. Saffy flinches, as though she feels each piercing shard in the woman's bare feet. *Crunch*. Inside the bubble carrier on Saf's back, Sandbag hisses, forgetting about the open can of soft food she'd been lured with. Maybe it would've been better to leave the cat behind rather than losing her here. I should tell them to turn around, and yet there's an animal need, an impossible compulsion, to finally witness what waits for us on the other side.

We've passed the last patch of solid ground, where people used to park their cars and drag coolers the rest of the way. I remember how small I felt in Aaron's truck, even after how I sneaked out from the trailer. I remember someone smacking my ass that night in the mad dash for the water but not who.

The cove opens to us, black rock rising high on both sides that narrow to a tiny entrance through which the water moves. Is always moving.

We are not alone.

There are bodies everywhere. Not the tired drunk people like you'd expect to see after a beach party, but lifeless forms slumped on the rocks, ripped to shreds. It seems impossible that there would be so many dead in one place. But when we step closer, we see no blood at all. Each husk is more costume than human. The faces, all transparent masks without eyes and frozen mouths without tongues. Muscle and viscera have relocated, or vanished. Like cicadas molting from their shell, these humans have left their crispiest organ behind.

A dreadful quiet has swollen around us. Mrs. Olivier walks through the bodies, and we can't make ourselves take the short, two-inch drop off the ridge to stop her. Sandbag meows, her paws scratching the bag's clear case. Saffy shushes the distraught cat.

"We've seen enough." Wilder tentatively steps ahead. "Mrs. Olivier! Please, stop. Come with us."

The woman halts so suddenly that her torso swings forward from the momentum while her feet bury into sand. Mud has splattered up her ankles and touches the ends of her nightgown. She must have been wandering outside since her disappearance. Centimeter by centimeter, she turns around.

In her fist is a knitting needle, a fluttering cord of yarn still attached.

The spit on her chin glints as Mrs. Olivier whispers, "Don't you want to take your skin off?" The bandages around her forearms are gone, revealing angry red rashes with spider-web veins. Her wounds secrete a clear substance, much looser than pus. My side starts to prickle nonstop.

Covey blocks us from view. "Don't let her touch you, in case it's contagious."

The observation is shitty, but Covey has a point. Maybe the scientist had found some incurable disease. Mrs. Olivier is unwell—on the verge of a breakdown. Her son had said so. But she isn't someone to be shut away in an old people's home or ignored on the streets. She is my librarian, my teacher, my one adult who didn't disappoint me in some way.

"It itches, doesn't it?" Mrs. Olivier asks. She's looking at all of us, but she's smiling at me. That cut of teeth sends a chill down my spine, but more uncomfortable is how it seems to gnash on the rash that has plagued me since Mom accidentally knocked me overboard into the sea. A coincidence, that's all; tell a welt not to itch and of course it will. Mrs. Olivier inserts the knitting needle into an open wound at the top of the rash on her arm. She digs underneath the skin at her elbow, then further down, as vigorous as a violinist in concert. She peels back one section of well-oiled skin and offers the flap to us. "If you all pull at the same time, it'll come right off. Don't you think, girls? Less painful than waxing, I'd say."

Saffy breaks away from us. "Please stop hurting yourself!"

Mrs. Olivier sways heavily and kicks through human husks before slamming into a wall. She drags herself across the rocks, leaving a chunky splatter. "It's algae," I murmur as the bits of Mrs. Olivier stuck on the wall are illuminated in the dark. It must be sweet relief to leave all your hurting parts behind.

As Wilder told us, everything from marine invertebrates to fungi have formed symbiotic relationships with algae. Algae provides energy to corals through photosynthesis, and the reef acts as its shelter. In salamanders, algae grow within the egg, exchanging oxygen for nutrients. What has it done with us?

Mrs. Olivier walks into the water. It seeps into her nightgown, a blood spill in reverse.

The cove's pool is no longer calm. It is boiling water. It is a tidal wave. In our horror, we haven't noticed what should've been obvious. It is so many hands and feet and torsos shifting into form, humans that drip like candle wax. They are hairless and indistinct, gelatinous except for the bones that have not melted away. It's everyone who's gone missing and probably many more we don't know about, flowing from the open ocean to the delta to the estuary to here. It's a gathering place of sorts, a spawning of something new and vicious. Mrs. Olivier has vanished completely into the tide. At the next surge, when the entirety of the pool is *alive*, Covey shoots a bolt. The entire mass screams when the bolt makes impact. Mouths or, rather, open holes in the hundreds moan.

"Noon," someone says close to my ear. "NOON! Come on."

"Do you hear that?" I ask.

LET US IN LET US IN LET US IN LET US IN LET US IN

It has a hypnotic rhythm, the voice that isn't quite a voice, and yet the meaning is as clear as a thought.

"The cosmic monster with a shitload of mouths screaming?" Wilder asks. "Yeah, duh."

"No, I mean it's *saying* something." Confusion passes over his face.

LET US IN LET US IN LET US IN

I clamp my hands over my ears but it does nothing to shut out the sound, because it's me. It's all in my head—a demand only meant for me to hear. Every time I sank deep or long enough in the water, it's sung to me. The voices, pounding headaches, and knocking were all signs I am connected in a way I didn't expect. My compulsion to stay close to the ocean has been stronger than ever, and this monstrous thing wants my body to nest within. Already the rash has been growing.

What will happen if I slit myself in half? What will climb in and what will climb out?

The monsters have always been human. I should've known that.

Amongst the writhing is a hazmat suit, torn and rippling over a languid body. Since our short encounter at the trailer park, Dr. Delgado has run themself on the rocks, desperate to be rid of suit and skin, but they are mostly whole. A thick pencil remains lodged in each ear. I understand now. I picture the scientist puncturing their own eardrums to stop the noise and halt their transformation. Despite all Delgado's efforts, the siren call got them in the end. As it did for Mrs. Olivier; as it will with me.

Pressure pulses behind my eyes.

LET US IN LET US IN

My arms go slack, body giving up as it had done once before in Mercy Cove. It's like seeing and feeling double: me now and me in the past, chest constricted by Aaron's arms from behind. I am kept still. I just want the world to stop. Neither Wilder nor Saffy leaves, even when all I'd do is slow them down.

Unlike the other husks, Delgado has an intact-enough form to advance toward us steadily. Everything happens too quickly. The riverine tide is powerful, threatening to swallow us whole. I am a fish bone in spoiled flesh, pushed apart by the ocean's tongue. Or is it Aaron's now? Delgado swings forward with the momentum, too, and snatches at Saffy's wrist. Wil kicks their chest, which caves in. Saffy twists toward escape, reaching for me still, but a gloved hand wrenches her backpack loop. "No!" she screams when Sandbag's carrier is pulled into the red tide.

The cat yowls as water spills through the bag's numerous air holes. The chorus of *LET US IN* overwhelms Wil and Saffy's shouting as they fight off the scientist. It's the type of party no one wants to be at, and I can't stand by watching it happen. Taking deep breaths, I wade deeper within the slime to reach Sandbag. The warm innards of neighbors and strangers alike slither around my thighs. It's like I've stuck my head in a bag of pork rinds—how heavy the stench of oil. They suck along my skin, determined to dissolve the surface layer. Fingers clutching the barely visible bag, I haul us ashore.

I unzip the backpack. Frenzied and sopping wet, Sandbag doesn't need a warning before darting into the night. Chunks of someone fall from her fur.

"I can't shoot with you that close to them!" Covey yells from the side.

The trio are still tangled. The rubber suit is slick with algae and viscous fluids, slipping through Wil and Saffy's uncoordinated hands. Pushing off from the sand, I heave the empty carrier and throw it at Delgado's head. The scientist stumbles back and in a breath, Covey shoots. The bolt slams between their shoulder blades. For a moment, the body appears suspended in air. Then it falls right on top of Saffy.

Without a stronger tide or a capable husk to drag us in, this pool of many mouths is scary but ultimately harmless. So long as I am myself, my friends are safe. I don't realize I'm anxiously twisting the key on my necklace until Covey's burst of incredulous laughter. "I did it? We did it!" I let go, and the key thumps lightly between my collarbones. Delgado is a mess of dead tendon but still a specimen we can bring back to Jimmy, well before the deadline. There'll be more freedom. We've saved Mercy from closure, despite the town never saving us.

"Ugh!" Saffy shoves the body aside as Wilder helps her up. "Sandbag got away, right?"

"I didn't throw your cat. Only the carrier," I say.

Covey turns around to look at me, mouth in a huge grin that immediately vanishes. A terrible sound leaves her lips. "Mommy?" Sweet with memory, sharp with hope.

Rising from the water is another body. One eye has been picked from its socket, leaving the hole bloodred. Algae. She is familiar. The woman slouches forward, calves deep in the writhing froth. She swipes away at the jellylike substance coating the curtain of dishwater-blond hair. I recognize the angle of her pale, peeling jaw.

Covey was the little girl afraid to jump from a high branch in my vision at the shack. The woman is her mother, the person whose memory—mind—I had slipped inside. Now Covey is a child wandering under moonlight, every step shaky. The crossbow is so low it sends ripples over the water. "Mommy," she says again, in her own dream or nightmare.

When Mack opens her mouth, only a horrible gurgling comes out. Her voice box has gone, melted into the tide from which she's returned. Her attention rests solely on Covey. They run toward each other, a family reunion that begins and ends in Mack seizing her daughter. She shoves Covey into the water, all the while her throat attempts spoken word. A thick blanket of algae throbs over where Covey should be, and I'm there immediately.

Movement flashes at the corner of my eye, and I screech at Saffy and Wilder. "No, get out of here!" They linger too long before bolting for higher ground. The water wants to claim us. It is sticky molasses and old honey, the residue on sauce bottles that tempts bugs to land. A shiny film has formed over Mack's remaining eye, but the way it flicks back and forth is reptilian. She doesn't need more than that to outsee us.

I sink my teeth into her shoulder, and I taste salt. Ocean, something grassy, a ribbon of oil. I don't think she feels pain at all since there's no response until I pull away. Distracted, she loosens her hold. Covey bursts upward, and I drag her to the rocks, which are closer than the shore. She shoves at me to swim back. "We can't help her like this!" I yell over the cove's collective crying. Her eyes are bloodshot, but she nods slowly. The wet, rocky wall is difficult to climb. Covey grimaces whenever her nails lift. Mine would've too, if I had any left. Wilder appears over the ledge and reaches down, his dark hair whipped in the wind.

Covey gasps when her mother grabs her ankle. She squeezes her eyes shut, and I whisper to her not to let go. Keep moving. Mack's non-mangled arm can get her only up so far, and her body drops into the ocean as we make it over the ledge with Wilder's help—then we are running, our chests burning with night air and heartache.

19

BY THE TIME WE return to the mansion, Sandbag's perched on a windowsill, half-done grooming herself. Saffy practically cries from happiness, but the cat jumps to an out-of-reach shelf with a murderous expression. I don't blame her resentment since we smell like the many-mouthed goo that tried to eat her.

We'd brought Delgado's body back in a wheelbarrow, then stored them in a spare bathroom to deal with later. Back in the main living area, Wilder lays some plastic bags over the armchairs. Covey's been shaking since the cove. We held hands the way home, our fingers not interlaced but close, and I keep them that way as we sit next to each other.

Saffy sighs. "That was really real, huh." She already has a kettle on the burner.

"Yeah. It's real. Living body—bodies—of water? The symbiotic thing again, but with humans. The algae was in Mrs. Olivier and . . ." Wil's voice trails off. "Did you guys notice the stink?"

"Pork rinds," I say, tongue testing the inside of my mouth. "There was some kind of weird oil all over them."

Saffy squints. "Sebum maybe? It's a natural body oil. Everyone has it. Ew, what if it eases their skin off . . . wait. Oh, Mack." Her eyes are full of regret. "I'm so fucking sorry about Mack."

"Her body was still warm," Covey says, then turns toward me. "Noon?"

She wants confirmation, of course, that her mother might be alive under all that waste. I'm the only other person who got close. I didn't know Mack, but I know Covey. Wilder and Saffy wouldn't have let just anyone come to their sanctuary either. Those are plenty reason to wish for the best. "Mack was warm," I say. "Like me." It isn't a lie. Mack is human as much as I am, right now.

Our friends don't argue. Neither Saffy nor Wilder saw Rosa there, but it would be difficult to tell one person apart from all the husks. Silently, they'd come to their conclusions. Regardless, the red algae is living and spreading, and that means one day those bodiless screaming mouths will be on shores farther north. It must be the true reason the government wants to shut the town down.

"We all need rest, food if we can stomach it, but definitely rest." Saffy doles out mismatched mugs full of lukewarm, chunky hot chocolate. "Game plan in the morning."

I'm thankful for the excuse to hide away. I don't know yet if I'll molt like a wiry grasshopper, or if this entire ordeal's a resurfaced trauma. With my free hand, I twist the key on my necklace three times, locking away that anxiety until I know for sure. Separately, we wash up best as we can with our limited supply of rainwater. I avoid glimpsing or touching the rash on my side. I need a peaceful night of sleep.

In the bedroom, Covey has flopped down over the duvet. I rummage through my belongings, tempted to call Mom and demand answers. Understanding is at the edge of my exhaustion.

"Do you think it was her that night at the shack, come to drown me?"

I turn to look at Covey. She hasn't moved from the bed, but now her forearm's thrown over her eyes. I let the radio go. I cross the rug until the bed squeaks under my weight. We're on the far opposite sides of the queen.

"Yes," I say, because the woman in my vision and her mother are the same. No doubt about that. Maybe it's instinct to return for those you love. *Sometimes when a person loves you, they can't control themselves*, but that's just another fucked-up excuse Aaron told me. This is different. Strangely, it's one of Mom's platitudes that springs to mind. "The water always gives back what it takes, even if they come home different. She remembers you. Each time, she reached for you."

Covey draws in a deep breath. She doesn't talk about her mom much, so I only listen. I think I would like Covey's mom, who told stories and made up games, who shared with her daughter the lessons she learned in life.

Slowly, I reach for a book on the bedside table and flip it open across my lap.

Tonight, I read to Covey.

. . .

Morning arrives as a cluster of clouds, thick with a humidity that suggests rain. Since before dawn, I've sat on a tufted ottoman by a cracked window and watched the river. Each wave seems to me a deep, patient sigh. Yesterday's events have all registered in my brain. From the skin suits we found to the missing people returning changed, I am beginning to make sense of it all.

Never go back to the cove, Mom had warned me at the lighthouse. I'd been so used to listening to my mom that I didn't question it. My assumption was about shame—she didn't want to relive the worst night of my life. But there's more. I never once really understood my body and its whims to know what changes are extraordinary.

For nearly two years, I have been changing. After Aaron hurt me, my hair grew in white; my skin took on an oily sheen; my nails fell out. I don't eat well unless it's raw. Stress, trauma, whatever it was—Mom covered it up. Perhaps this sentient algae had been there during my assault in Chelsea's Cove. More than one unwanted thing had come inside me.

I bury my head in my palms and breathe. Dangling from my necklace is the boat key gleaming silver. Even magic can't erase away the soreness of my heart and body, the clipped flashes of memory in my mind.

When I am finally ready, I check that Covey's still asleep. She's curled into a question mark, hand on the edge of the book I'd read to her. Then, I stand before the full-length mirror at the far end of the room. With the sweater lifted, daylight reveals the deepening rash. Purplish-red and spread like a vine, it looks exactly as Mrs. Olivier's had. I must have scratched during the night because the edge of the original cut has detached, skin lightly moist. With enough patience, I can de-skin myself in one flawless pull.

The husks and I are similar but not all the same. I'd had years, whereas they transformed within months or days of their disappearance. Only one person knows why.

I pass the library where Saffy and Wilder are asleep on their respective sofas. Sandbag watches as quietly, I leave the mansion. The humidity envelops me as soon as I am outside, but the storm isn't here yet. I can feel it on my lips—that fresh, saltless water. I can feel it in the bounce of the aluminum boat as I leave my new and old friends behind.

The water simmers. The water cooks. It will not drown us today.

I might though. Like the undone—the word that pops up when I think about those unspooled bodies—I may be next to bring another person in. The worst truth is I *do* want to hurt something other than myself.

Why haven't I considered that I might be the dangerous thing? Jailbait since puberty, monster since ruined. I am the hateful witch whose wish right now is for sharp claws. Let's get the murdering over with.

At the lighthouse, I cut the engine and hastily tie the boat to the docks. They must hear me because Mom spills out the cabin's front door. She'd removed the sling again from her arm, but her condition has improved from when I last saw her.

Here she is, moles hidden as her eyes widen in surprise. Her voice, clear without a radio wave. Her feet dinging on this metal island toward me. My body is drawn to her like a magnet, but I throw fast and clipped Vietnamese as a wall between us. *"You lied to me."* Mom freezes in place. *"You knew something was wrong with me. Besides being sad or"*—I grit my teeth—*"an embarrassment you have to hide."*

She looks behind her to see if Vinh and Jenn are coming. *"Calm down."*

"No!" A bitter laugh bubbles from my throat. It's my turn to be reckless. *"I visited Mercy Cove. We caught one of those 'monsters' everyone's searching for, but it's a person. You knew, didn't you? But it's the cove that's special."*

"Nhung, I told you not to." Her composure has broken, desperation weighing on her brows.

"You should've said why then." For a long time, I've had to read between the lines. Dad loved me most until he got his son. Mom is ashamed of what my girl body has done, as if I had asked for it. I do not feel right in my skin because it's a lie. None of this should matter, and yet it does.

"Everything I do, I do for you," Mom says.

"No, you don't," I say. *"You're supposed to be my mom, but you just let things happen to me."* She was never going to be the mom bringing apple pie to the classroom bake sale, but she had other answers, important ones. My body is mine alone, but it came from her. It took calcium from her bones, fed from her blood. Doesn't that mean she had a responsibility to teach me how it worked? Shouldn't she be the person to tell me to value myself? Or that, even violated, I am loved and should love.

Wondering "if Mom only . . ." is younger Nhung's bad habit, but the questions run rampant.

I furiously dry the hot tears, because part of me believes I am only making myself a bigger disgrace. I speak anyway. "*You let me go back to Mercy alone. You know what Aaron*"—she flinches at the name—"*did to me.*"

Everyone had to have known at school. A freshman hanging out with a senior. The way he draped an arm around me during pep rallies. Did they see me and think I'm not someone worth saving?

Not worth the trouble.

Not worth the paperwork.

Not worth leaving for.

For as long as I remember, I measured myself against boys. In elementary school, we had boys versus girls. In middle school, it was boys and girls in separate spaces, a delicate balance of body odor and perfume. Then in high school—a turn of events, it's all about girls *on* boys, boys *on* girls. I just wanted to know how it felt to make sense. To be normal, as people put it. I pretended to be what everyone else saw: a teenage girl who could fit in if she really tried. I slipped into a type of skin.

I didn't know how to say no to a nineteen-year-old's phone call.

Chelsea's Cove was a rite of passage for people born and raised in Mercy. Survive a night and you'll add yourself to the legend. In my case, you become a cautionary tale. "What did you find at the cove, Mom? Tell me."

She lets out a shaky breath, defeated by our torn-open secret. "*I came right when I realized you were gone from the trailer. Your dad was away shrimping, so I had to leave Jay sleeping at home. I locked the door behind me.*" She starts the story too early, taking time to build the courage for every word. "*It was close to morning. I was so mad. The cove . . . everyone smelled drunk. Sleeping. That son of a bitch was right there.*" I had never heard my mom curse before this, but she barrels through it because if she stops, she may never finish telling me the truth of that night. "*And you . . . your clothes were shredded. You didn't look right. Almost as clear as ice, like you were going to melt away. I was so confused. What did he do to you? My daughter, she . . .*"

The word stings, as though there had been two of me, and I am the lesser one now.

"*I felt it then,*" she whispers. "Sông." The river, the ocean, the water—the family myth about what keeps us alive through famine and war. A shiver rakes my spine. This is a name I didn't expect. "*I don't know why* Sông *wanted to take you like this, but I begged it to let you stay with me. The color came back to you. You were* con gái của Má *again. I brought you home.*"

Nauseous, I imagine the scene: my fourteen-year-old self, barely clothed in my mom's arms, then laid down to recover. Body changed. Little brother still dreaming. Mom trembling with the certainty that only a god could save her daughter from vanishing in shame. "And the algae?" I ask, forcing myself to look toward the stretch of red-tinged blue at the horizon.

"Algae?" She sounds confused.

I yank my sweater off and roll the raggedy tee to show the fast-growing rash where underneath, I'm certain, the bloom has been growing. Startled, she attempts to wrestle the sweater back over my head. I break away from her reach. "A sweater doesn't keep me safe!" Birds scatter from the lighthouse and become scribbles in the distance. "*A sweater doesn't keep me safe,*" I repeat. "*It doesn't make it hurt less.*" I've worn heavy clothes in hot weather long enough to know it doesn't stop men from teasing me or me blaming myself.

"*The algae didn't come until after the hurricane,*" Mom says as Vinh and Jenn emerge from their house, moving urgently.

My understanding cracks and reassembles. The time I fell from our trawler, I'd felt a behemoth force hold me. A cut marked my torso, where algae can seep in. The second time in the water by the shack, I rescued Covey without knowing how to swim, my eyes darting like an animal's. I experienced a memory that wasn't mine. Maybe it isn't many monsters but one all along.

It started with Aaron's assault on me during my first and last party in the cove. I don't remember. I *can't* remember. Sông must have answered *my* cry for help, the only one to do so. I was meant to survive beside it, not as this partly transform-ing creature living boat to boat, but Mom had pleaded. Then, Mom chose the word "reincarnated" strategically about our family—a secret hope that they can be recovered, too. After being submerged in algae, my transformation escalated.

It doesn't matter to her that I am the survivor here. Mom's keen on staying near Mercy, even if it puts me at risk of being taken back or Aaron finding me again. She thrusts the sweater at me again and says, "*No one can know.* Come on. *Now.*"

Ambiguity lies in her statement. Does she not want people to know that I put myself in a position to be violated, or does she not want people to know the monster I will become because of it? But my changes hadn't happened right away—they trick-led in over the two months after Hurricane Arlene took the rest of our family. She'd been hiding me before that. She withdrew me from school. She never asked if I was okay. I'm not; I'm really, really not, and I'm done keeping it together for her.

"*You were supposed to protect me.*" I rip the necklace from my throat and throw it at her. "*Take it,*" I say. "*I don't care.*" She catches it against her heaving chest.

"*I am. I—*"

"*You're embarrassed by me. You don't see me at all.*" My entire body is shaking as I turn to leave.

Joining us in a flurry of linen, Vinh warns, "Don't treat your mom like that."

"Don't talk to me when your own kid doesn't want to see you," I snap. He swivels as though I've slapped him.

In the tiniest voice, Jenn asks, "Wil's around?" Bright color blooms across her cheeks. Tears glimmer from her thick lashes.

I hadn't meant to bring him up, not without his permission first. Clenching my fists, I answer, "He's healthy."

Vinh and Jenn appear so normal, not at all like the lighthouse keepers that brave the waves shored against Louisiana's coast. They were afraid, so afraid that their son liked to pierce his ears, dye his hair, and wear nail polish. They worried he would look out of place, and that would somehow reflect on them. Mercy is an echo chamber, and even when your family comes from somewhere else, it will swallow you.

Adults having their shit figured out is an illusion of childhood. You wake up one day and the mirage is gone. The soft gold sunlight now appears too yellow, too harsh. Your parents aren't bickering cutely but arguing, their faces red. Even when you're hurt, they will tell you your wounds aren't real. Better yet, put a sweater on it and hide away.

"You should feel stupid," I say to them. "You pushed your own kid away over accessories. Was it worth it?" Wilder's parents appear stung, but I'm not done. Rage breaks all my boundaries. My eyes meet Mom's. "You never taught me how to survive. Worse, you never taught me how to live without hiding." Her hand catches my wrist when I turn to leave. "Let go," I tell her in English, not bothering to check the moles on her eyelids for her emotional state.

Her fingers squeeze harder, but I do not back down. My mind is set, the surest it's been for a while. Reluctantly, she releases me. I return to the small boat and turn the motor on. The last thing I look at, so I can keep that memory with me as long as I can, is *Wild Things*. Dad loved this boat so much he went into debt to have it. Mom loves him and Jay so much she would sacrifice me to keep it. In it is my box of small treasures, which I leave behind because I must put myself first for once.

Too powerful, too everything—balled up in this skin, I'm ready to take shape.

20

I ROW THE SKIFF back north, away from the lighthouse and my mother. The wind carries her screaming far from me. I like not hearing her right now. Old her would've gotten right on *Wild Things* to follow, but maybe my words have stuck. Maybe it's Vinh and Jenn stopping her, afraid that if my mother pursues me, that she'll scare their child off too. As if Wilder has any intention of returning home.

My heart longs for the mansion, our little neverland, but Wil, Saffy, and Covey will realize something's wrong. I left without telling them. We should be celebrating our survival together. Wilder would break out the fruit juice, Saffy would pull us in for a team hug, and Covey would plan our next move. It's cowardly but I can't face them yet, especially because I hid the rash and there's much I've yet to discover about this gift or curse from Sông. Convincing myself that I'm brave for protecting them from afar doesn't work, because my mind is riddled with cruel faces. Like students and teachers from the past, they would only see a dumb girl who got herself into this mess.

So I spend a few slow hours on one side of the levee, listening to my neighbors pack for the evacuation. Inside trucks hiccupping under the weight of all that's important, they drive away from the incoming storm. No one will be back this time. Fat welts form on my arms as mosquitos eat me up. Apparently, I'm delicious even when I'm not all human. I flick them whenever there's a pinch, leaving blood streaks and legs as thin as eyelashes on my body. Nothing about me has begun to glow yet.

Because I cannot return to the lighthouse, Port Mercy, or our abandoned trailer, I go back to the one place that felt like safety—or at least, a liminal space within another liminal space where no one can find me. My first cabin with Covey, the one with the hole in the floor. Sông or the algae had made me a creature of the water, so there's nothing to be afraid of anymore. By the time I reach the broken pier, my muscles have strung themselves out from rowing aimlessly. The sky is tangerine orange and clipped with approaching darkness. I stalk toward the door, *thud thud thud*, and open it.

Covey is sitting on the cushionless couch pulled over the gape in the floor. She is facing me because she has been waiting—maybe even since I left this morning. Covey does what a hunter does best, after all. She observes. The crossbow was settled on her knee, but now it's in her arms. Rising to her feet, she says, "I'd rather just get it over with." It's a throwback to our conversation right in this room after she almost drowned.

You must do things you aren't ready for, or else it'll become a pattern. Look at me and Mom, how one missed conversation became two and three. Ignoring the problem created more. "I was awake this morning before you left."

Ah, so she saw me.

She tilts the crossbow at my abdomen. "May I?" It isn't a threat.

I nod.

Slowly, she rolls up my T-shirt to uncover the pulsing rash. Her fingertips, light as they are, pool little sweat droplets on my slick skin. In a single breath, she has withdrawn from me, hand back on the crossbow.

"Are you going to shoot me then?" My emotions have been bleeding steadily since confronting Mom. I am surprisingly calm, somehow amused as I add, "Jimmy did say dead or alive."

Covey has one monster. What will her dad give her if she brings another?

"I guess I deserve it," I say, and hold my arms out wide. "We were never meant to be friends."

She doesn't move. Her blue eyes are sharp and wet. I don't smile because she'd feel guilty killing something that can smile. Her mom taught her that.

I step forward until only the crossbow holds us apart. The bolt's weight rests against my breastbone. I feel it so clearly: my shock, the mystery, the violence of wanting to show Covey that I am the same underneath all that skin. I must be Covey's dream, the kind Mrs. Olivier asked us about at her house, about what violence can be awakened inside of a person when confronted with danger. I lean in more. "Do it then," I say, because

I'm still searching for validation. I want to know that I'm worth saving, without explanation. It's unfair and entirely selfish to put it all on Covey, but fate brought us here to this strange shack with the hole in the floor.

All we do is stare at one another. Then the crossbow clangs on the ground, immediately forgotten, and Covey steps into my space. Her arms wrap around my shoulders. The world around has darkened considerably. The only light in the room is from my watch, which ticks as loud as our hearts pressed together.

It is my first true breath of September, and it smells like her. It's a metal scent, twisted with grassy notes. In her rush to find me, she'd left the mansion without a hint of sunscreen. The small detail siphons all the fight and self-hatred away. I melt into the embrace. If I had died before this moment, I wouldn't have this warmth, Wilder safe and happy back in my life, or the joy in knowing a person as complete as Saffy. It's good to be alive and breathing, even when the air is toxic and the water can kill you.

Face pressed on her shirt, I confess, "I'm one of those things. Husk, monster, whatever."

Her answer is muffled against my hair. "You're a person." More quietly, she adds, "My friend." The word is electric. As much as I resist letting it light up every synapse in my body, I fail.

We untangle because we're bad at being vulnerable and our faces are red. We've never touched this much outside of a life-or-death situation. Together we sit on the couch, carefully a foot apart and looking at the wall ahead of us. I ask, "How did you know I would come back here?"

The couch squeaks when she leans back, tucking her hair behind her ears. "I didn't. I hoped to see you, that's all." She could have just taken Delgado's body straight to Jimmy and told him about Mack. With how much he loves Covey, he might have sent real help to get her mom back. I'm easy to leave behind, but she waited.

It makes me want to cry. "I have a story to tell you," I say. "Will you listen until the end?"

Covey considers my question seriously because this is the kind of vulnerability we're not used to. All the world's natural horrors do not compare to our humanmade ones. She nods.

I first piece together my family myth for her. Luckily, I've learned a thing or two from listening to Covey read at night. It's easy to pretend this part is someone else's history rather than my ancestors'. "It began when Great Grandma left on a wooden boat, thin as a bow, with her husband and two kids. Great Grandpa had been a South Vietnamese soldier, and he was the only boy from their village to come home. They were already hungry that first day on the boat, and every day it got worse. Their lips peeled from dehydration. Her kids begged to drink the saltwater, but that's a trap. They longed for a rescue, or a shipwreck on an island, but on the fifth day the clear skies turned deep gray. Thunder was the closest sound to their chests. Each wave grew taller and taller, and this boat that was not meant to carry so many lives broke." At this point in the tale, Dad would subconsciously rub the spot on his chest where he had a tattoo of a ship. I place my hand over my heart.

"Scattered like seeds, they did not know right from left or up from down—only that they were drowning, and fast. The ocean was dark and ravenous. But they all woke up on a ship, blankets around their shoulders. Alive. Later, Great Grandma said she remembered a dream. A promise, really, between her and the water that wanted to swallow her family. They named our savior Sông. We've always lived off rivers and streams, but now there is another force to pray to: something that listens and answers."

This is the section of story I can't pretend is someone else's.

My voice trembles slightly. "Last night wasn't my first time in the cove." It comes out disjointed, likely making zero sense, but Covey listens intently: the party that shouldn't have happened, the invitation to swim, and the fingers on my drawstring shorts. The fragments rewind in time, too.

I acted how I thought girls were supposed to. Curious, I believed what others told me. I had been at the edges of woman-shaped; enough. He first approached me down the road from our trailer, where I liked to pick wildflowers. He was not beautiful or ugly, just so ordinary—like table salt, yellowing grass, dust on a forgotten shelf. I thought I was being kind when I became his friend.

"He was . . . my boyfriend?" I say because if I make it sound normal, maybe it can be—but it isn't the right word. It has never been the right word. It will never be the right word, and yet I can't say anything else through the nausea in my mouth. The memories are too much, and I want to curl in on myself. Carnations, a telephone, a song on the radio that he said made him think of me. It is a fucking joke. I was only ever a wound he wanted to stick his dirty fingers into. "It's my fault."

Covey does not hesitate. "He groomed you. Then he— fucking creep." She tries to hold herself back from saying more, the sheer effort creating heat to roll off her body.

"Everyone makes it seem so normal, you know?" I pick at the sofa's loose threads. "You get into high school, you're old enough. You pair off, you know who you are, you graduate, more school, get married. Like life's mapped out, and you pick or you get picked. The worst thing is to be alone, and I started behind everyone already. I didn't understand myself."

The mysteries of the universe should be this: why the ocean is so deep, how crumbs are the most delicious part of a chip bag, why some animals travel together and others apart, when a female spider decides to eat her partner.

It shouldn't be about your own body. It should not be a mystery how you should be loved.

"My mom is the one who found me after, on the cove." The shame descends on me again, but I wade forward. "Sông apparently answered my cry for help. Like the sea witch for the Little Mermaid, you know? It tried to make me something else so I could forget, but my mom begged for all of me back. I've been changing for some time without knowing. Not until the algae made it worse. Sông's here now, everywhere." I laugh. "Is it terrible that I feel better in this messed up world, because I don't have to face most of the people who saw how pathetic I am? Am I a bad person for preferring it this way?" My voice shakes. "I'm sorry."

I wait for her to say I'm making a big deal out of nothing. I wait for all the nasty things I've told myself over the last two years: you deserve it, you walked right into the trap, you never fight hard enough. Worse, she'll just say "I'm sorry," like those two words even have meaning anymore.

"No, you're not," Covey says. She reaches out with her hand. Her eyes are so blue. "Noon, you survived. You don't ever need to apologize for that."

That's when I begin to cry. Really ugly cry, sobs heaving through my body, as I hold onto her hand. Tears collect in her palm, and I want to say I'm sorry again, but she has already told me I don't need to. Covey presses her hand back into mine, and I wish that we had nothing between us. Not even skin, the barrier that's meant to protect us but, for me, has been a constant source of pain long before the rashes infiltrated my insides. I have lived in confusion and shame, those feelings rooting from my guts to my thoughts. Apologizing for Mom. Denying myself everything I could be and living off the scraps of someone else's love.

Covey, Wilder, and Saffy have given me a valuable lesson, in their own ways. Sometimes we need people to hunt the things inside of us that need to die but that we aren't ready to kill.

21

WE STAYED THE NIGHT at the shack since it was too late. A critical, insecure part of me thought maybe Covey might try to catch me off guard after I sleep, but she started snoring as soon as her head hit the pillow. She wasn't afraid. She isn't afraid. The next day, we return to the mansion. We approach slowly, past massacred boats and dying trees. Covey had asked Wilder and Saffy to borrow a boat first, though she'd been mysterious about the reason. They let her—after all we'd been through together, and of course because the scientist's body was still stored in the bathtub. They know how important it is to us to bring the body back to Jimmy.

A light flashes from the loft window: they see us. It is safe to stop at their docking station. We tie the boats to the balcony and slip through the window. Covey and I had discussed telling them that I'd been infected by Sông or whatever is connecting the husks at Mercy Cove, but there was no script. I'm still making sense of my skin before and now, so maybe they'll have to sit through a story as Covey had. It would feel incomplete otherwise.

The mood is already somber when we step inside the mansion. In the hall, Saffy and Wil frown, their shoulders slumped in defeat. Every explanation wilts on my tongue. "What's wrong?"

"You have to see it for yourself," Wilder answers. The door to where we kept the scientist is ajar. It smells like a store-bought-candle version of the sea, heavy on the seaweed and salt. The hazmat suit is rudely bright against the pale-gray backsplash the Sharps chose for their guest bathroom. The shape of it is entirely wrong, deflated.

I kneel next to the bathtub to study what's left of Delgado. The gear's complete with the headpiece still, but nothing solid is under the tears Delgado had made in their attempt to de-skin. The crossbow bolt is slanted down, the grip loose. Immediately, Covey gets a knife from her boot and slices open the suit. Pinkish suds pool inside, like the innocent aftermath of a fizzy bath bomb, but this oozing liquid reeks of bloated animals. Chunks of algae rest at the surface.

"They dissolved," says Saffy.

"In case more supernatural shit happened, we kept the door barred from the outside while we slept," Wil says. "But by the time we got up this morning, the body was that." He gestures at the stinky goop.

"I . . ." My jaw aches from holding myself together. My tear ducts have completely dried, with nothing more to give, and I am so, so tired. "They turned into sea foam," I say. My day just got that much worse. It makes cruel sense. Those who survived and congregated at the cove became a living entity in the water, their bodies and memories indistinguishable. But Delgado had been killed. They could no longer do the work of amassing husks. The algae or Sông had no use for them.

Wordlessly, we reconvene in the library. As soon as Covey chooses a spot on the sofa, Sandbag plops down on her lap. The cat snuggles up to Covey, who gives in to petting her. The silence is deafening, crammed with the things we cannot say.

Mack. Rosa. Mrs. Olivier. If they die, there will be no body to bury or time to mourn.

Me, of course.

There's no good time to break the news, so I rip the bandage off. "I need to tell you why I left without saying anything yesterday." From the sexual assault at the cove to finding my mother at the lighthouse, I tell them everything. The pain, the shame, the changes I couldn't understand in my body, the clues that accumulated with the red algae, how I think Mrs. Olivier lured us to the cove. "I don't think I know what it means to be a girl," I say, "so nothing ever felt too weird, because everything always is weird."

Wilder and Saffy share an unreadable look but don't yet speak. Maybe they understand. Vinh pushed Wil to be the same kind of man like his father, who survived the Texas fires and racism in Mercy. My parents said girls leave home to become part of other families but never thought to say that, perhaps, they were forced. Mom loves Dad, but even their marriage had been arranged at first. Saffy was given the choice to lie about her gender or get kicked out. She chose the truth.

Sông and the algae are guest stars in all our stories because the people who hurt us most, who forced us here, have been those responsible for our care. This world is after that fact. Still,

I've put them at risk in my naivete, then with blatant purpose. I want to be accepted. In zombie movies, this is when people reveal who they truly are. Some kill first and ask questions later, and others wait, not knowing if it'll be a mistake.

Neither Wilder nor Saffy jump for the baseball bat leaning against a bookshelf.

"We don't shun people because they're sick," Saffy says finally. Her soft socks pad over to me. "We shun people when they lie about something they have a choice about. When they hurt us." I deserve the worst, I think, as Saffy stands in front of me. "You lied to me, but you haven't hurt me. Got it?" She sticks her pinky out and almost glares at me until I take it.

Wilder stops fidgeting and reaches over to grasp my other hand. "That stuff about being a girl, or boy, or maybe nothing? That's normal." I blink rapidly. This is the millionth time since our reconciliation that I wonder how differently things would've gone had we talked to one another rather than hide away. "The rash though. Sông." He lets out a breath. It's probably a name he hasn't heard since our dads spent their evenings drinking together. "How long has it been?"

Since I'm still processing, Covey answers, "Days." It honestly feels like a lifetime has passed since we began working together, but she's right. The rash started a little over a week ago.

"If what my mom says is true, about Sông 'saving' me after Aaron," I say, "then I've been changing bit by bit for two years. The algae's sped things up."

"But why?" Saffy asks, thinking face on, as she pulls a mini whiteboard from a bookshelf. "How are they related? Is it like divine shit, or biological shit?"

"It's shit-*shit*," I say. "Here's another thing." All of them curse. "I recognized Mack from before the cove. When I pulled Covey from drowning at the shack, I had a vision. I was Mack and Covey was in a tree, afraid to come down, and Mack said—"

"*I'll always catch you,*" Covey finishes for me. Her expression is stunned, marred in bittersweet pain. "I was four."

I chew on my nub of a fingernail bed. "So it really was a memory."

Wilder hesitates before adding, "I thought I'd gone nuts so I didn't say anything, but when we were in the cove yesterday, I had flashbacks in the water. Not mine."

"This sounds like a hive mind," Saf says as she writes the two words with a question mark. "Shared memories and shared bodies, that's kind of bananas. I didn't see anything. Do you think Sandbag saw something?" The cat meows in response, then puts her head back down on Covey's forearm, where itchy patches have begun to form.

"From what we've seen so far, animals are changing physically inside or otherwise. People are, too."

"Jellyfish are like ninety-five percent water," I say. "Maybe the husks are becoming like that but with a mental component."

"So what, they're becoming primordial soup?" Wilder says. "Sorry Noon."

"No offense taken."

He scratches his chin. "More exposure to the algae makes you change. For a symbiotic relationship, it doesn't *seem* mutually beneficial for a human to become a puddle."

"They're almost like cadaver decomposition islands," says Covey. "Dead bodies have a lot of concentrated nutrients. Universities study the decaying process for forensic science because the growth of certain plants and insects tells you a lot."

Saffy mouths *true crime girlie* to the rest of us.

Covey continues, "But the difference is they're alive, with memories floating around, making sounds even. There's got to be stages, right? Mrs. Olivier, my mom, then . . ."

"The undone," I cut in. "The husks remind me of Mrs. Olivier undoing her knits. Back to basics."

She nods slowly, then says, "I believe my mom's still in there. If this theory about exposure's correct, she might get better once she's out of the algae. I want to bring her back on land. If the bloom's only a mechanism or whatever, then I'm not above begging Sông to spare her."

Saffy chimes in, "And Rosa too, if she's there."

This is the imaginary Pandora's box I'm most afraid of opening. I see the grieving hope that Mom indulged in and that I ignored. I see it lurking within me too, wishing for Jay and Dad back in any form. The pain is too rooted in my gut; these dreams are too big for my ribcage.

Wilder ruffles his messy hair. "So we need to trap your mom, maybe also Rosa, leave on a boat, park at some other harbor, then go as far inland and away from the bloom as possible. All the while maybe being tailed by a god. Sounds really easy."

I clear my throat. "We need Jimmy." They stare more at me now than they had during my confession. "Resources are limited. He has them all." Until Mercy is shut down, Jimmy has his hands in everything. He's the reason Covey and I started this pursuit, against my will. "The undone are strong. We have to take Mack in without killing her. We need more time and sturdier nets. Fuel for the getaway boat."

Covey looks uneasy, unprepared to face the man who ran her mom off and who controls her life. She grasps her knees, steadying herself.

"Family is a choice," Saffy says in a soft tone as Wil nods. As I nod too, understanding all too well.

And although Covey has never been fully aligned with her father, she's been under his protection. We're asking that she abandons that relative safety for the unknown. "The emporium has tranquilizers too. He uses them to sedate the untamed animals. If we do this, we can't let him know my mom's alive," says Covey. Gaining resolve, she decides. "We go see Jimmy, get what we need, and leave all this behind."

The gravity of the situation sinks in. I face them. "I have a favor to ask."

The office is impersonal, decorated in rich mahogany wood and plush rugs. The shelving on the left boasts several Best Mercy Business awards, all gold trophies given by the local association. A central piece to the room is a large blown glass statue of water flowing, with a bright orange koi leaping. Never mind we have no real koi in our waterways.

Wilder lays a beat-up first aid kit on the desk before shuffling aside to a cabinet teeming with fancy bottles in all shapes and sizes. Given the lack of any sedatives or painkillers, they

opt for a more traditional approach. Some bottles are half full
of clear liquor, others amber. The dust is a thick shawl on their
delicate necks. "This is older than us," he says, reading the label
on a round bottle in a bad French accent. He unscrews it before
handing it to me.

The whiff almost makes me gag.

Next to me, Covey says, "We really don't know how painful
it's going to be."

"Do you want to risk it?" Saffy asks, thoroughly squeamish
as she sets a bucket down. She'd taken the most convincing of
all of them, reluctant to agitate the wound further, but she had
to admit that the risk of it becoming infected is already there.

Of course, I don't tell them that if it were this easy, Dr. Delgado probably wouldn't have shoved pencils in their ears. They
must've had plenty of training to pick specimens from open
wounds. Still, I must try and remove the variable that sped the
course of my transformation, even if Sông will always want me
back. The rash on my side is a fiery red, flayed as though by a
million needles. I can't help but remember Mrs. Olivier shoving
the knitting needle into her arm, sawing away at the skin there.
She hadn't seemed hurt, so maybe there's hope for me. I take
the whiskey.

"First time?" Covey asks.

I shake my head. That night two years ago, the cove had been
covered in coolers brimming with beers and drinks so sweet
you'd mistake them for juice. The bottle of hard lemonade
sweated against my fingertips, which were painted purple. One
of Wilder's old polishes. I wonder if the Sharps' supermarket
had sold the alcohol to the underage teens in the first place, and

that perhaps Best Business doesn't always mean *best*. Just who is well connected. "No," I answer before taking three gulps. The alcohol burns down my throat and immediately warms my belly through. I set it down with a smack on the table.

Saffy fusses with the large office chair, pulling and pushing on knobs until the back lies fully flat, as close to an operating table as we'll get. I guess money can buy convertible business furniture as well. Covey helps me onto the chair, which is raised high so it's easier for them to reach my side. We'd talked about it, but it's surreal to see them whip out an assortment of scarves and ropes to tie me down with. Saffy secures a long piece of fabric across my chest to hold my arms flat, while the others section off my hips and legs.

"You know," I say to them. "Praying mantises can get these parasitic worms that grow and grow in their guts until the worm is matured enough." The warmth has reached my extremities, fuzzing my brain. "It releases a chemical that compels the praying mantis to jump into water. At which point, the worm escapes through its back end orifice, leaving behind an empty husk of its host."

All three are apparently stunned by this piece of information.

Saffy's long and very pronounced sigh breaks the silence. "I'm going to need a drink too." She takes a swig of the amber bottle, face contorting, then hands it to Wilder.

"If anything comes out of Noon's ass, I'm leaving ASAP," he informs the group before sharing in a sip.

Covey gives a little shrug, which charms me because my self-denial is eighty-nine percent tipsy.

Wilder disinfects his hands, then the tweezers, with a spray. They roll and clip my shirt up, revealing the rash splattered on my torso. Chin to chest, I can only glimpse the shiny sebum on the outside of the rash. It has grown since our adventures in Chelsea's Cove. Their expressions are, in a word, horrified.

"Come on, y'all," I say. "It still looks better than Saffy's spaghetti Bolognese from the other night." With a choked laugh, she hits me on my shoulder.

"Are you sure about this?" Wilder asks.

I nod because giving up is not an option. I can't live in the same denial as Mom, or look away when the evidence presents itself. If there's a way to live, I want it.

"Okay okay okay." Wilder breathes in and focuses on my side. His hand is remarkably steady. Maybe he'd watched his mom stitch his dad after accidents. Maybe she'd treated his cuts and splinters, comforted him when things hurt. He carries this shared trait, even after all this time.

The metal touches my wound, the unnaturally perfect cut, and it feels *good*. The sharpness itches where I dared not scratch before. In my buzzed state, I want to say *dig harder*.

The feeling does not last long.

Like the worm in the praying mantis, the algae in me has responded to outside intervention. My entire side seems to pulse. They brace my shoulders down. My hands turn into fists as a cramp wracks my side, a force that twists through. Wilder's begun to pull with the tweezers in a gentle and firm manner, and the edge of a red thing—I first mistake it for an actual vein—squirms.

"You're about to lose—"

"I know. Shit." His free hand shoots out and grabs the string-like algae, yanking it from my skin—so much of it, an impossible amount loosening from my side. He's not supposed to touch it since we don't know how it truly occupies the body, but he's determined to get every strand. He dumps a handful into the bucket, then goes back to yanking threads from my body.

After another intense twenty minutes, we are done and they untie me from the chair. Self-consciously, I splay a hand over the large bandage. The restraints have left red marks on my skin, but it's nothing compared to the thing in the bucket that resembles a shredded organ, a long-haired ginger scalp. It does not look as though it should have come from me at all. "It was spread out like web under your skin," Wilder says. Saffy looks sick to her stomach but stays firm at my side. "I think I got everything?"

"You don't sound sure," says Covey.

An argument seems imminent so I cut in. "Thanks for doing it at all."

The rawness hasn't subsided, and I can't tell if it's from the algae's absence or its usual behavior. I'll find out with time whether it's helped, or if this, among so many things, is unfruitful. I'll find out if the cove will one day be my grave.

22

WHILE WE STRATEGIZE THE entire afternoon, the two-way radio crackles with my mom's pleas and, by extension, Wil's parents trying to reach him. I'd already confessed to Wilder that during the big argument, I'd thrown it in their faces that he's alive and well. His choice not to see them is a consequence of their own failures. He hadn't been happy, but he got over it pretty quickly by pettily drawing me as a stick figure with a shark head on the whiteboard in every iteration of the plan. Even I had to laugh.

It's strange, how little love you can survive on until you experience the warmth of people who choose you despite everything. They tease me when we break to add to my sad fuck-it list. As Saffy told me before, life is too precious now to be overly careful with our hearts, and so we willingly take the chance that this might last long enough for simple happinesses. It all hinges on us outsmarting Jimmy and outrunning the bloom.

Late that evening, Covey leads the way back to her dad's emporium, which is located on a bayou a few hours north of Mercy. She brings us to the mouth of her swamp, a big great gaping wound in the earth that's swollen with rain. Trees rise from the water, thickly corded and veiny. She points at them when we pass. "My mom calls them witch throats," she says. "Because they're like giantesses walking the bog, cursing the men who wronged us. Careful, or they'll swallow you down in a way you don't like. She loves a revenge story."

I glance at the water. "So do I."

There are eyes in the swamp—real ones, like green and yellow marbles. The alligators cling to remaining patches of land, bathing in the dying sun. They are tired and lazy. Wearily, others watch us pass. "They don't like the motor," says Covey, waving at the back of our little boat. "Keeps them away for the most part."

While I've always been fascinated by marine creatures, I have always been afraid of alligators. The way they kill just seems mean. Their long jaws were made to grasp you in the water, and then they spin rapidly to dismember you. Probably the only thing worse than drowning is getting your limb ripped off as you're drowning. I flip them off.

Finally, we arrive at Jimmy's Gator Swamp Tour and Emporium, which is bigger than how I imagined it. Most buildings accidentally survive floods, not get expanded after flooding. While the main facility is a mellow yellow, the other buildings are newly painted and sitting on stable stilt legs.

"He really thinks this can be the eighth wonder of the world," Covey mutters. Unlike many others, Jimmy has planned to stay and make money off it—the premier spot for those who dare travel so close to the coast. Mercy is only an extension of his scheme. At the sight of us, a worker calls in on their radio to announce that Jimmy's daughter has arrived.

Over the last two weeks, Covey's body had relaxed. This is reversed in moments. Her bones take on a rigidity, making her look taller. Her face doesn't shift in emotion; it doesn't read as anything at all. She is as elusive as our first meeting. Almost imperceptibly, she distances herself from me.

I knew it would happen, but it stings nonetheless. Jimmy must believe he's in control of the situation, which includes his daughter's loyalties. I should be nothing but an obligation to her.

We leave a dockworker to secure the boat. Without a word, Covey leads me farther in the wooden structure. I stare at the back of her short dark hair, then at the walls decorated with animal bones, cleaned and strung up as trophies. There are the tiniest of birds and big animals whose shapes I can't decipher at all. Higher up are animal heads, preserved with their shiny eyes observing us. They smell like mold and insecticide.

I imagine my own head mounted there, skin stretched out with wood-wool, eyes replaced with glass replicas, if Jimmy were to find out what I'm becoming.

"Girls," Jimmy greets as soon as we enter what looks to be a cafeteria. His smile hasn't faded, but his gaze shifts between us, obviously discontent. "I don't see my specimen, and as I'm told, there's nothing else in your little boat." His eyes sharpen on me. "Where's your momma?"

"Injured," I say, not the full truth. "You did dislocate her arms and slam her on some nails."

Covey throws a sharp glance at me. "She was also hurt when"—her head turns back toward the older Boudreaux—"we caught one of the monsters. But there's a hiccup."

"A hiccup," Jimmy repeats.

"The specimen's body doesn't last longer than twenty-four hours. It just dissolves into a pile of gooey foam."

Despite our lack of evidence, the excitement is palpable. He is finally getting answers to what's scared off residents and officials alike. Jimmy rises to his feet. "So what exactly are we dealing with here?"

"It's human." I use my most dispassionate voice, but Jimmy appears more elated by the news.

Covey takes the rein now, more used to tricky conversations with her father. "We found the scientist actually—Dr. Delgado, but changed." She leaves out the part about Mercy Cove as discussed, not because we worry he would get hurt there, but that he might try to go there himself and accidentally see Mack. He wouldn't let them get away. "It's hard to explain, but the composition of the body changes. They get this urge to shed their skin, and they're alive when they do it. They want others to join them. We think that's why there've been so many disappearances. But if they die, they melt into nothing." For this next part, Covey pauses expertly and plants the idea. "There's absolutely nothing we could have brought back to the emporium."

He rubs his chin, considering all of the information. "And you're sure?"

Covey nods. "We saw signs of others changing. This is why we're here to talk to you about it." She's careful deciding which details to share. It strikes me that Covey's done similar exchanges before with Jimmy. "Mrs. Olivier went missing last week, but I think I can set up a trap to lure her out. It's almost like a new instinct for the changed people to bring others to the same conclusion. But to bring her in alive, I need the tranquilizer gun."

Jimmy rebuffs this idea. "If this is our only shot, it's better to send everyone in at the same time and get her."

It's not the reaction we wanted, but we prepared for this. I speak up. "That can't happen because her son Travis will notice if more strangers arrive in Mercy with a bunch of weapons. He's not going to let you take her, so it needs to stay quiet." This is a trickier part of the plan—convincing Jimmy that only we could do it in this time frame, rather than his goons.

"I need a better reason than Travis to not go in big now."

"I'm going to act as bait. If our theory's right, it should be an appetizing set-up." I reassure him, though the truth is Covey will put herself at risk. She's the one Mack wants. Twice she's been dragged into the water; she's confident she can survive once more.

Jimmy looks impressed. "This is the first parameter of the deal: you get thirty-six hours once you're back in Mercy to do this."

Anger sparks in my chest as I argue, "There's a week left in the original deal."

"Have you not listened to the news lately?" His grin is vicious. He snaps his fingers at a nervous-looking man, who immediately switches a radio on. A weather report seems to be on loop.

Forecasts indicate that Tropical Depression Sixteen will make landfall in four days' time at the current trajectory. Winds have picked up over the warming Gulf and analysts expect the storm to strengthen into hurricane status ahead of landfall. The governor has issued a mandatory evacuation order for Plaquemines Parish. The potential cost of life is—

Jimmy stamps down on the off button. Despite the severely fucked natural disaster we're in, none of us had paused to consider that the incoming storm might be more serious than our usual. Satisfied, Jimmy continues, "So, the timeline is being compressed as necessary. Like I said, the government's not going to let people return, and I want my daughter back before the storm comes. Here's the other parameters: you will report immediately to me what happens, and you'll have to take one of my men." An ill feeling seizes my gut. "You've already met Aaron, I heard."

"Absolutely not," Covey snaps. "He's a shithead." She doesn't shoot a glance my way, but I know she's thinking about me. Us. Mercy Cove. Though I'm back to being clothed head to toe in the same sweater and jeans Mom insists on, I am exposed. Aaron has told Jimmy whatever he wanted. If they didn't enforce the law before, no one will enforce it now.

"Explain," Jimmy says. "I would rather help my constituents prepare for the upcoming storm, but if I have to take time out of my schedule to personally attend to the matter, I will. Everyone else is busy securing Port Mercy."

In addition to unpleasant company, both options add a complex layer to our plans. For one, we don't want to expose Saffy and Wilder to more scrutiny. Secondly, we must subdue Mack without divulging to Jimmy that she's alive. It's too unpredictable—and the point is Covey wants to escape with her mom.

She takes a few steps closer to Jimmy, voice dipping a register. "It's like you said. Everyone needs you to lead them through this mess. You can't take time away to just lay some traps, and Aaron is no replacement for you. He's thickheaded. He'll just get in the way waving his big gun everywhere. The key point is we need Mrs. Olivier *alive*. Trust me, Dad. I can do this myself. Noon listens to me."

His dark eyes lie heavily on Covey, trying to find the cracks in her act. She holds steadfast. Eventually, he strikes a compromise. "You'll get the tranquilizer gun. You'll set things up like I taught you. You're in charge, but Aaron will be on standby at the harbor. The minute it goes wrong"—Jimmy's gaze lands on me—"you radio him."

Although our plan has gotten complicated with Aaron being clued in, Covey and I rehash the details in the privacy of her bedroom. It was too late to go the long way back to Mercy, so we'll make the trip first thing at dawn and collect other supplies from the harbor. It'll leave some time to update Saffy and Wilder, but for the most part, not much else has changed. Bait, shoot, run. Don't think about what happens if it doesn't work.

While Covey eats a strained dinner with her dad, I pick at the plate of shrimp po'boy in her bedroom. It tastes like chewy cardboard, though the smell keeps enticing me to try. Hunger grips me in a strange way. I want fresh seafood—oysters twisted from their shells, fish sluiced off their thin bones—or even meat, not just bloody at the bone but dripping red all over. Remembering why makes my appetite disappear. The rash hasn't bothered me all day, but I'm afraid to check.

Instead I walk the perimeter to Covey's room, past track-and-field ribbons, pencil drawings in Mack's style, and photo-booth printouts of mother and daughter. Covey's lived a whole life before me, even if Jimmy kept her and her mom caged. I was free, and yet I always tied myself to Mom.

After Jay was born, I used to hide around our trailer to see if she ever noticed. If a monster took me, would she come? She never did, even after hours and hours. When I cried about it, she would laugh and say, "But I didn't know we were even playing a game!"

Now, I don't want Mom to find me at all. I'm leaving that pathetic Nhung behind.

A little later, Covey reappears at the door, her mouth set in a grumpy line. "Come on, let's go."

"Huh?" I'm already in her bed, nice and cozy.

She rolls her eyes. "We're going for a night swim."

We tiptoe out to a building reserved for recreational use. It's more like a basement in which everything goes in, unorganized. I'm wondering if swimming among alligators is a white-person activity I haven't heard about. We head out toward the back where large barrels are stacked against the wall. Comical DANGER signs sticker the outside. "Ah yeah, the algaecide," Covey says when she notices me looking at them. "When the bloom first came, Jimmy was very gung ho about settling it for himself. Government visit nipped it in the bud."

On the wooden deck is a raised circular pool, black tarp sealing off the top. A second-level deck hugs its back, obviously meant to be a jumping off point. Covey pulls the tarp away, revealing clean, chlorinated water.

"I know it's ridiculous," she says. "But it's useful, like right now. You need to learn how to swim."

My mouth opens, then closes. This is an improvement from swimming in the swamp, but quite honestly, given my impending transformation to oceanic monster, I was banking on instinct kicking in. It worked once.

Covey crosses her arms. "Consider 'teaching Noon how to swim' at the top of my fuck-it list. You're doing me the greatest favor by getting your ass into the pool."

A long sigh tugs at my lungs. "Fine. I don't have a swimsuit that, uh . . ." I wave all down my side, where there'll be leftover irritation from the rash, even if Wilder had removed all the stringy bits. It would not be good for Jimmy to witness.

"Take your jeans off and you're good," she says matter-of-factly before stripping off a layer of clothes.

I raise my brow but follow her lead, with the sweater too. My undershirt stays on. I climb the stairs to the upper deck and timidly slip into the lifeless water. Standing, I'm a good foot higher than the deepest section. That makes me feel only a little bit better, since maneuvering around with your head tilted back just looks uncool. Especially because Covey does a backstroke across the small pool. I splash her. "Show-off."

"I'm only showing you my qualifications to be your personal instructor," she says when she comes to a stop.

This time, I roll my eyes. "What's the first lesson then?"

In a very serious voice, Covey says, "Bubbles." She lowers herself into the water, her dark hair a halo in the water, and blows with her lips. Bubbles rocket toward the surface. I don't even know why that would help someone swim—I certainly can't imagine Dad teaching Jay like this—but I too sink the tiniest bit, bending my knees until half my face is wet. I blow out. She laughs. We move on quickly.

Little kicks with our feet, floating on my back, her fingers guiding my spine. I watch her swim, too, because she's missed it. From the butterfly to the breaststroke, Covey is a seasoned swimmer. We stay in the pool, talking and laughing. We don't talk about what comes tomorrow. The pool is our bubble of a world, where fireflies light one by one above our heads. The water is gentle in these fake confines, the swamp quiet compared to the cove.

Tomorrow, we'll try to bring her mother home. Tonight, we have this. A simple swimming lesson between friends. Teasing each other but trying to keep our voices low so the parents don't come looking. I've barely moved in the water, and yet I'm exhausted.

We sit on the steps that lead into the pool, legs resting half in the water. I lean back on my arms and watch the blue-black sky. I'm cold all over but don't want to go back inside, in a place that's truly Jimmy's, where false eyes will follow me. Naturally, we scoot next to each other. The swamp flickers with incandescence, the predators restless.

I let our knees touch first, those caps that have borne so much pain from falling and rising, the scraped skin healed over but now warming by degrees. Covey's looking at me. I deserve a memory from a beautiful night. I deserve good things. I keep reminding myself this.

"Do I scare you?"

She smirks, almost nonchalantly. "I wouldn't say that's a bad thing."

I laugh. Wilder had asked me if I wanted to be kissed, and I'd hesitated but I've been thinking. I want to kiss Covey, but I'm also not ready. And that's okay. "Can I get closer?" I ask.

"Yeah." At this hour, her eyes are a deep blue. I'm reminded of an ocean I love.

I rest my head on her shoulder, and she puts an arm around my waist. There's gentle heat every point we touch.

We stay until the skin on our toes wrinkle. We stay until we're ready to be apart.

23

TWO OF MY TEETH have fallen out overnight, a canine and a molar that I roll in my hands again and again. There's a soreness all around my gums, especially in the holes left behind. I can't help but dip my tongue and taste the salt of my own blood. Apparently, what they say about fluoridated water is true—without it, tooth decay rapidly sets in. But a gappy smile is my lowest worry today. I leave the teeth under Covey's pillow in the rare event, but not impossible in this strange world, that the tooth fairy is real. It's a true sign of friendship that I'd share money with her, not that we plan on returning to Jimmy's Gator Swamp Tour and Emporium.

Once Covey's up and her dad puts in the supply order at the port, Covey and I head back to Mercy. The tranquilizer gun and sedatives are in their own hard plastic container. The weapon resembles a rifle with its long military-green-and-black body. I don't like it at all. It's different from the crossbow, but Covey handles it with confidence. The darts and vials of trank, on the other hand, confuse us both. Since they're meant for large animals, there's no dosing information for humans. That's a problem for later.

Port Mercy is less busy than usual, as people evacuate from town before the incoming storm. It'll be the first in a quiet hurricane season, which means everyone expects the worst. Tension hangs thick in the air, and the workers are anxious to see us off so they too can leave for safer ground.

"You sure you can handle that big thing?" Aaron asks Covey for the fiftieth time.

Coldly, she replies, "I don't know. Should I test it out?" She unlatches the container as if to take the gun out, and Aaron tries to play it off as a joke.

His attention slides to me. The more I ignore him, the more aggressive he gets. He flicks at my hair and tries to goad me into speaking. As we load up the premium nylon nets, Covey's jaw tenses. We'd agreed to get in and out of the harbor as quickly as possible, without drawing scrutiny. We can't get into a fight. Everyone at the harbor watches this happen and says nothing. They even laugh at a few of his jokes.

"You're gonna make her cry." Skidmark grins.

I stick close to Covey's side, and as much as she can, she tells them to shut the fuck up. We're almost done loading up new food stores when Aaron brushes Covey's bare arm.

My reaction is automatic. I dart from behind to pull her away from him.

The flash of annoyance across his face is soon replaced by derision. "Don't be a dyke, Noon." The first time I'd been called a dyke was sixth grade, when I told an eighth grader that I did not like him *that way*. His friend had yelled the word at me down the school hallway while everyone watched. I looked up what "dyke" meant after.

The world has been awful for a long time, churning out people who hear *maybe* when a person says *no*. They respect nothing and no one but themselves, always blaming others. The difference is now I'm certain I can rip out this one's tongue. The bloodlust and pure rage are incandescent, and yet I hold myself steady, buoyed by the sound of water.

"You're kind of old to be fucking around with teenagers." Travis Olivier steps onto the pier, looking far more exhausted than when we visited their house. Thick, purple bags line the space underneath his eyes. He looks as though he hasn't slept since his mother went missing.

"I'm not fucking around. I'm supervising," Aaron snaps defensively before taking a step away from us. He has to lean his chin back to catch Travis's gaze, shoulders squared. He flicks a glance back at our boat. "Looks like we're done here anyway." The dockworkers follow at his heels.

Travis mutters "asshole" and hikes his duffel higher. "I'm catching a ride with a buddy of mine before the storm hits," he tells us. "I'm better alive than dead. I'll come right back after, but maybe someone picked Ma up already and she's at an evacuation center. I hope. You two ought to go too. This storm's a bad one."

His sliver of hope hurts because we already know what happened to his mom. Mrs. Olivier is in Mercy Cove. She's peeled fresh, probably down to the bone now, and fully surrendered to the bloom. Solemnly, he joins his friend at the end of the pier.

Covey and I share a pointed look because maybe Travis needs to know the truth about his mom's whereabouts. We would want answers for ourselves. When we don't bring back a monster to explain away all the disappearances, Mercy will close for good. Travis will never get to come home to his mother in any form.

Still, we keep quiet. Wilder and Saffy are relying on us too. By the time we get back to the mansion, they've buried the scientist. They decided against cleaning out the gooey foam, formerly Dr. Delgado, from the hazmat suit in the bathtub. Instead, they duct-taped any rips and dragged them out back. The only things they saved are the two pencils, brown with blood. Judging by how much it covers the wood, I'm shocked Delgado had lasted that long. Sông does something to our bodies that make them more durable.

"We don't have to listen to his deadline," Wil says after Covey fills the pair in on her dad's conditions. "We have the tranquilizers, and if worse comes to worse, we escape on a boat as far as we can and deal with everything later." It's very much like Wilder to do first and think after. He's gotten this far and smiled this much following that motto.

"Yes, but we know my mom's approximate location *now*," Covey says. "That can change. So we need to set up and get her ASAP, then run before Jimmy realizes."

Saffy nods in agreement. "This is like alligator-strength tranquilizer though. If we get it wrong for Mack . . ." Getting Mack safely and in non-foam form hinges on us getting the right dosage to knock her out, but we've no clue.

Wilder speaks again, "I'll radio my mom." It hadn't crossed my mind to ask Jenn. She's not in veterinary practice, but she's probably dealt with similar sedatives as a nurse. Still, Wil shouldn't have to get in touch with his parents unless he really wants to.

"Don't feel like you have to," says Covey. Of course, all of us here understand what it means to want to cut contact with family.

"Can't we make an educated guess about the dosage?" I ask. "Err on the side of being too low than high."

Wilder stands up. "No, I should talk to them. I'll ask, and I'm going to tell them to leave the lighthouse too." He borrows my radio to call them; they answer immediately. Their staticky voices echo from the other room, and I can hear Mom in the background, trying to ask about me. Wil keeps it short, almost businesslike in how he gets Jenn's most educated guesses on safe tranquilizer dosages for a person. He's quieter than normal when he returns, but we have a viable starting point.

We study the map Covey and I had previously marked up. In the end, we choose a location from the scientist's sampling list since Covey and I had scouted it before. It's the houseboat unironically named *Seaz the Day*, partly sunken and abandoned in a secluded area of the swamp. The sediment, junk, and relatively low water would impede movement while the abundant trees give us cover. Since Rosa hasn't been spotted at all, we agreed Mack is our top priority. Once she appears, Wilder and Saffy will unroll nets across the biggest exit points, hopefully deterring her enough that Covey can get a shot in. From what we witnessed at the cove, Mack, Delgado, and Mrs. Olivier didn't need water to move. They are faster in water, yes, but as long as they have functioning limbs, they can travel on land. It would be our advantage if we can get Mack out of the water.

"This sorta feels like bullshitting a group project the day before it's due," says Saffy, arms covered in dry-erase marker. Sandbag helpfully stretches out on top of the whiteboard.

"We're kids," Covey says, shaking her head. "We're not supposed to be doing any of this. Adults are. We should be in our rooms playing loud music and making out or watching responsibly made, women-led soft porn—"

"That is super specific," Wilder says.

"*The point is,*" Covey emphasizes, a hint of pink on her cheeks. "They failed us. They're always worried about the wrong thing."

"It'll be dark soon," I say finally. "We can't waste any of the shots, and visibility will be better during daytime, so we should set up very early tomorrow."

Saffy gets up, brushing fur and dust from her tiered skirt. "Let's make the most of this afternoon together."

And we do. That day in September is perfect—distant winds sweeping away the rotting stench. Clean, fresh air fills our lungs. We spend the cool afternoon draped on the soft sofas, listening to Covey read a fairytale retelling. Wil's mom calls in with a more conservative dosage for the tranquilizer. From my sparse fuck-it list, I tackle "do three double-unders" with a rope lying around and fail spectacularly. In the morning, we manage to scrape together pancakes with the few ingredients we have, Saffy ingeniously replacing a mixture of ground flax seed and water for egg, and applesauce for butter.

The batter sizzles to perfection. They eat them plain. Then, we each kiss Sandbag on the head.

At our designated corner of the swamp, we get to work. Radio reports indicate that Tropical Depression Sixteen has officially become Hurricane Isaias. The water swells under a deceptively breezy day—all signs that the storm is on its way. We wear high waders to protect our bodies from the algae bloom, though only Covey's fit right since she's tall. Options had been limited at the port, so Wil, Saf, and I tighten the shoulder straps and clip any excess fabric. *Seaz the Day* is half-submerged in the muck, lying at an angle that blocks access from the northern side. Mold has eaten away its white paint. The brackish water, thick with eelgrass, tapers to a stretch of land that will serve as Covey's back-up point.

Between the houseboat and thick trees, we lay down a net that's sized smaller and lighter than my trawling ones. Fiber cords are released from gear tethers on either end. Retracted, the net will tighten over whatever's stepped or swam in it. It's not meant to trap something as big or agile as a human, but it'll give Covey time to take a shot at close distance.

Saffy and Wilder watch from their vantage point on a wide branch as Covey slides a sanitized blade on her upper arm, enough so there's a steady drip of blood into the water. We'd debated this part since the last thing we needed was an algae infestation in Covey, but she insisted, "I mean it when I say *bait*."

From *Seaz the Day*'s slanting roof, I poke my head over to make sure she's keeping the wound high above the water. The four steel traps set underwater in a line ahead of Covey, in case the net fails, are barely visible from this height. I lose my grip when I shift back out of sight, face-planting into the metal roof. My mouth is filled with brine as a tooth slides right into the swamp with a delicate *ping*. Giggling bursts from the trees, and I flip my friends off.

Hours pass where the only visitors are Great Blue Herons, offended when we *shoo* them away. Covey gets more anxious as time goes by, but I simply observe our surroundings. The swamp, a declared dead zone where the bloom supposedly depleted all oxygen, teems with life. The herons snap up fish in their beaks, flying between cypresses held by thriving strangler figs. Frogs skip rock to rock. There are few flowers, but they punch the green landscape and grow from waters as red as burned blood. It's stunning here, aside from the refuse that's floated from the sunken boat.

Steadily, and from far away, comes a sound, breaking the surface of the water with rapid movement. No motor, no engine, just a body cutting through. We whistle to signal each other. My hand is sweaty on the gear tether, ready to retract the line at any time. From her spot, Covey glances at the tranquilizer gun hidden in a bush. With only a handful of tranquilizer darts, she needs patience to get the best shot.

A skeletal hand emerges from the distant water. It pushes ahead, followed by another arm. Someone is swimming toward us at an alarming speed. They swim fast enough that red algae ripple outward. They stop about ten feet outside our net. The swamp is deceptively still, all other animals gone.

Slowly, the wet creature shows herself. I know by the gray hair barely hanging from the scalp that it isn't Mackenzie

Boudreaux. Inch by inch, Mrs. Olivier returns to us, her shape no longer frail. With her skin gone, the outer membrane is dark pink and full of pulsing suckers, like an octopus's muscular arm.

No, no, no—it isn't supposed to be her. The undone should want their loved ones most, and Covey scented the waters with her blood. Do we have it all wrong?

"Mrs. Olivier," Covey says in a shaky tone. "Please come toward me, and I'll take you to Travis. Promise." I get her new plan immediately. We must hold off on the sedatives, but the net's free game. We have another net back at the mansion.

The librarian moves forward. "Oh, my baby boy," she cries, voice distorted as if there's a marble under her tongue. "He's not here anymore, is he? My baby." The suckers along her body contract, as if writhing with emotion. I don't know what Travis will do if he sees his mother like this. Stopping just barely inside our net, she suddenly swivels her head up. Right at me. "Don't you hear how the water calls you home? You've waited too long."

My stomach drops. While I process this voice that's not completely hers, someone yells "Now!" from the other hiding spot. I reel in the cord, which quickly zips up out of the water. I'm on my feet for leverage, but Mrs. Olivier has dived in, patches of algae and murky water shrouding her exact whereabouts. I focus on the weight in the net until it thrashes, throwing me aside. I dig my heels in, and that becomes a mistake. The houseboat's roof collapses in pieces, whittled down by mold and rot. Splinters and dust fall alongside me into the water.

People are shouting outside but the chorus of *let us in* has begun. "No!" Perhaps it'd been there all along, but I've been too stubborn to hear it. I dog-paddle through murky green water toward a rectangular opening of light, but something yanks me beneath. The grip is relentless. Water fills my throat, and yet I'm not drowning. Nothing about me aches here, except for the bruising at my ankle. I pry at the cool hand reaching through the hull, where jagged rock has long ripped a hole in this houseboat. When that fails, I try unhooking the suspenders to the waders.

Mrs. Olivier pulls me down before I can escape. The aluminum cuts into my arms, and then I am in hers—wrapped in a net meant to save her. The water is frenzied with memory. There are so many happy ones: book fairs, gifted drawings, and warm summers. A few sad ones, too, like Mr. Landry, the former high school principal, standing too close to a fresh-faced Grace Reed straight out of college. Then, Mrs. Olivier falling in love with a sailor who meant to blow through Mercy. Travis as a toddler enjoying his first sliced cucumber. There's me, too. Sitting in a sunbeam at a library table tucked away, sneaking bites from a granola bar since I was missing lunch. She saw it all in her incredible, blessed life.

She loves me. That's why she is here.

In a rush, memories are siphoned from me. Dad gifting me a snow-white teddy once, which I promised to keep forever. The rainy but fun afternoon I taught Jay how to ride a bike with my old pink training wheels. All the days I locked inside so I wouldn't miss them. The images end abruptly when Saffy and Wil haul us toward dry land. Instinctively, I reach out, as if memory has a tangible shape to hold on to.

Covey's busy disarming the metal traps before we can escape, leaving Wil to cut through the nylon with her knife. Mrs. Olivier's jaw opens, and it is a tunnel of sharp barbs that protrude inward from her gills. Only suspension-feeding fish like mullets and whale sharks have such gill rakers to trap food, and hers is the biggest I've seen. She closes her mouth on the person closest to her.

She rips a chunk from Wilder's hand. His scream penetrates my ears, and I ache for his pain, his suffering, and I'm yelling too. Saffy immediately pulls him onto dry land, where she uses her bandana to tie a tourniquet around his hand.

I wriggle from the net just in time to see Covey shoot a dart at Mrs. Olivier. It lands square on her shoulder, but she doesn't react except to untangle the net.

"You've waited too long," she says again.

"For what?" The humid air tingles strangely on my neck. I run my fingers along that soft curve, and the slits close again, their use limited out of water. My voice shakes. "Sông?"

The body that is not only Mrs. Olivier's smiles. Her lips don't move, yet I hear each word as clearly as a thought: "*Let us in. Live in their memory.*" The dam full of ridiculous hope breaks inside me; my family is gone. Sông intends to give me a homecoming. It smells like rot, tastes like the sea, and sounds like an engine. That noise is as familiar as breathing.

From the corner of my eye, my mother yells "Nhung!" just as Mrs. Olivier launches at me. Covey runs into the fray, caught by the net as I am. The suckers pulse and squeeze. In seconds,

Covey's out, and another scream is at my throat. I want Mrs. Olivier to leave them all alone because the damage is too much already.

The tears build up in my eyes from the pressure. I can't see it, but I feel her nails dig into the cut on my side, already tender if I were to tell the truth. She yanks at the scab, then the fresh skin—this, I know, by how hard she must rip. Moisturized skin doesn't make that much sound, actually. We're both slammed by a momentous force.

Screaming, Mom shoves Mrs. Olivier from me and keeps pushing her away until Mrs. Olivier's leaning into a houseboat window. The woman—the undone—gapes at the sharp glass puncturing her chest. Mom steps back in shock, shaking her head repeatedly. Mrs. Olivier lifts her torso from the sharpened point in a sickening squelch. She stares at us, the bloody foam from her mouth bubbling a word—or name—I don't catch, until every bit of her dissolves. Like she never existed at all.

24

WE LEFT THE SCENE of the crime. Mrs. Olivier is less than ashes now, dispersed in algae. It was always likely to end this way for her, but still, it feels like our fault. My fault, to be precise—since she had come for me.

Mrs. Olivier had cared enough to find me, after searching for her own son. It wasn't all Sông's doing. Mrs. Olivier had treasured the memory of a younger Nhung in her library.

I'm too rattled to argue when Covey leads Mom back to our cabin. Half an hour later, we spill inside. A mixture of river, sweat, and blood drip from our aching bodies. Saffy and Wilder, who'd been clutching his wounded hand inside a thick wrap, split to the mansion earlier, after I promised to radio them. It goes unspoken that the mansion is ours alone. Mom was never part of the plan.

"How did you know where we were?" I ask as I rip the waders off.

Mom wrings her hands together, as if to stop herself from covering my lack of modesty. My undershirt and boxers are soaked through. Blood tinges the fabric on my side. She answers carefully, "*When Jenn and Wil talked, I heard. I couldn't leave you to do it alone.*"

I try to hold onto coldness, but I am too exhausted. It's futile to stick to my conclusions when new information keeps coming. I turn to Covey instead. "I'm sorry our plan didn't work," I say.

She looks at her empty hand. During the fight, she'd dropped the tranquilizer gun into the swamp. "I don't think there's anything we can do for them," Covey says softly. Given the extreme tissue changes, the whirlpool-shaped suckers all over Mrs. Olivier must've be permanent. "My mom's already half gone." There's grief in her blue eyes as they shift my way.

I wish I can tell her to take the time for herself instead of worrying about me. I lift up my shirt. The rash has exploded again to its former size. Deep red tendrils are rooted in the tissue, some skin already missing from Mrs. Olivier's peeling. The cut on Covey's arm hasn't changed at all. "Rashes are not the most important thing right now," I say, then dig into my neck until gills flare out.

Covey and Mom suck in air at the same time.

"The transformations don't stop," I say. "Maybe removing or avoiding red algae will slow things down, but it's not the same thing as being fully human." My neck relaxes, though thoughts and worries race throughout my throbbing head. I gesture for Mom to speak with me in privacy. "I'll be a few minutes," I tell Covey.

In the back room, Mom and I face each other, tense and quiet. Mom had saved me from death or full transformation— whatever happens when a monster finds another—by impaling Mrs. Olivier on a glass edge. She wouldn't have done this a week ago to any monster from the water, but she did it to save me. It's a sign that maybe she's changing, too.

"Jay and Dad are not alive. Not as reincarnated creatures, not as monsters or ghosts; they're gone. What you have is me." I know that without submitting myself completely to the bloom. Sông had let me in, in a way. "Live in their memory"—spoken directly to my synapses, then the feeling that they died in the hurricane, without intervention.

She buries her head in her palms. *"You are a miracle. It's why I believed so hard."*

"I didn't ask to be your miracle," I say. *"I wanted to be cared for, properly. Looked at like I'm not someone you're ashamed of."*

"I didn't want us to leave because what if Mercy is what's keeping you alive?" Mom says, turning to look at me. *"I wanted you to forget. You still can."* She offers me the necklace with our boat key on it, our silly magic trick. Count một, hai, ba, then pretend all is well again.

I saw a dead bird once, in a rare snowstorm that reached its fingers this far south. The roads were slicked beyond any-one's imagination; it was easy to drive too fast. The weather had begun to outpace the birds' migratory instinct. I found a yellow-rumped warbler on the road outside our trailer, its blood still warm enough to melt the dusting of snow.

I learned then how fragile life is. We do our best to survive it, but sometimes it's not enough. Not alone, at least.

"Sông is here," I confirm, to her surprise. *"Making the impossible possible. You know, even with the world like this, even with Aaron back in Mercy, I've been happy these last few weeks. I never liked my body but at least it has its advantages now."*

The moles on Mom's eyelids disappear as her eyes squint. Confused. *"I don't understand. Why wouldn't you like your body?"*

The feeling is hard to articulate. How does a horse know at birth that it is a horse? That with its gangly legs, still wet from its mother, it can stand and run and do what it's meant to do. "I don't want to be a girl," I say. The way I should've phrased it is, *I don't want to be human*, but this suits my tongue. This is right, and I am relieved.

"Would it be different if he hadn't hurt you?" Mom asks. I tilt my head. "Would you *ah*"—she takes a shaky breath, rephrasing in English but still not understanding—"like yourself?"

"No. That's wrong." I turn to face her, determined, because it's difficult to convey that others' treatment of me doesn't change who I am. It took a long time before I figured that out myself. "Má, girls are like some of the best things about the world." I love them: the ferocity, the softness, the friendships so close you wonder if it's healthy. I love boys too, like Wilder and his sparkly nails, his humor. What I hate is anyone who scorns us for not being cookie-cutter versions of Boy or Girl. I'm ashamed how I parroted those beliefs, when I told my little brother not to cry because boys just don't do that, as if their tear ducts are for fashion.

In a way Mercy is my mother too. I was raised on these roads, covered in its dirt, then taught in its schools. I knew everyone in my grade, and our parents knew each other by sight. In every way, Mercy taught me to fear.

I never had the choice for who would be my mother or where I would grow up. I was born loving her and not knowing anything but Mercy. It feels as though I'd been born in a caul, then never cut out from that amniotic sac. I'd walked around with a part of my mother around me, obscured by what she and others demand I be. Before, it was hard to see clearly.

Now it's easy to understand: my skin has always been uncomfortable. I tell Mom this.

"Sorry," Mom says. "Sorry." She opens her palm to me, waiting to see if I'll take it, and at first I'm not sure I want to, but then my hand slips over hers. It's a tenuous touch, brand-new. We do our best to understand each other.

After the closeness gets too awkward, when I'm truly spent on sixteen years' worth of emotion, I crack open the door. "Covey?"

"Yeah?" she says, and she's in the room, looking tall and imposing as if she's prepared to throw my mom out.

"I think our time is up," I say. "We don't have Mack. We don't have another body to stall Jimmy." And even then, would I be able to hand over anyone whose memory is still there? No, definitely not. No matter what bodily organ is missing, or growth has happened, they were a person who mattered.

If we stay, we will lose everything. Covey will be forced to follow her dad.

If we go, maybe we'll always be chased by Jimmy or the undone, but there's a chance for happy, peaceful days. What's blood compared to water—the thing that runs the world?

"We run as soon as possible," I say, renewing my attention on Mom. She gave me breath once, and now she can offer more: escape, another life, a way to start again. "You'll transport us out on *Wild Things*. You owe me this."

25

FOR YEARS IN OUR small trailer, I slept on the mattress beside Mom. Then, for many more months, I slept in the bunk right by hers, our breathing falling in tandem. She always sang me to sleep. I don't let her this time. She sleeps in the back room, her expression as dejected as I feel when I shut the flimsy door. The talk has narrowed some rifts between us, but like my skin, our relationship is still tender. I can't shake off the resentment so easily.

Covey's hovering at the end of the hall, duffel bag open. There's a cut of a smile when she sees me. Instead of knives, she flashes a series of gold compacts, mascara tubes, and eyeshadow palettes. "I grabbed some things when we were at Jimmy's," she explains. "They're all my mom's, so it's probably expired, but I don't mind. Do you? We can check one more thing off your fuck-it list."

Her tone is light, but so is the sky hours before a storm.

"We don't have to," I say. "Covey, you were expecting to be with Mack by now. Don't hold it together for me."

"I'm not together at all," she says breathily, melancholy flickering across her face. The wound is still fresh. "I need this too—something normal before we go back to running and hiding and thinking about what comes next. Turn my brain off, please."

The rain has begun outside, a beat faster than my heart. Hurricane Isaias will arrive tomorrow, a whole day early. After the danger blows past, we'll scramble onto *Wild Things* and search for a haven away from Jimmy, who will be enraged, and Sông, who wants me home. None of us—me, Covey, Wil, Saf—have explicitly promised to stay together. The future is uncertain. Right now, Covey's not looking for a magic trick to make it all okay; she's asking for a reprieve.

"Okay," I say, because she gets to choose when to face her monsters. Covey lets her exhaustion go. She tosses makeup at me. I catch it clumsily against my chest. Though the makeup is old, the packaging is still pretty and shiny. Distorted, blurred versions of us are reflected on their surfaces. Opening one package sends a waft of sweet peach up my nose. I cough.

We settle onto the cushionless sofa. She fingers through other palettes and waves a very colorful array of gem-colored shadows. "I always liked this one. She let me use it once when I was a flower girl. Shit, these *really* are ancient."

"You were a flower girl?" She shoots a "what the hell does that mean" look my way. I shrug. "I just mean, it's hard to imagine you in a cute white dress tossing rose petals when I've only seen you throw bolts."

Covey flips me off. "I was six and forced into the dress. The ring boy got to walk a dog. *A dog*." This decade-old indignation over a missed dog-walking opportunity explains a lot about why Sandbag likes Covey so much. Cats always know who they need to conquer. "My mom, she—actually, let's not talk about our parents. Just us."

I understand because we have been forced to change. Like the bride who marries into other families, a child is meant to grow up and take care of their parents in their old age. They wanted us because they're afraid to die alone or leave no legacy, but here we are—forced to survive in a world with strange rules and now an uncertain future.

I pick up a palette. "Let's pretend we slopped out fully formed from the primordial goo then." Covey makes a face when I laugh at my own joke. "Come here, I bet this shade will look good on you." The label indicates it's called Botanical Eggplant, which raises too many questions to figure out.

Covey scoots closer. "All right. Make me hot." Her skin is dewy from at least four layers of reapplied sunscreen. I reach out and brush her brows up with my fingertips.

"I've always thought you were pretty," I say, and don't regret it when her blue eyes widen in astonishment.

Night is for the shy creatures, for the people who don't need fanfare, for the stars. Night is when the truth is most likely to come out: in the blue-black of a bedroom, with a girl who is finally your friend, where anything is possible because it is impossibly lucky that the two of you are alive at the same time.

I slip a makeup brush into my mouth, then open my palms like a book, mimicking Knife Girl's posture at the port. I drawl, "I'm so intellectual and hot. Femme fatale babe."

A shrill laugh escapes from Covey as she throws a powdery puff at me. A blush has suffused over her cheeks. "My god. Stop making that face."

"It's *your* face."

"And what about you? Your core is like short, surly grandpa who is, against all odds, cute."

This time, I throw the puff at her. It's hard to believe our first impressions lasted up to two-plus weeks ago. Brush fallen, I gently hold her chin and paint a wash of Botanical Eggplant across her lids. Immediately, I can tell it's too dark. I keep a silent *oh shit* for myself.

"What?" Covey immediately tries to see the deep bruises swiped on her lids.

I pivot to distraction. "Where are you going first?" The implied "after all this" is there. It's probably better to leave as a mystery, but I haven't had a friend for so long. Not knowing where Wilder was all this time qualified as its own kind of torture; I don't want the same with Covey.

"The wind phone," she answers. She wants to go to the half-sunken phone booth that lets you speak to the dead.

I swirl Bitten Fig over the previous color. "I thought you said you never wanted to use it."

"Circumstances change," she says. "Sorry, we aren't supposed to talk about all that." She waves her hand. "If I'm going to leave Louisiana for good, might as well stop at another tourist trap first. Get my thoughts out. It's silly."

"It's not really silly," I say. As the last few days have proven, there's more to the universe than we understand. Who am I to say her words won't be delivered to Mack? These booths might not have been put down with sincere intentions by whatever nonprofit, but if we believe our deceased loved ones watch over us, then maybe that's enough.

"All right, my turn," she says, swatting the makeup brush away. Covey snatches the glasses from my face and moves close enough that I feel her breath. She goes for the peachy palette and gently strokes color on my lid. Out of habit, I keep my eyes open, which means I get bristles in my eye until she yells at me to stop.

I close my eyes and let her do her thing, though it makes me a little anxious.

"Time for a lighter question," Covey says. "You can have any meal materialize in front of you. What are you eating?"

I snort as she spreads a sticky substance on my face that feels and smells suspiciously like sunscreen. I fail to tell her that it's literally nighttime and that my days as a human with human skin are probably limited. "A hot dog."

"A hot dog," she repeats. "Like not even a bratwurst or kielbasa?"

"I don't know what either of those words means, but I'm driven by my immediate needs, and right now I want a hot dog. That beefy, nitrate-filled stuff, topped with sweet relish, fresh onions, and mustard and—"

"We're not at the cannibalism stage of the world dying."

"But I *am* at the craving-white-cuisine stage. I've been eating my mom's cooking for two years," I say. "Let me punish my body."

She laughs. "You are ridiculous." Covey's clearly thought about her answer since she goes on a ten-minute description about her desired meal: a buttermilk biscuit, red pepper jelly, fried green tomatoes, two eggs over easy, and a tall glass of ice-cold orange juice. No pulp.

I pick up a creamy blush that reminds me of watermelon and slather it on her sharp cheekbones. I blend it out more with my fingers. She uses the same one on me—each of us coloring the other's cheek at the same time. Her touch is softer than mine. "I barely feel anything."

"I'm keeping it very light so we can still see your freckles," Covey says. "Skin damage looks adorable on you."

I break out in laughter. "Doesn't matter much in hell, yeah."

We turn a compact mirror our way. Horrendously pink circles cover our cheeks, and our eyes are little orbs in a sea of paint. The sunscreen also makes me unhealthily pale, several shades lighter than my neck. We look like clowns. The only thing missing are poofs of blue hair on either side of our dumb skulls.

In another timeline, we would be sitting with different friends in a world that isn't slowly burning itself out. We'd be gossiping about the first weeks of school. Maybe I'd still be tormented by mistakes, but I like to think not every universe would be so unkind to me. There are universes in which Nhung Lê is allowed to be weird and happy. Still, there are good moments to be found in this one, too.

Wilder and Saffy, both old and new friends.

The vegetation, new blooms and growth overtaking old spaces.

This night, with Covey.

I can lose all this. I *will* lose all this once I escape toward the ocean's horizon, back to the timeline in which I'm alone.

We lie back on the only part on the sofa that's still soft. Our heads are turned toward one another, shoulders relaxed and bony elbows grazed. It's too hot for much else.

"God, it looks like you have sunrises on your lids." Covey does her best not to laugh, but the corners of her lips cut deep into her cheeks. "Or, like, grapefruit slices. What did I do wrong?"

"And you look like I punched you repeatedly," I say. "Actually, this is kind of spiritually healing for me to see." A fresh peal of laughter overtakes us both before we finally settle in for the night—only quiet between us. Common wisdom would have us scrub the makeup off before sleeping, but at the end of the world, neither of us gives a flying shit about acne.

I can't sleep and I wonder if it's because I've changed. Maybe my brain has rewired itself as the cells in my body do, becoming that which can survive in this world.

The water calls me. I feel it seeping into the stilt legs of the cabin. I hear its restless mumbling before the coming storm. It's different from before, when the only thing I could hear was *let us in*, because now I must be close to my next shape.

What will I become after all of this?

I follow the call to the window. Someone—no, something— is there, lit by the moon and hovering over water. A dream. I haven't seen Jay's face for twenty-one months, and it is the same: childlike, with Mom's chin and Dad's eyebrows. I can't see it from here but I know he has freckles like mine.

A cynical part of me says this is a trap, one to finally drown and turn me into another kind of monster, but this imitation is weightless. As quietly as I can, so I don't wake Mom or Covey, I leave the cabin. The boardwalk is cool but wet under my bare feet. In a blink, Jay has moved from the water to the pier. I pick my way over to where we've tied off the boats.

On the opposite end of the skiff, my brother waits for me. The boat doesn't shift at all, because he isn't real. *Let's go see your house*, the thing wearing my brother's memory says. The voice is inside my head—thin, watery, only a shard of what Jay's was. This is not my brother or a person undone.

"Sông?"

The imposter tilts its head. *Many names for one.*

I wonder how many families have a story about Sông and all they lost and gained from it. They must have given this creature of the water different names, maybe even in languages now gone. It is certainly ancient, by human years.

I'm almost sure it hasn't come to claim me by force. It's been patient this time. I step onto the boat. The water moves us slowly toward Mercy—a place I love and hate. The rain has slowed to a drizzle for now, but the wind is strong. The boat stops at a stretch of levee I would know in my sleep. I pull the boat somewhere safe, then wander up and over to the Magnolia Springs trailer lot.

There used to be a fence perpendicular to our home. I stained my teeth red every summer with the berries that grew there. They took the bush down a long time ago, but the berries scattered elsewhere. In a nearby oak, I would place my collection of rocks at the base. And though many species are not thriving now, other plants are: algae, the darkest green of moss, and vine. New life persists amidst all the dying. That's always been true.

I pull myself into our old trailer, the air damp. This should feel like home, and yet I'm hollowed out. I've never believed in Mom's delusions of reincarnation, but having seen the trans-formations for myself, the tiniest slice of hope has dared to light itself. It must've been painful for Mom to wait for a miracle, only to never get it.

"Are they in the water somewhere too?" I ask, to be sure.

Standing at the center of the wrecked kitchen, Not-Jay offers its hand. *Memories.* Tentatively, I step forward and grasp it, but the sensation is running water, a rush of cold in my palm that seizes me. I'm thrown through memories, as if I'm wading in Mercy Cove, and see from Jay's perspective. His worry for me when I stopped smiling my freshman year. The pressure from our dad to be the next man of the house, when he only wanted to be young and soft for a little longer. Then there's a flash of stormy skies some decades ago and the desperate pleas of a refu-gee mother—*my* great-grandmother—to save her family, and Sông was curious about why so many risk dying on this path.

It had slumbered long enough, and it wanted a taste of this America too.

I understand then that this is the ocean that nearly drowned my family, personified. It is the rivers flowing from it. Its true mouth is bottomless and unknowable, the shape of it miles and miles beneath us, maybe even around us. It chiseled at our shores, flowed through faucets, and cried within our filters, parted itself from itself. It heard my crying at the cove. It needed to be in us, wholly soaked in our cells, the memories scraping in our throats to the pits of our bellies. It was sick of death. It needed to be part of us and us part of it—to understand, to survive. It bled itself for us.

Like a scientist, it does what it can to try and save us. It experiments. It morphs some wrong. It connects our memories but doesn't know how to ease the suffering it's inflicted too.

I withdraw my hand. I'm overwhelmed by a deep sadness that isn't all mine. Nameless memories, but known ones too: Covey's, and that moment she knew Mack was truly gone; Saffy's, over the fear of packing up and searching yet again for another home; and Wilder's, learning that sometimes love forces you to choose either yourself or others. The buried grief resurfaces: Dad and Jay are gone. My tears are fresh and taste of old makeup.

Not-Jay's jaw opens, and it's a whirlpool of darkness. It wants to save me. Water rushes over and over itself, and the voices are crying as one. *Let us in let us in let us in.*

"No," I say. "Not yet." I back away, then run to the boat. Not-Jay has vanished by the time I chance a look. Immediately I start the engine, not caring if others hear, and drive through the rain.

When our strange little cabin finally comes back into view, everything seems off.

Wild Things is gone. The door is open when I'm sure I left it shut. I jump from the skiff to the pier and step into the shack. Empty, empty, empty.

Mom and Covey have disappeared.

26

"MÁ!" I SCREAM. "COVEY!" My voice echoes through this empty shack, through the cracked windows and over surging tides. Desperate and too loud. I want it to be an anchor that can reach far enough to hook them to the river floor. *Stop.* Does it need to be said? *Don't leave me.* Endings are inevitable, but it doesn't have to be like this.

I keep breathing, emptying my mind with every exhale until I see clearly. It's a mess inside the shack: makeup scattered and crumbling on the floor, overturned furniture, and a streak of blood on the wall. The door to the bedroom is open too, showing nothing but abandoned sheets. I turn the whole place even more upside down for any hint of where they went, but their things are still here. Covey hadn't taken her crossbow. The only knife she has on her must be tucked in her book. And the blood on the wall is fresh. I can't tell whose it is. They either rushed themselves or someone else rushed them along. I wasn't gone that long, but every moment had lined up perfectly for them to disappear without me.

Rain beats down my back as I kneel on the pier. Mrs. Olivier had no care for her body's welfare when she tried to return me to Sông. I don't think the undone would have done this so delicately. Besides, I am the one they want, and I had been alone in Magnolia Springs with the entity itself. It had learned to ask for permission. "Did you know someone was coming?" I ask the river, feeling ridiculous even though I'd spoken to Sông minutes ago.

My reflection in the water is a stranger's. Greasy haired, rounded nose with her nostrils flaring, and makeup partially melted. She bares her teeth in question, and there, in place of the canine she lost, is a sharp white tooth. Rain droplets disturb the surface as I run my tongue on sore gums and find a few more triangular teeth meant for ripping meat.

Sông had lured me away, and now nothing answers.

Rushing inside, I search for my radio, the same one Mom and I used to communicate while apart, since the other one must be on the boat still. I find it lodged under a broken chair. Fingers sweating on the black plastic, heart crushed with hope, I speak into it. "Mom, where are you?" I sound like her from those days she begged me to talk to her, to listen, after our confrontation at the lighthouse. "Is Covey with you?" The line is only static. I press the hot plastic object to my forehead and think about praying, about throwing my thoughts into the world for any ounce of luck in return.

Maybe I have come to the wrong conclusion. No one took or attacked them, but they left of their own volition. After witnessing how sweet Mrs. Olivier deteriorated, they decided to leave me while they still could. Going our separate ways was the plan anyway, so why does it hurt?

The radio bursts to life.

Through the haze, I think I'm mistaken. It can't be, and yet—

"I hear you, Noonie." His voice, my nightmare.

"Aaron," I whisper.

"So you're still around," he says cheerfully. My brain struggles to accept this reality. My finger hovers over the OFF switch, but this is my only connection to Mom and Covey right now. There's no other way he could've stolen Mom's radio. "Did you really think Jimmy was gonna let y'all get away without collecting what he's owed?"

"Mrs. Olivier is dead," I say. "There's no body to bring back."

"But we have another fledgling monster on our hands, don't we?" He continues. "You see, I'm good at supervising. You were being weirder than usual at the harbor. I followed you. I saw the fucked-up mess Olivier became, but mostly, I saw you."

The word *you* invokes a wave of nausea. I am sick and trembling. Like a predator, he'd hidden amongst the wreckage and observed. The foremost feeling is violation since he must have seen us laughing with Wilder and Saffy at the mansion too. I imagine Aaron amongst the shadowy trees, drinking up my skin. Preying on me, until the changes took over. Aaron has cataloged a *before* and *after* of my body. He knew enough to start documenting the changes. And now, he has Mom and Covey.

Swallowing down bile, I ask, "Where are they?"

It's noisy as people shuffle on the other end, then Mom's muffled shouting gets louder. Her voice resembles the high pitch in her songs. And though I don't hear Covey, she must be there too. The voice on the line changes. It grows deeper and pauses as its owner blows cigarette smoke. "Aaron told me all about you and the algae," Jimmy says. "The problem *is* algae, right? Mutating everything in it. You know, I was gonna take care of it myself when the bloom first came around. I got the hookup on industrial strength algaecide, but then I let those officials tell me they got it all under control. They care more about a bunch of tree huggers than they do about people who want to work."

My patience snaps cleanly. "I'm not here for your monologue. What do you want?"

Jimmy chuckles. "I get rid of all the algae. Fuck the EPA. I turn you in, little monster. It's a win-win situation for them that I'm manning up and doing what they can't do. I get my businesses back in order. Fishermen fish, shrimpers trawl, and the tourists come back. The whole parish wins. So this is the only deal you're getting: Come to the emporium before sunrise, turn yourself in, and your mother goes free. It's that simple."

It's my turn to laugh. *Simple*, as if the bloom hasn't been spreading everywhere wet and dry. An ancient being watches us, and yet it's *simple*. Only men like Jimmy would look at nature and think it can be controlled. "And Covey?"

This time, he snarls, "Covey is where she belongs. You best realize where you belong too. Sunrise, Noon."

I clench the radio in my fist. "Don't count on it," I say.

There's endless space on the line, as Mom's muffled cries end suddenly. I hear only wind whipping through the trees, growing stronger as Hurricane Isaias draws nearer. It will rip through Mercy and its port, then make its way farther inland. It will swallow the emporium and its surrounding swamp, perhaps with Covey and Mom and Aaron and Jimmy all inside. They won't be my problem anymore.

Saving myself would be so easy. No one needs me in Mercy. I'll be easily forgotten. I can steal a boat and go anywhere else. My body has changed and it will keep changing. Some animals like humpback whales and crocodiles eat only once every few months, and I'm not even hungry anymore. Sông must possess a certain wisdom from all the collected memories, from the flow of water throughout the world. It believes I can survive, or else it would not have tricked me away from the shack.

I am no longer a person to Jimmy Boudreaux. Maybe I never was to begin with. Jimmy deals in numbers, where everything is cost and profit. I'll be a rat in a cage, surrounded by his taxidermy trophies, until he trades me in. Then I'll be studied as the next in line of the human species—or eliminated, because it wouldn't be the first time someone is killed for being different.

Squatting against the sofa, arms wrapped around my knees, I press myself as small as I can. If I disappear, it would be so much better. I'd not have to think. There's the easy choice to run and live the time I have left. This new me can have no mother. No friend. No crush.

And yet why must I be the one to hide?

I feel fourteen again. Only fourteen and tasked with protecting herself. She alone is responsible for finding ways to walk without shame, places to go where no one knows how she's been ruined. Long before the bloom tucked us in, I have needed help. I scream, letting loose all the rage and self-pity that's hardened me over the last two years. Mom's done enough damage by wishing away the truth. I said it before: a sweater doesn't keep me safe. This costume that everyone else sees can't protect me either. Hiding doesn't help because I am the one existing in my skin.

27

SOMEHOW THROUGH THE STORM, I found my way to the mansion. I climbed through the designated window, then called for my friends. For a terrifying moment, I was gripped by the fear that they were taken too, but a lamplight switched on, shining on their sleepy faces. Delight over my running makeup causes them to laugh, until they notice that it's not only due to rain. They usher me in. Saffy serves unintentionally chunky hot cocoa, and Wilder clumsily heaves a fluffy comforter around my shoulders. Both patiently wait for me to tell them what happened.

Once I'm done, Wil rises off the sofa. "Mercy isn't all we have. This shitty, imperfect place that has rejected us over and over again? It isn't all there is."

Saffy gets up too, as Sandbag hops from her lap, tail curled. "We'll whiteboard it out. We just have to get your mom and Covey back. Then we'll *all* live somewhere else. That doesn't have to change."

I set my untouched drink down. "No," I say. Although I've never imagined myself as someone who stays in Mercy forever, I also don't want to leave the coast. For all its problems, I love being this close to the ocean. Even though Dad never nurtured it, I miss *Wild Things* and the bounce of waves beneath my feet. My love for what surrounds Mercy doesn't change just because people have done bad things here. My body is not bad, either, for all it has lived through.

There is no other home for me.

I look at my friends—my lovely, ridiculous friends—and decide, finally, what I want. "Do you trust me?"

My body is taking me to Chelsea's Cove. There has been a pull inside my body this entire time, like the water's call and my intermittent headaches, that I've valiantly ignored until now. My story doesn't begin or end here, but both cove and town have left imprints on my pages. We can't pretend this trauma doesn't exist.

The water has receded into the soil, soaked deep. Body-shaped husks are left along rocks and the sharp points of trees where people snagged their skin, itching it off. Clothes in all sizes lie abandoned on the ground. Baseball caps, sundresses, fatigues, baby shoes. No one was safe. Mercy Cove has always been a cursed place. Even before the algae bloom seeped in, many bodies were ripped apart on this shore. Countless girls, I'm sure, starting with Chelsea. Then others, coaxed by people who claim that this is all normal and expected, a rite of passage. Me. *Boys will be boys.* What did I know about being a boy or girl?

"This is far enough," I tell Saffy and Wilder, near a rocky ledge that blocks the windy brunt. The water stirs in anticipation, too distant to try enveloping us. They glance anxiously toward the cove's low moan. Wilder's cheeks are wind-chapped, glistening with fresh tears. I smell the wound in his hand. They take in a shuddering breath and soldier through the discomfort for me. There's only a few hours left until sunrise. Facing them, I warn, "No matter what you hear, don't come closer. Okay?"

They nod. Saffy's trembling hands hold mine and massage the palms. Smiling, she tries to reassure me. "The future is trans. The future is non-binary. The future is soup." Despite the long, hard day we've had, and the pain, I can't help but laugh. I laugh until tears gather at the corners of my already puffy eyes, until they're crying too and snotty with laughter, and we're a damn mess.

"The future is soup," I say.

They wrap me in a bone-crushing hug. Goodbye for who knows how long. A bittersweet emotion, because why did we find each other at the end? Why do we have to leave each other? It's not fair, it's never fair, but at least I get to see their faces now. I hope to see Covey and Mom again, too.

Under a beautiful sky, terrible things can still happen. And yet through the horror, there will be moments like this, when a drizzle replaces a downpour in the lovely night and bioluminescent pops light the world all around. I let them go and walk toward my future.

The undone are a mass of skin and loose teeth, tangled condoms on a dusty road. They are melted candle wax, too cloyingly sweet, a pool of remains to be sifted through. The cove holds them, rock curving like hands. They are water but also skin, folding into one another—all waves, all crying *let us in let us in let us in let us in*. The temptation to puncture my eardrums as Delgado had done grows, but I simply slip my shoes off and place them on flat rock. I take one step after another into the dark pool. They hug me firmly from all sides. They seep into my clothes, over my scars, and caress my cheek. They soothe the burning rash in my side to a dull ache.

The skin on my neck splits into proper gills, trembling underneath my fingertips. It's almost like petting an animal—a horse, maybe—and feeling its restrained strength and potential violence. I sink into the water, toes scraping away from the sand, that sensation that I hate so much. My body jolts into a free fall, dragged farther than the cove's actual depth. The pressure squeezes all around. I am an overripe orange, threatening to spill out juicy fibers. I fall, and fall, and fall, until I'm suspended in the deep ocean where there's mostly black. I am held in place.

Every now and then, something skeletal flickers at the edge of my vision. Bright violet or blue, body as transparent as bridal lace. Animals have evolved to survive these freezing waters in all manners of ways. Some rely on gigantism, growing far larger than related species; others possess eyes so mismatched as to function separately on different tasks; and a few dangle their own lights to attract prey.

I don't know whether Sông is genuinely benevolent or just bored. All I know is that it's here, dissecting me and my possibilities.

"Let us make a deal," I say to this primordial beast, though no words come from my lips. Something other than language connects us. It's instinctual. Maybe a cosmic presence as tenacious as algae has filled the crevices of my brain. No matter. Wilder once taught me that the first step to getting a good deal is to insult the product. "Your plan so far has been absolute shit." For full effect, I fervently visualize the poop emoji.

It wants to save us by completely undoing us. Is that different from killing an entire species?

"The people you undid are suffering. It hurts them to continue like this in the bloom. For someone—something—with a lot of patience, you rushed." This close, I feel their remnants. Their bodies may be gone, but bits of them stay. Sông made me and Mrs. Olivier, perhaps even Delgado, different. In her transformed state, Mrs. Olivier had been supernaturally strong; it's what I need in order to save Covey and Mom. "Let them go into me. Let their memories be mine, and mine be yours. Maybe we can figure out another way to do things after."

The dark space cleaves open.

Sông resembles a great, pulsating eye, a roundel creature with a mane of thick-bodied worms. Those are not the right words to describe it, but its body is incomprehensible. No pupil stares out from its immense form. I do not think it has a body in the way humans understand anatomy. We're limited by shape, then imagination. How silly of me to think that Not-Jay's manifestation was its entirety.

I open my mouth, and Sông flows into me. Warm cider down a cold throat. A bag of razors. Sông doesn't know what hurts yet.

It is magical; it is not; it is magical. A childhood spent somewhere will always impart a bit of magic. You pass a road and you remember the food stand your dad stopped at, sneaking you a nitrate-filled hot dog. You got food poisoning, but it was kind of worth it. You look outside a window and see the same leaf-shaped shadows on the opposite trailer as the day before. You remember heat, but not uncomfortable sweat. Riding your bike down a winding road, your neighbor in a car behind you. They don't honk. Maybe they remember they once did the same.

The thorns behind your house hurt, but the roses smelled sweet, softer than his thrifted shirts.

Your sister finds you in the laundry basket, like every hiding spot that came before it. *Gotcha*, she always says, then you're in her arms. Safe. You want to always find her too.

You remember taking your children to the town's only playground to ride rusty swings.

You remember when you were a boy and the river wasn't so angry and how you and your parents could ride its waves all day.

This is what it means not to be alone. They grieve for us. They worry over our ongoing destruction. They beg to save us. They live their happiest moments, and they are not alone in their most torturous memories. Their emotions connect in a way our brains weren't wired for.

An intense pressure starts within my chest, cracking each rib slow from the sternum. It's not painful; it's meant to be. I bloom.

My first thought when I wake up is, *I don't itch*. The discomfort has been culled, though the rash is still a torn mess. Everything is as it was and yet I feel, with certainty, that I am finally the right shape. My glasses have drifted away, but I don't need them anymore. I see the world clearly now. The water is calm as it slinks over my feet, mouths sated. I was wrong before, because the undone are not suffering. Nor are they the decomposition cadaver islands Covey speculated about. They are alive—the body of bodies, moving as one. And the rest are harbingers of change, as busy as worker bees.

I did not sacrifice myself at all.

So many days before, I felt like apologizing for being me and making mistakes. I felt small from how everyone looked at me, as if they knew—and if they did, how they calculated whether I'd put myself in harm's way. They played a game full of blame, without knowing that their world is so small. I glance down at the water. My reflection stares back with strange eyes, the complete set now of ice-blue slits through pitch-black.

I wade to the beach, where my friends are already rushing over, and put my shoes back on.

Who gets to decide what I deserve?

Only me.

28

THE STORM FOLLOWS AT my back as I go the same way Covey showed me to Jimmy's Gator Swamp Tour and Emporium. It's comforting to feel the strength of the current beneath the small boat and not be afraid of drowning in it. I am alone—as alone as I can be, with all these memories and voices inside me.

I made Saffy and Wilder stay behind because it's too complicated to have more people I care about within reach of this greedy man. When I arrive at Jimmy's emporium, it's the men outside that unnerve me rather than the alligators and their marble eyes watching from the swamp. Alligators might attack to defend their territory, but men attack to make their territory. Every body is a conquering ground.

A generator-run bulb splashes raw light across the green-hued water where alligators lurk, the algae settled along their back ridges. They must be changing too, little by little, down to their very cells. Greasy-haired workers pull my boat in, and I climb onto the docks, damp from my swim in Mercy Cove and the ongoing rain. Skidmark, who's here instead of the harbor probably due to Hurricane Isaias, shoves a flashlight right into my eyes. "What the fuck happened to your face?" He's wearing a slimy grin, which means he's seen only the clown-like makeup melted over my cheeks. I tilt my head back and smile widely, as people have often told me to do. My gums ache deeply with shark teeth that haven't all pushed through. Skidmark stumbles back. "Fuckin' hell!"

Keeping as much distance as pride allows, they lead me to the main building. The wind is nearly fierce enough to bowl us over. The pool's cover has been slipped back on, and the memory of Covey's knees touching mine warms my chest. All algaecide barrels have been moved, so there are pale outlines where they used to sit, moisture creeping into the wood. Inside the dank hallways, the dead eyes of Jimmy's previous kills accompany me until we reach the cafeteria. Jimmy sits on top of a table while Covey stares stone-faced besides him. She gets up immediately, mouth dropping open. The message is clear in the angle of her brows. *Why did you come?*

It was inevitable, fate as I've come to believe it.

My head whips toward Jimmy as he speaks loudly, so he can be heard over the raging storm. "Damn uncanny. Just look at how her eyes move." The wonder on his face is unrivaled.

I raise my arms wide. "I'm here now. You got what you want. There's no reason to keep my mom and Covey here."

"My daughter belongs with me," Jimmy says coldly. "You're just the beginning, sugar. What kind of person thrives while others die? Not a person, that's for sure. A monster. A fucked-up catch. And why settle for one when I can have many?"

An ill, foreboding sensation lurches in my stomach. "What are you talking about?" I look from the foreman to Covey, whose hands have curled into fists. There's no sign of Mom anywhere.

"Jimmy's will be *the* premier spot for anyone looking to explore the mystical wilderness of Mercy, Louisiana. And you," he says, "are the star of the emporium itself. You and your mother get to live right by each other. That's a kindness even the government wouldn't grant."

I'd overlooked the fact that he doesn't actually care about Mercy or the docks or any of the disappearances. He was only ever supposed to be a contractor for transported goods. We were a pit stop in his contingency plans. If his original businesses resurge in popularity, he doesn't need Mercy to be habitable. In fact, it's better that it isn't. Exclusive experiences make good marketing.

"Asshole," I say, disgusted by Jimmy's false altruism and grandiose schemes. "The sunrise deal was a bluff. You were never gonna let them go."

Jimmy wears a brutal cut of a smile. "You reap from your own stupidity."

From a side door, another figure in a flannel shirt joins us. Aaron is a shard of light. An alien. A gash in my eye, unseen but felt, that pain plunging in. He never deserved me. He never should have had me. A square bandage covers his cheek, blood seeping in the pattern of teeth.

In a split second, Covey has sprung to her feet and punches him in the face. There's a *crunch* to the impact, and he doubles over, clutching his face. "You goddamn bitc—"

"Watch your mouth," Jimmy warns Aaron. Satisfaction rushes through me as I watch Covey nurse her knuckles. Suddenly, Jimmy turns on me. "I don't like how you look at my girl, Noony." There's an unwarranted venom in his gaze, more so than when he'd looked at the man who cursed his daughter. He signals the workers to move. They break from the line behind me to flank Aaron as he stalks forward.

Swearing, Aaron digs his fingers into my neck, deep inside the gills. His strength knocks me off my feet, which scrape uselessly over the floor. He drags me backward to the outside hall. Jimmy has an arm out to keep Covey from running after me.

All down the corridor, the taxidermy animals on the walls seem to send their condolences. Aaron grips me harder when I try prying his hands away. His fingers down my throat makes it hard to breathe, but it's him touching me at all that enrages me most. I am a fish stolen from water, about to be tagged and measured for a trophy. I am nothing to these people, though it seems hardly new.

He throws open swinging doors to a room that smells wet and foul. Tanks and cages are stacked along all four walls. Bright red snakes coil in one while large lizards lay lazily in another. He and Skidmark hoist and toss me right into a tank, replacing the lid with a loud snap. The water is warm and dead. I kick up, bursting through the filthy surface, and gulp air from the five-inch space. I hold onto one of the metal bars across the top. Across from me is another large water- and algae-filled tank. Pale and exhausted, Mom hangs from a metal bar as well. She perks up when it registers who I am. "Nhung!" she cries. Her lip is split open, and her left arm is bent at an unnatural angle again. She'd not gone without a fight.

This viewing room reminds me of the scientists in the gymnasium, of the animals left to rot in their tanks. There had been algae there too, sticking to glass as if desperate to escape. At least Delgado had wanted to help. They believed this remarkable discovery could save the coral reefs. There's no honorable cause here.

Aaron taps my tank. "You won't be special for long." Every line in his face is unkind in a sneer. Mom struggles in the tank behind him.

"You can't *make* the undone," I say with a dark realization about how far these men will go to get what they want. There's no rulebook on who or what the algae roots in. Jimmy and his company can't replicate a cataclysm, this one-in-many lifetimes event. Sông will let the bloom run its course.

Before leaving, they turn the main overhead lights off. The bulbs in our tanks stay on, the glow sickly. Rain pummels the roof, so constant that it sounds like a bucket's been turned over all at once. Throughout the building, there's a banging too—not the undone's knocking but people nailing wooden boards over delicate windows.

From Jimmy to the workers, their anxiety had been high before I arrived. They're running behind schedule because Isaias is early. It is not a day for big moves and yet, it must be done.

There's just the hum of a generator, of other animals rustling, and my mom fighting her cage to get to me. She's perfectly sealed in. *"What happened to you?"* Mom asks. In the hours since our talk, I've changed. The eyes have fully snuffed to a deep blackness, wedged through with ice. My entire body thrums with instinct.

I decide on the easiest of truths. "*I followed Sông back to our old trailer. I guess it knew they were coming for me. It looked like Jay but was not at all Jay.*"

She appears stricken, unused to the reality that Jay is truly gone. She pulls herself higher on the bar, ragged from hanging there for the last several hours. "*That fuck ambushed us with some of the harbor workers. They beat me, demanding to know where you were. I was so thankful you weren't there. You should've stayed away.*"

Despite the situation, I giggle. Mom flinches at the unexpected sound. I've never heard her curse in any language before. "Did you bite him?" I ask.

She throws a look toward the exit, her long black hair fanning out in the water. "*I should have killed him.*"

It's my first time hearing her rage expressed this way—fiery instead of shame. Thunder cracks, throwing a cypress's shadow across the floor. They deserve a reckoning. I check the tank's length, pushing against the lid to see if it'll pop off, but holes have been drilled into the lid and glass, then wired through with aluminum. The only opening is a small entry point for food to be thrown in.

I let myself sink as I abandon my clothing piece by piece. It must be a sad, alarming sight—the floating clothes, like it's a crime scene. I'm never dressed the way people like. I kick to the surface as Covey had taught me. Before Mom can say anything else, I press myself to the small tank opening and begin to molt.

29

PICTURE A TARANTULA TEARING away from its old legs, leaving behind hair still soft to the touch. A snake slipping from its too-small scales. Or maybe it's more comforting to imagine something dead—even though there's no decay in this body of mine—being processed, like sausage meat cut from intestine or a hen with her throat slit, her feathers damp in your hands. But the dead don't move, and I am, limbs twitching as a cricket's might.

This process can take hours, but I've no time. It is indelicate work. I see what Mrs. Olivier meant when she suggested we pull from one flap to unveil her. Through the dirty tank, I glimpse Mom clamping a hand over her mouth, drowning out a scream that would attract guards. My hand slams against the glass. I dip my head into the filthy tank water, teeth gnawing on loose skin. I get a hangnail as far down as I can before emerging from the water.

The tank's edge is within reach. I haul myself upward, feeling stranger out of water than within it. I am an animal in flux; there's no name for me yet. I press myself again into the opening and maneuver my head through.

Monsterhood is a girl's body you don't belong in.

The tank scrapes rind from sinew as my body compresses, everything clicking or breaking apart. The layers of me that never made any sense fall. Long before I'd started shedding skin, I've been slicing pieces of myself away.

I was quiet so I would not draw more attention.

I was no trouble because I thought I'd caused enough grief.

I listened to the teachers, the adults who should know everything, about what it means to live in the world: make money, buy cars, poison the land and air. Let it be my child's problem some day because it's *too much* now. The deep dark space is where we belong next, as if we aren't all made of stardust right here on Earth.

Life started in the ocean.

Water spills onto the floor as I land with a thud. Humid air touches this newborn skin for the first time. I study my arms and its patchwork of scales and exoskeleton. No blood drips from me. In the tank is the vaguely feminine shape that others saw, a tan-beige suit containing only water. The eyes and internal organs are missing. It's a vessel for no one. I have left her behind.

Turning around, I face my mom. There's no trace of fear in her expression. Sadness wells in her eyes, the pupils no longer a twin to mine. I pry at the lid of her tank, but it barely budges since it has the same aluminum wiring through drilled holes. A padlock keeps the hinges shut. I'd been able to squeeze through the tiny cutout, but I can't free Mom that way. A frustrated groan slips between my teeth.

I step down and grab a footstool, swinging it against the glass. The pointless impact sends shocks up my arms. Jimmy had invested in professional-grade aquariums for the long term. I beat it with my fists, wishing my anger was enough to shatter everything.

"Stop it, con," Mom says. "*Just go. You're hurting yourself.*"

"Do you know where the key is?" I ask. Pliers or another metal tool should be easy to find for the wires, so the lock's the big problem.

She ignores my question. "*The storm will trap you here.*" This close, all the injuries on her become easier to see. She has far more cuts and bruises than before. As in Covey's case, the bloom hasn't found its way under her skin. It floats in the murky water, because Jimmy cannot command it. He can't fathom not being able to manufacture the undone for public consumption. In the old world, Jimmy's words mattered. In mine, they don't at all.

The door slams wide as Skidmark marches in, our commotion gaining notice. He doesn't see me at first, it seems, judging by his confusion over the tattered husk inside my former containment. Slowly he shifts, sight on the wet footsteps until, finally, he's staring at my animal body.

I am not a boy or a girl. Do you know the shape of water? Do you know clouds, and mountains, or every bud of wisteria at the height of spring? Your eyes follow me but you've never really seen me.

Skidmark and I move at the same time. He goes for the weapon at his belt buckle, but I use my hands. Nails have regrown in place of my stubs, sharp as a shell. I'm careful to remove the gun from his possession, kicking it far into a corner. In the aftermath of our tussle, the room smells like spilt beer, tangy blood, and muddied feet. No one is dead yet, but he won't be bothering us for a while. I unhook the dangling key from a belt loop, then climb back up to help my mom out.

Once she is on her feet, Mom holds onto my shoulders. A sob wracks her chest.

With my fingers, I stretch both her eyelids so the moles show. A constellation. "It's usually okay to be upset, but right now I need you," I say.

Blinking rapidly, she takes in a deep, long breath until the sob dies in her throat, then nods in new resolve. Mom raids the small supply closet for a weapon, but there're only aquarium cleaning brushes and nets in different sizes. Giving up, she pulls a raincoat from a wall hook and slips it over my shoulders, as if to protect my modesty now that my clothes and skin are in tatters.

"It doesn't matter what I wear," I say. "They see what they want to see."

We tiptoe slowly down the hallway to avoid detection and because Mom's hurt all over. She tries hiding her pain, but she softly grunts whenever she moves too quickly. The storm has begun in earnest. Hurricane Asswipe is here, and we're getting a thorough cleaning. Rain beats down on the slate roof, thwacking against windows whenever the winds shift directions. Pale daylight is thrown across dreary walls, and dead animals cast shadows larger than what's left of them.

I rebuild the place in my mind, trying to remember everything about my last visit. There are four buildings total. This emporium area is new to me, but the private suites are on the other side of the main receiving area and gift shop. We just have to slip by unnoticed, which should be easy because people are sheltered in place.

"*Where are you going?*" Mom whispers, frantically waving me over to a side emergency exit. "*I think I see boats out this way.*" Through the closest window and rain outside, there are vague shapes resembling boats. She's probably right, but I have other goals on my mind.

"I'm not leaving without Covey."

The space between Mom's brows crinkles deeply. "*She will be okay here, with her dad.*" Although they may have spared Covey during the kidnapping, she's obviously not compliant with Jimmy's wishes. Punching Aaron will have repercussions, considering his humiliated anger.

I shake my head. I was okay just living with Mom too, but it had hurt. If I had another choice, if I had the sort of hot bravery running through me now, I would have done things differently. I'm not going along with her whims anymore.

I enter the gift shop. She pads gingerly after me. There are T-shirts and baseball caps boasting JIMMY'S GATOR SWAMP TOUR AND EMPORIUM and its ludicrous logo of an alligator eating its own tail. Behind locked glass are gator-skin purses and belts. Cute shot glasses and tumblers are lined on towering shelves. On a spinning rack of keychains, rubber alligators and other animals have names imprinted on their spine. There's Brittney, Ash, Logan, but no Nhung. There's never one with my name on these things.

Wandering the halls of Jimmy's home is a bit like a fever dream, a funhouse of kitschy furniture. When I reach Covey's room, a pang of disappointment strikes. No guards are posted. But then again, when Jimmy is used to everyone being afraid of him, why would he expect anything different? Just because someone refuses once doesn't mean they'll always say no, is what a man like him thinks.

I wiggle the locked doorknob. Softly, I tap in the same rhythm we experienced at the shack. It's a charming but grating pattern—*knock knock knock*—that stays in your head. I imagine her freezing on the bed. But Covey being Covey, she answers the door. Suspicion loses out to surprise, and she pulls us both into her bedroom. "How did you get out?"

It should be obvious, even in the raincoat. I flourish a hand over my body. "I let them in."

Covey reaches for my hand. "Tell me it's a lie." She's so hopeful that it hurts me, but even with my scaled palm in hers, she doesn't let go.

I tell her everything from Sông luring me away from the shack and knowing who was coming with bad intentions, to our friends accompanying me to Mercy Cove, where I willingly stepped into the water. I don't need to elaborate on how different I am now, when the whites of my eyes are gone. "I couldn't leave either of you with Jimmy and Aaron."

"Who saves you then?" Covey's ragged whisper is marred in rage. "Who saves you, Noon?"

It's the same as when I unknowingly rescued her from the river by the shack. She's angry I risked myself.

"Not everyone gets saved," I say gently. "Not everyone lives. I'm not a fairy tale. Saving yourself, putting yourself first . . . I get it, but sometimes it's not the right answer." We can work hard all we want, but if the bootstraps are barely holding on by a thread, it snaps anyway. I'm tired of following the lessons set out by others. I want to find a new way forward, even if it takes deconstructing down to the marrow.

I'm learning I've been loved this entire time, in small and big ways. Mom complained about my messes but never threw my treasures away. She tried to be present, even if it was not enough. Dad wanted to protect me. My neighbors watched me walk toward the wildflowers, into the wildness I often disappeared in, to make sure I came back.

They just couldn't save me the one time. And one time can never define me.

This town is my mother, but I don't have to be what it wants me to be.

Saffy held my hands, despite the trembling in her own fingers. Wilder liked me before I liked myself. My brother loved me enough for two. Disregarding the rules, Mrs. Olivier let me haunt the library during lunchtime.

By giving myself over, I am not alone. They who wait in the cove aren't alone either, warning us of the times to come. It's mercy they offer, however bitter and strange. I share in their memories and experiences, and so do they in mine. The algae bloom is a part of us and vice versa; we'll survive as so many animals have before, in these symbiotic relationships.

"If this is the end of the world, I don't want to be careful with my heart, my body," I say, sure Saffy would be proud. "This is my choice. It's me."

Covey's eyes are watery, but she doesn't cry. "Okay."

Sensing the end of our conversation, Mom gathers next to us. "You know way out," Mom says. The storm howls on outside, but the worst of it isn't even here yet. When the hurricane hits shores, we will feel it rumble through the walls, climb up the stilts, and spill swamp water against the tall windows.

"Everyone's holed up inside right now," says Covey. "There are a few boats without a motor, but you know we're not going to get far in this weather. Neither can they. We can get far enough to a hiding spot—I've been cataloging them on my trips out—and stay low for when the storm lets up."

"*We have to leave* Wild Things," I tell Mom in Vietnamese, though it should've been obvious. Neither of us has the key anymore. The words are a strike on her face, but she softens when she notices how Covey's holding my hand. Reluctantly, she agrees.

The slate sky is rumbling when we reach the wraparound porch. We stick low to the floor as we make our way toward the docks. The air smells fresh and clean, as if the hurricane is tempting us. As if it's offering to wash the blood and sweat off my body. Clusters of boats bounce up and down from the disturbed waters. *Wild Things* is at the far end, swaying in the wind, and I wish there were time for goodbye. A few smaller ones are completely waterlogged and hold on by ropes linked tightly to the docks.

The storm is so loud that we don't notice the occupants on the largest airboat. In their raincoats, Jimmy and Aaron have loaded large barrels turned on their sides. Caustic fluid spills into the fast-moving water in giant gulps.

"The algaecide," Covey mutters.

Leaking fuel is not uncommon in Mercy. A purplish sheen often covers the surface of our waters, especially by harbors. This is different, a liquid designed to destroy and so casually spat into the waterways that sustain us. Decades of pollution have taught them nothing. Jimmy is a slot machine villain—predictably driven by money and more money. Aaron is his right-hand man, all to secure life with a seventeen-year-old girlfriend until something better comes along.

People are often frightened by the night, but it is in daylight where the real monsters hide. They wear smiles, and they are loved—or else, believed. Those are the most dangerous.

"I should've done this to begin with," Jimmy announces as his attention pivots to us. "Oh Covey, I'm so disappointed in you."

30

THE STING OF DISAPPOINTMENT from an adult, even one
you don't like, is real. We're conditioned to fear their dismay
because they know better and they're always right, so Covey
flinches under her dad's words. Her shoulders rise tensely, but
then she steps in front of me—a tall, broad shield.

"Fuck you," she says. "You're the reason Mom left, why we're
always trying to get away. She didn't have a boyfriend. She just
hated how controlling you are, and selfish." His normally wide
grin is downturned as he moves closer, Aaron right behind. "She
actually wanted to help people. You could too! Just let us go."

Jimmy leaps from boat to dock. "You ungrateful little shit."
He stalks toward us. People are insignificant things in weather
like this, where every draft threatens to take you off your feet.
Jimmy and Aaron cast a long, big shadow that starts to eclipse
us. "This is for our family. You want to be some pencil pusher
answering to a boss? Or a stay-at-home momma collecting food

stamps? The Swamp Tour and Emporium is how we make money, Covey. I'm carving a future for us while you and everyone else waste time with crocodile tears."

"I don't want this," Covey says, gesturing all around her. "I never did."

Like so many parents, Jimmy thinks his daughter is fit only for his hopes. But when we inherit those, we also inherit the mistakes. We are the ones to live the consequences. Every generation before had a semblance of a chance, but we have the end of the world. *This* end of the world. It's beautiful, it's crushing, and I wish we could think of a future without a thousand ways of how we must change to endure it.

My eyes dart after Aaron as he departs from Jimmy's side. The soft flesh under my gills still hurts from where his fingers dug. He peers at the churning swamp, the vein in his neck pumping thickly with adrenaline and terror. The familiar curve of our boat key hangs from a necklace that has often rested on my breastbone. The swamp emits a low moaning that had blended in with the thunder. Lightning flashes, and the water is alive, come to reckon. Too many undone are here now to escape notice. He staggers away immediately, hand clamped over his chest.

"The key to *Wild Things* is around Aaron's neck," I whisper to Covey and Mom. "That's the fastest way out." Since we're already caught, it doesn't matter how much noise we make. Of course, Aaron is between me and the goal. Despite the pain Mom must be in, she tenses her hands, ready to strike. Covey withdraws a tattered book from a side pocket and from within, a knife.

The three of us move at the same time, as if they—rather than the undone—are part of my mind. Nails curled, I swipe at Aaron's throat while Covey slices his thigh. Her aim misses in the rain, knocking the staticky radio from his hip. Mom has shoved Jimmy aside with a wild scream, pummeling him as best she can. It's hard to focus between the beating rain and groaning water. My body twists in the compulsion to change more, and I try to hold back. There's no time.

Aaron slams Covey's wrist repeatedly into a pile beam until the knife drops and spins on the slippery dock. Yelling obscenities, she tries to punch him with her free hand. I'm fighting against an insistent urge, as strong as nausea, to fall over. I won't forget that there's power in this body as I watch the worst person try to wreck someone I care about. Before I can help, someone yanks my hair from behind.

The wooden docks are hard and unforgiving against my spine. Jimmy blocks out the sky as he hovers above me, limp hair dripping rainwater in a half-circle around me. Mom's hysterical, pulling on his arm. I realize why.

Covey's knife is in his hand.

"You're too much trouble," Jimmy says. Lightning strikes overhead, then the blade enters my body. Cold, and foreign, but at least my clothes are on.

A girl is often told she's better on her back; I hate thinking about that.

Covey is screaming. I turn my head, glimpsing only legs and feet. Aaron's boots go *thump, thump, thump* down the pier as he gets away, once again, from a sad scene.

I have survived a drowning. I have survived abandoning my own skin. Only scars remain in the places that I have been damaged. I'm learning I can survive so much—both emotional and physical, but it's not a limb that Jimmy's stabbed.

It is my heart.

He pushes me into the water.

31

THE WATER ENVELOPS ME. It swallows me whole. The wound from my chest leaks blood redder than the algae that has infested the rivers and the estuaries and the lakes. It streaks through the water, a bloody shooting star, and I'm falling away to the swamp's depths.

There's trash, the dead, and things abandoned here, rotting away.

But there's also life: bioluminescent fish, reptiles that have hints of warmth under their scales, and flowers and plants not native to such environments. Each beautiful and strange.

The algaecide *burns* us. It eats its way through shredded skin; it buries itself in my gut, acidic and deadly. The pain is intolerable, but still it won't be enough to kill us.

Those from Mercy Cove who followed the knocking and voices are here, their memories a balm to this pain. In a way, they are like Mrs. Olivier since they've come to save me. I remove the foreign object from my chest, and the wound is not so angry anymore. They remind me that some jellyfish can regenerate themselves over time, so why shouldn't I try?

I'm Sông's child as much as I am my mom's, and Mercy's now. It is raising me well. I burst through the surface into a world of sound. Chaos has unfolded on the docks. More voices have joined the fray. Blood scents the air. The water ruptures on either side of me as two undone bodies emerge. An elder with algae growing thick within deep wrinkles and a teen with a photogenic smile torn right to her triple-pierced ears.

The new folks on the docks finally notice us. It's probably that tingle at their necks of being watched, that feeling that you might be ripped apart. A spark of confusion ignites, then spreads. Hearing about a monster is one thing. Seeing many is another. The swamp is alive with more than just alligators. Most workers retreat into the emporium, as if it can keep us out. Mom screams my name as she and Covey tussle with Jimmy.

Rain-slicked, Aaron takes one look over his shoulder before running again toward a boat. I know which one, because it's my key he's stolen. It flutters around his soft throat, a bright bait. I dive in, the other bodies close behind. Swimming comes naturally now, unlike my ungraceful movements under Covey's tutelage. It requires no thought. I simply move, eyes wide open, until I spot the familiar *Wild Things* paint.

He is where he shouldn't be.

Lurking in the water, we bang our fists against the boat's hull. Standing on the deck, we bang our fists on the walls and windows separating us from him. Inside the cabin, the man trembles and tries to put the key into the ignition. We ask to be let in. Our moans are low, torturous, squeezed through broken or restructured tracheae. *Let us in let us in let us in let us in.*

There are more walking undone than I originally thought. Their bodies haven't yet been stitched into something new, or abandoned in favor of the collective form. Yet I feel them as strongly as the ones whose memories I've swallowed into the pit of my belly. They feel me too, or else they wouldn't have followed me here. Connected through the bloom and Sông, our instincts are aligned.

We are horror movie villains, shunned for being grotesque and different. If only people would look closely, they'd see that our blood is like starlight. We are not the monsters in this world. We are the undone; the basic black tee; the beginning and the end. Transforming and living, evolving to fit the future they wrought.

Sink in and be free, give in to the scorch of your tongue.

But not Aaron. Aaron does not deserve a tongue, much less starlight and infinite memory.

For the very first time, I'm not possessed by fear.

It's easy to break down a door when you know its weak points, like which screws Mom didn't tighten enough. It hangs uselessly on the hinges. Inside this tiny cabin that Mom and I lived in for the last two years, it smells a bit like home: dried shrimp, watermelon shampoo, and minty medicated oil.

"Knock knock," I say.

Jumping in surprise, Aaron drops the key. He falls to his knees in a desperate search. It's disappeared on the dark flooring, probably in a crevice too small for his fingers. He curses frequently and loudly. He turns around to watch us approach. "Those aren't . . ." He's stuttering. He's afraid. "You aren't . . ."

Here is my definitive list of things I am/was or am not/wasn't wearing:

Suede cowboy boots. Onesie. Short skirt, long skirt. Nothing.

Wide-legged jeans. An expensive top from Old Navy. Mom's dress. A T-shirt with a clown on it. Fishnet stockings stolen from a dollar store.

A 550-fill goose down parka. My little brother's bedsheet. Gym shorts. Plaid.

My age.

It doesn't matter. He's decided what I am from the start.

He throws our large rice container. It bursts on impact, scattering white grains across the entire cabin as a wedding party might outside a church.

"That's wasteful," I say.

Next he drags out a shoebox—my box of treasures—and hurls it at me. The lid flings open, and so many small happinesses spill from it. The #1 SISTER pen lands at my feet, still caked in filth. Mom must have put it away for me. Normally this would sustain me for a bit, but right now it's not enough.

Monsterhood is a girl's body you don't belong in. Didn't I tell you that?

There's a type of monster you don't know about until you do. They wear normal human skin and smile and say neighborly hellos. They cleave apart ankles to execute their depraved wants. They humiliate your mother and hurt your friends; they'd do it again, and again.

He's in my shadow now. "Open wide." I smile as I break his jaw, forearm inside his mouth, then press. "Good boy." I empty him, undo him, until he is less than nothing. I let him scream as loud as he wants.

32

A MERMAID TURNS INTO sea foam. That's how the stories go. At least that's what Covey told me. I worried that would be my ending, too, but there's never been one like me in those fairy tales, a kid of the Deep South born from immigrants and watched over by a primordial beast. I was never destined to be a princess or a bride. My family has abandoned many homes to survive, so I'm not leaving this one.

Aaron is a blood stain at my feet. Spilled from his jean pocket are money, a condom, credit cards, and a picture of a teenage girl. He's incapable of hurting me or anyone else anymore. The wound in my chest knits itself slowly, bleeding into the iron pool on the floor. When the undone die too soon, they dissipate into sea foam but are still absorbed by Sông. Their memory is held among us. Treasured. He's not there because he's always been so painfully ordinary, and he was never part of Sông. We remember what he did.

I leave behind the key to this boat, to my trauma, as I step into the raging storm. It lashes against my bare legs, threatening to bowl me over. The undone have righted the barrels to stop the vicious chemical stream. Only Mom, Covey, and Jimmy remain on the docks, clinging to the railing to stay on their feet. Muddied handprints are all over the emporium, their owners unseen. Screaming joins the wind's howl. If only Jimmy had talked to people in Mercy, he would've known what they wanted. Clean water, air, a community living in harmony. Sông will give us that.

"I am your dad." Jimmy's voice is as loud as thunder, cracking like a whip on Covey. "You listen to me. *Only* me."

My body feels unnatural out of water, but I hang on, not ready to lose myself completely. Mom rushes to help me stay upright as I close in on the group.

"Just go," Covey tells her dad. "You've done enough damage."

"Go where, Covey?" he asks sarcastically. "Our family has been here for centuries, and I built this place up myself to what it is now. I'm getting life back to normal while everyone else wants to run. Even those Sharps hauled ass outta there. You and her, and her, should be grateful to me. You're going to risk your future on this Asian girl? It's a phase, Covey. Ain't nothing special."

Of course, Jimmy would have it all wrong. If I survive him, he'll probably think it's because he pitied me. I tilt my head. "At the moment, I'm not a girl."

He sneers. "Fucked-up little monster then, how about that?" He's a man backed into a corner, about to lose his trade but more prominently, his relevance. He is desperate to succeed and willing to ignore the evidence around him.

"Better than being a whiny bitch," I say.

He charges and knocks me clean off my feet. Mom scrambles to get him away. Rather than wielding a knife like earlier, he uses his hands. He wants to feel the life slipping from me, proof that I will be gone. My soft, translucent shell seems to frustrate him, so he presses his thumbs deeper into my pulse. He's telling me to die, even when he doesn't know me at all.

Both Covey and my mom try prying him from me, but he only strangles me harder. My head's limp, feeling like it'll burst with pressure. At the far end of the deck, a bone-white hand has wrapped around the railing. It pulls and pulls until the rest of the woman appears, standing. She has craters for eyes, and yet her gaze settles on us like a weight. Mackenzie Boudreaux sees. Since our encounter at Mercy Cove, she's scraped more skin away, exposing tendon and bone.

No sound leaves my lips as a headache pounds deep in my skull. I slap a hand against the wooden planks, trying to warn Covey that her mother is coming, but they're all preoccupied with either hurting or saving me. Slowly, Mack makes her way toward us. She swipes Mom aside first, then Covey. She seizes Jimmy's torso without hesitation, stronger than her fading body appears capable of. I'm lifted a few inches until Jimmy releases me out of shock. He recognizes Mackenzie; he looks almost human.

Covey's lost in this familiar dreamland and once again steps forward to meet her mother. As if motivated by some maternal instinct, mine stops her from getting closer. A breathy rumbling emits from Mack's chest. Words. Feeling. Whatever it is, it connects, and an anguished cry leaves Covey's mouth.

Mack's arms are tangled tightly around Jimmy's bulky torso. His boots squeal their resistance as she throws them backward over the railing.

He screams when he hits the swamp. Algaecide bubbles against his skin. His eyes redden from the humanmade poison. A vicious urge to see him drown rises, to hold him still for the algae to work into his skin, but I gain control of these impulses. This algae-ridden water will not make home of his gut. I will not let his memories foul mine. I leap after them, but Covey's mother is faster in the water, even with her ex-husband in tow. Flickers of her thoughts shuffle into my mind.

If Mack had tried to fold Covey into the water out of love, she does it for Jimmy out of hate. She won't allow me to drag him back. The bloom is weak here, too far away from the cove, and the chemicals have agitated the swamp's other residents. He struggles against her grip, but she's immutable to the hurricane's pressure. She drags him closer to nearby ground, where the alligators have burrowed mud caves to hunker down. Maybe they remember the way this man skinned their brethren, or maybe it's within their nature to see food and not let it go to waste. Either way, with a glint in their eyes, they converge on the pair. Teeth find Mack's remaining flesh as well, but she doesn't let go.

Task done, Sông wants to coax me back to the cove, where I can more quickly become something else. Give in to the deal. But it's not enough to only survive anymore. I don't want to go. I still have my mother, Covey, Saf, and Wilder, and I've had them for so short a time. I need more. I've also never wanted to keep a body as much as right now. I'm in the right shape, a creature split between water and land, untethered by fear.

The storm is strong, so I must be stronger. The swamp is a blood- and chemical-filled mess, and gators continue to roil the surface with their death rolls. I am myself, utterly wild, cutting through tumultuous water in my electric skin. At the deck, I reach one hand up. Neither Mom nor Covey hesitates to help, falling onto their knees to grasp my hand and wrist. I hit the deck floor in a sick slop. So many parts of me are not as they were. They melt away, like a snake's shed skin. Covey's sitting on the balls of her feet, completely broken and sobbing openly.

Kneeling right beside me, Mom reaches for my neck and I think she means to search for the keys to *Wild Things*, but instead her hands rest on either side of my face and massage my cheekbones as she begins to cry. "Con ơi," my mom says. *Oh, my child*, she says, and it doesn't sting because she's really seeing me now. She knows what I am. She kisses me again and again on my forehead and cheeks, as she had done when I was small.

33

THREE DAYS POST-HURRICANE

"IT'S PRONOUNCED CORNFLOWER," COVEY tells Mom, very earnestly propping her book open so my mom can see. Unlike me, Mom loves to read and had gone through the small Vietnamese collection at the library years ago. After everything went down at the emporium, Mom just sat down one evening next to Covey and pointed at one of the books. I think both were glad for the distraction.

Wilder and Saffy are safe, too. We picked them up after the storm died down and explained everything. Wearing that soft, concerned expression that's never limited to herself, Saffy had asked, "What will happen when it finally comes for all of us?"

I said the only thing that was true. "We all begin again."

They understood what Sông's intentions were, as much as a human could anyway, and decided they would leave Mercy. There were more items on their fuck-it lists to check off, after all. But first, they want to stay with me. It won't be forever, but it'll be long enough.

Now I'm steering a hunter-green houseboat named *Best Wishes* downriver. The motor's not meant for long distances, and the extra bedroom makes the boat obnoxiously wide, so it's been slow progress. On the dashboard, Sandbag sleeps on top of a picture of Dad and Jay. There's a metal can full of rice and ashes, the last whispers of incense sweeping against my cheek. I'm wearing Covey's clothes. I like the soft fleece and how it smells like Covey the night she came back to the shack to wait for me, sans sunscreen. I like that it's her size, so the sweatshirt ends closer to my knees.

Today, the ocean is soft—all rolling blankets and loose plush. Our boat tips and dives, moving with the water. It sings gently under my feet, patient. It lets me pass to the broken rocks. The lighthouses' skeletal metal rises from the drift like a sleeping beast. I stop by Wilder's parents' so he and Saffy can visit. His mom will check his injured fingers or lack thereof, supply another round of antibiotics, and maybe they will heal other wounds. It's his decision.

"Remember to come back," Wilder warns, before he lets me go.

Beyond the damaged but still standing lighthouses, the horizon is split, broken by the rise of an old phone booth on jagged rock. Amazingly, the wind phone that calls to the dead hasn't sunk to the bottom of the sea, but this is probably the last time it will be visited. It won't last much longer.

I turn the engine off. Mom has leaned back to look at me with her brown eyes. Though I am whole, I am different and she knows it. "We should have done so many things," Mom says in English. "I am sorry." Her voice tugs at my heart, almost the same way that the water does. I understand what she means. For many months she had me, and all of it had been spent searching for the dead. Still, there'd been fun days—finding rainbows rising from the middle of the ocean, seeing blooms of jellyfish near the surface, and playing too many rounds of Thirteen. It wasn't all bad, or sad.

I hug her tight. "I won't be away long." On the wall is the portable whiteboard, on which we convinced Mom to start her own fuck-it list. "See the Statue of Liberty" is the first bullet point, and I think she will finally be okay. Mom hugs me tight, too.

Out on the boat's deck, Covey stands for a long minute just watching the wind phone. I wonder if it's living up to how she imagines it. Half-crashed into the rocks and partially underwater, it's a sight to behold. She glances over when she hears my steps. I drop down the side of the boat, landing on the rocky island.

"You ready?" I ask Covey, reaching for her hand.

Her eyes dart at the lopsided phone booth. Algae paints its side, and long ago the sign had faded to nothing, but this is the phone believed to connect us to those who have passed. Her mother is really gone now, and Covey needs to say goodbye. She takes my hand, stumbling a bit upon landing, but I anchor her against my waist. This close, I can see the bit of sunscreen on her ear that's not spread out.

"Not yet," she replies.

I incline my head toward the higher shelf of rocks, where we can sit while she gathers up whatever courage she needs. We linger so long that Mom peeps her head out to make sure we are still around. She doesn't bother us again.

There are many things I've yet to experience, and I don't want to let this moment go. "You know," I say to Covey. "I don't really like anyone, but if it had to be someone, I guess it's you."

Covey laughs until she's practically snorting. "That . . . that was not romantic at all."

I smile with my shark teeth. "Then let me say it differently: I'm glad this close to the end of the world, I am with you." It's a little embarrassing to say, and it makes me feel vulnerable and bare in a way that sloughing skin doesn't, but it warms me. Until I'm completely gone, so drowned out by the voices that sustain me, Covey, Wilder, Saffy, and my mom are staying. Even if it might hurt, because some of the best things in life hurt just a little bit.

"All right," she says after some time. She takes out her knife and nods, gesturing for me to follow. We climb down until we're right by the wind phone. Her fingers graze the wood there, testing it, then scrape the sharp knife against it. It only takes a single letter to figure out what she's doing. Though it won't last, we carve our initials into the wood.

NL & CB were here!!!

Too hot for summer, and yet our hands meet. We grin at our penmanship. Covey holds my hand for several minutes, the bones in her sharp fingers surprisingly gentle. She isn't scared at all. "Now I'm ready," she says with a nod. I release her, and I miss her, and she goes to the phone booth. Her legs dip entirely into the water. She leans on the single wall that's still intact.

I sit on the moss-wet rocks and splash water all over my face and neck. Inside, she picks up the receiver and lifts it to her ear. For a moment, the water below pulses with my reflection, ripples distorting its surface though nothing has fallen in. It calls me, it loves me, but it can't have me yet. The wind whips my hair into a frenzy, calling my attention back to the horizon. The day is hot, in that way September should be, the settling afterstorm. I can taste the season to come.

I'd thought everything human would bleed out of me, but it was the opposite. My core is the same, untouched and filled with the memories of those living in the water and those who passed. Not everyone meets their end in the water. Not everyone becomes something else. But I am here, and Sông is with me. So maybe it isn't so bad to be so different, to have your core cored and split to a thousand pieces so a creature billions of years old can understand you and others.

At the end of the world, there is still Mom's singing, Saffy's laughter, Wilder's antics. Covey's hands pulling me into the night. There are birds and trees, revived flowers. Friends. From the red algae come monstrous forms, but there is also life in the animals returning where they were once extinct. This world and its sharp, intense beauty.

There is me too, scars and all, freckled and peeling.

I was beautiful. I am beautiful.

ACKNOWLEDGMENTS

As always, thank you to the entire Bloomsbury team for shepherding my books into the world: editors Mary Kate Castellani and Kei Nakatsuka, publicist Faye Bi, marketing hero Erica Barmash, and school and library marketing duo Beth Eller and Kathleen Morandini. My agent Katelyn Detweiler deserves all the flowers for her incredible care.

I must now say sorry to friends Clare Osongco, Lindsay Fischer, Wen-yi Lee for having to deal with my terrifying early drafts and my whining about it. I owe you like 1000 beverages of choice. Jen St. Jude, *They Bloom at Night* would not exist as is without your insights. Thank you so, so much for seeing me and Nhung. You made me brave.

Alex Brown, Courtney Gould, Liselle Sambury, and Andrew Joseph White are all amazing, generous people who also write amazing books. Go check them out!

Shoutout to Writers' Block, my fierce writing group that throws the best writing retreats. Your community brings me endless joy.

Daniel, thank you for being by my side. You've saved me in so many ways. One day I'll let you teach me how to swim too.

To Laurie Halse Anderson, thank you for writing *Speak*. It found me at the right time and has stayed with me since.